Justice
FALLING

Justice FALLING

BOOK THREE
AUDREY CARLAN

WATERHOUSE
PRESS

Sarah Saunders

*You single handedly made me a better writer.
What an incredible gift to an author.
I wanted to impress you and in the end I impressed
myself. Something I know you would applaud,
because that's the type of person you are. I am so
honored to have a friend and critique partner that's
not only epically gifted, but strong, talented, and
loving. This novel is for you.*

Namaste

CHAPTER ONE

Ten thousand dollars. That's how much my silence cost me. In my defense, I had no choice. Eighteen. Pregnant. No money. No family. No concrete place to live. I did what I had to do.

When it happened, I thought it a joke. Who gets a woman pregnant, asks her to abort their child, and when she won't, buys her off? One person did, and I was the messed-up girl who let him. For me and for the life I carried inside of me, it had been my only option.

Thinking back, I should have pushed harder, made him take responsibility. Even though my life was hard now and I barely had enough to pinch two pennies together, Tanner was worth it all. In spades. The room started to change as I thought back to that day four years ago, when I approached my son's father for the last time.

"You're nothing but a two-bit whore. I should have known the sweet and innocent thing was just an act. You are a gold digger. I'll bet you planned this to trap me!" he roared.

"I…I d-didn't." The words left my lips on a choked sob. I tried to reach for his arm, anything to hold onto the man I thought I loved. He shucked off my advance as if revolted. His face held in a menacing scowl.

"Oh please. The moment we fucked you got pregnant? I've been with my wife for five years. Five. Fucking. Years! We've never

so much as had a pregnancy scare."

Wife. He had a wife? That one word rang like a gong in my ears, deafening, blocking out all sound. Finally his words came back, "You and I fucked a handful of times, and you get pregnant?" He shook his head and scowled. "It's probably not even mine!"

"This is your child! You're the only one, Tyler, I'd never be unfaithful. I was a virgin!"

"Well not anymore, sweet cheeks. Now you're going to take that tight ass right down to the clinic and purchase an abortion. Here's the money." He pulled out a handful of hundreds.

"I'm not killing our baby, Tyler. Let's be reasonable. We can work through this," I pleaded, tears streaming down my face, wetting my shirt. I placed my hand over my abdomen protectively. He scanned me with a grimace, noticing the same pair of jeans I wore every Friday, the one pair of shoes I owned, scuffed even after I scrubbed them clean in the hotel bathroom's sink.

"Are you fucking insane? You must be." He flicked his index finger hard against my temple as if knocking on a door. I winced, realizing in that moment that he was not the person I thought he was. How could I have been so stupid? Naïve. His eyes blazed with white-hot fire. I stood still, trying to be strong though I was petrified. "Get it through your stupid-fucking-little-itty-bitty brain. I do not want you. I do not want your child. You will get rid of it."

"I will not!" I held my chin stiff as he gripped it painfully. I stared into his blue eyes. They were squinted together so tight I no longer was able to see the ones I so loved. Now they were glacial, cold, with intent to harm.

"I'm not going to take care of this bastard child or you." He walked over to his desk, opened a drawer, and pulled out an old-fashioned cash box. He counted out ten stacks of crisp, one hundred dollar bills. He piled them up, grabbed my hand, and slammed them *into my palm so hard I stepped back, afraid he might do something and physically hurt me. After my last foster parent, I was used to taking a beating, but now that I was pregnant I'd do anything to avoid one.*

"You'll take this money and get rid of it. I don't care what you do or where you go. This is all you're ever going to get out of me. Do you understand, you fuckwit?"

I couldn't believe his response. It was my nightmare come true. I gripped the money tight, holding onto it as if it were a talisman, a way out of this hell. I didn't know what I was going to do beyond this point, but I had to figure it out and fast. I stared at the ground and nodded.

This was it. My path chosen in the blink of an eye. I was going to be a single mother.

A shudder rippled through me as I sat at my beautiful, solid oak desk at the front of Jensen Construction. I had been working here for the past three months, a quasi-receptionist/secretary/personal assistant to Hank Jensen.

The job was a dream come true. More than that actually. It was everything. My ticket out of poverty. Well, almost. I still had the *other* job. I wasn't proud of my after-hours employment. Would never tell Tanner I'd done it, and would lie through my teeth if he, or anyone for that matter, found out about it. Only my roommate Jin knew, and that's because she did it too.

Sometimes you had to do things you wouldn't ever see yourself doing. Drastic measures had to be taken when you were providing for a life. My four-year-old son, Tanner, was worth every bit of hell I had to go through to take care of him. He was my world, and I'd do anything necessary to make sure he had a good life. Growing up, I'd been bounced around from foster home to foster home for as long as I could remember. Some were okay, most of them were unbearable. Once I turned eighteen, I took what little savings I'd been able to scrounge up and left New Jersey behind for the Big Apple.

I didn't know what I'd do when I got there. It wasn't as if I had any special talents, but I figured I'd work retail, go to school, and become a school teacher. It was my long-term dream. Still is. Though, of course, meeting Tyler Thornton and being swept off my feet by a rich loser hadn't been part of the plan. Then again, getting pregnant at eighteen wasn't planned either. The pregnancy definitely halted my immediate goals of jumping right into college after high school.

That first year I worked at a diner. Back-breaking, pain-inducing manual labor, but I never complained. The owners kept me on even when I was ready to pop, knowing I needed the money. It's where I met my roommate Jin. I was living out of a crummy hotel, and she had a place and needed a roommate. I was a few months pregnant at the time, and knew I had to save every dime of that ten grand for my child. Turned out she'd already had a one-year-old of her own. Together, we shared a crummy apartment on a dingy side of town, worked like dogs for scraps and raised our children as one happy family unit. It was the best decision of my life. Jin and I get along famously, and our children treat each other like brothers. It's the family I've never had.

Our apartment wasn't much, but we kept it clean, warm, and stuffed with food for the boys. Her son, Zach, was a five-year-old fireball, where my Tan Man was an angel child. Polar opposites those two, but the best of friends, just like Jin and me. They say God only gives you what you can handle. I don't know if that statement bears any truth, but as far as children go, I definitely had the best.

"Hey, sweetie, do you have that purchase order from Bill's Lumber?" My boss knocked his knuckles on my desk, the sound unusually loud, due to his size. The man was huge. All muscle and man in a hunky cowboy package. Even his southern drawl made my belly jump a time or two.

"Who are you calling 'sweetie'?" An agitated voice from behind him proclaimed as the door opened and closed. I knew that voice. Without turning around, my boss, Mr. Hunky Hank Jensen himself, grinned wide and shuffled a paw through his sandy brown hair shaking his head.

"Angel," he said wistfully, and then waggled his eyebrows at me. I beamed a smile back at him, knowing he was about to get an earful.

God, these two made me believe true love existed. I had seen it every day for the last three months. Hank spun on his heel and there she was. Hip cocked to one side, long blond hair flowing like a golden wave over her shoulder. She had on a sexy formfitting siren-red dress that hugged every curve. Most specifically, the huge basketball-sized baby bump. Aspen Jensen was a knockout. Pregnant or not, she'd make any man drop to their knees and worship at her feet, which is exactly what Hank did. First, he fawned over his wife, and then he got down on his knees and rubbed and kissed the bump. It made me wish I had a man who loved me and Tanner that way.

"How's my baby girl doin'? You comfy in there, darlin'?" he asked Aspen's stomach sweetly. She allowed his overt public display, running her fingers through his hair and smiling as only a woman completely in love would do, regardless of who was watching them.

"She's good, stud. Rolling around like crazy, but that's to be expected."

"What week are we in?" I asked, knowing what was coming next.

Hanks eyes lit up as he covered his wife's belly with both hands affectionately. "We're now a head of lettuce, baby," he said happily, looking up at Aspen. "Twenty-six weeks and counting. Whoa, Nelly!" Hank spoke to his child. "You be nice to your mama now. Don't be kickin' too hard." He stood, shook his head, and pulled his wife in for a kiss.

It boggled the mind how hands-on my boss was with his wife. He did not care who was around or what they were doing. He was constantly touching her, kissing her, and overall being the most doting husband I'd ever seen. It was pretty storybook. It didn't seem possible that a couple so different in every way could be so perfect for one another. For them it worked. I'd never been so lucky, but I had Tanner and he was all I needed to be happy.

"How are you feeling, Mrs. Jensen?" I asked as Hank stood, rubbed her stomach and held his wife close.

"Sleep deprived, need to use the restroom every five minutes, hungry, and then stuffed. It's all encompassing."

"That's because you're growing the world's most perfect little girl in there!" Hank palmed her belly again. I had to give it to Aspen. Hank couldn't keep his hands off her and she handled it like it was the norm. I couldn't imagine a man putting his hands all over me all the time. It made me claustrophobic thinking about it. Then again, if the man looked as good as her husband I might have a change of heart.

"Have you guys picked out any names?"

They both nodded and smiled. "We have, but we're keeping it a secret. We don't want anyone to sway our decision. I hope you understand." Aspen rubbed her hand over her belly.

"Oh I understand perfectly. When I was preg—" Both their eyes widened, and I realized what I'd almost admitted to. "Um, what I meant was, I understand the need to be private." Aspen squinted and tilted her head to the side to assess me. Those crystal-blue eyes were sharp, the kind that saw everything, especially when you didn't want them to. That's probably why she was a gazillionaire and owned the entire skyscraper Jensen Construction was housed in.

"Cami, do you have children?" Aspen asked point-blank. Hank's eyes widened in surprise at the question. I know my face turned completely white. I could feel it going numb around the edges. Before I answered, Oliver, Aspen's personal assistant and BFF, rushed in, saving the day, just like he did the day he found me in that diner three months ago and told me he was going to change my life. Oliver's pointed pristine features were set in a scowl, and his manicured hands in fists. I was pretty sure I had never seen him so flustered.

Crisis averted. *Thank God!* My private life needed to stay private. These kind people, ones that were rich, solid, and loving could not know about Tanner or my second job. If they did, they wouldn't want me working here. I'd tarnish their good names and successful businesses, not to mention the shame of them finding out what I did at night.

"There you are! Our baby's doctor is not going to wait while you two play kissy face all day." Hank had taken to kissing along his wife's neck and rubbing her back.

"*Our* baby, Oliver." Hank pointed to his wife then himself. Oliver stood in his immaculate suit looking bored to tears. He even put his hand up to his mouth and mimicked a yawn. Hank continued, "Stop trying to take credit for my hard work."

Aspen grimaced. "*Your* hard work? You mean *my* hard work. I'm the one who's missing out on sleep. Throwing up at God all hours of the day and night. Let's not forget about the back pain incubating *your* giant child, Mister." Hank turned his wife and moved her along toward the door while she ranted.

"I'll be back after our baby appointment," he said over his shoulder so I'd hear him.

"…swollen ankles, giant knockers."

"Hey, don't be talking poorly 'bout that last one. Those were a happy surprise. I'm not complainin' none about that one," Hank said as they made their way down the hall.

The phone rang, and I grabbed it on the second ring. "Jensen Construction, Cami speaking, how may I help you?"

"Yes, hello, love, is Hank available for a chat?" a smooth, British voice spoke through the receiver. Just the tone of the voice, not to mention the sexy syllables, uncharacteristically sent a little trill down my spine. He spoke again before I realized I'd not answered him. "Hello? Cami?"

"Um, yes, I'm sorry. No. Mr. Jensen is out of the office and won't return for another couple hours. Can I take a message?" The words left my mouth in a jumble, sounding halfway professional.

"Really? He told me I could call today to schedule a meeting. Shall I ring another time perhaps?" The man's tone was like lotion over dry skin, smooth and silky. I had the insane desire to keep him speaking to me.

"Yes, of course you can. Uh, schedule a meeting. Not call back." The stranger laughed on the other side of the phone. The sound tumbled directly to my belly, heating and tightening in equal parts. "I schedule all of Mr. Jensen's meetings," I finished, a tad breathless. My response to this caller was extremely unusual. Rarely did I feel so…attracted to a stranger. Rarely being never.

I hadn't felt desire or any form of pleasure from the opposite sex since being with Ty all those years ago. That loser remains the only man I'd ever slept with. Now, hearing this sexy foreigner's ragged breath over the line, his lusty tone, I crossed and re-crossed my legs to staunch the ache between my thighs. It unnerved me.

"Well, aren't you just Ms. Efficient?" he cooed.

"I try. Let me check his schedule." I clicked a few keys to bring up Hank's calendar. "Mr. Jensen has a slot available at four this afternoon. Does that time work for you?"

"It suits just fine, love." God, the way he called me "love" made me *feel* loved even though it was insane to be thinking such crazy things when I'd only shared a few minutes conversation with the stranger. I didn't even know his name, and I felt off balance and warm in a way I hadn't been in years.

"May I take your name and information?"

"Of course, love." The way he said it that time made me feel less special. Maybe he said it to everyone. He was British. "My name is Nathaniel Walker of Stone, Walker, &

Associates."

"And what will this meeting be in regard to?"

"I'm not certain that's any of your business." His tone was cool.

I shook my head and apologized. "Oh no, I'm so sorry. I didn't mean to pry. I typically prepare whatever items Mr. Jensen may need for his meetings. Excuse me for being so—"

"Cami, love, I was just fooling about. I'm Mr. Jensen's lawyer." My face heated.

His lawyer. Wait a minute…I'd met his lawyer. His name was not Nathaniel. It was Collier Stone. "I don't know what you're trying to pull, but Jensen Construction's lawyer is Collier Stone."

Another belly-jangling chuckle came through the line. "I wasn't trying to diddle you, love. Collier is my brother. He's the Stone in Stone, *Walker*, & Associates." I gripped the receiver until my knuckles turned white and tried hard not to slam my forehead onto the hard desk. *Stupid, stupid, stupid!* I could feel embarrassment burn my pale skin scarlet.

★ ★ ★

The precious Cami over the phone line was quiet for so long I feared she may have rang off. I was rather enjoying the chinwag with her. Something in the tone of her voice, the breathiness of her words as she spoke made me want to talk to the young thing all day long. At least I imagined she was young.

"I'm sorry, Mr. Walker. I've only been here three months. Please don't be upset with me. I need this job—"

"Love, whoa. Whoa. Hold your skirt." I cut her off. "No

worries. No harm. Just a bit of jolly banter between soon-to-be friends. Right?"

"Thank you." I could hear her take a calming breath. "Um, right. Friends. Sure. I'll schedule that appointment. Is there anything you need me to prepare for your meeting with Mr. Jensen? Anything at all? I owe you one," she added sweetly.

"I do love a spot of tea and a biscuit in the late afternoon," I joked. Unfortunately, she took my words seriously. The Yanks really needed to lighten up.

"Biscuits? There may be a local bread store that would have biscuits. I'll do my best. We have tea and cookies, though."

"Oh, love, you are too precious. I can hardly wait to make your acquaintance. While you're preparing, look up the British terms for 'biscuit.' We'll discuss at four. Cheers!" I rang off and sat back into my chair.

Curious thoughts about the sweet Ms. Cami filled my mind. I'd not been to Hank's office in a while, and now that I'd spoken with his lovely sounding receptionist, I looked forward to my four o'clock. Never hurt to make new friends, particularly if those new friends were sexy little vixens. I imagined her petite, blond, and curvy with that breathy small voice.

I finished my last meeting early and made it to the AIR Bright building with time to spare. When I stepped off the elevator and stole a glance through the glass, I plumb lost my breath and the ability to walk. I stood stock still and watched the elegant beauty for a moment, taking in her edible attributes as she rounded her desk. If this was the precious Cami I'd spoke to, I was overjoyed at my good fortune. She was most certainly not petite or blond. This woman was tall, at least five foot ten to my six-foot-three-inch frame. Brown hair cascaded down her back. Not quite curls, but that wind-swept beachy look American girls did so well. The only word that came to mind was stunning.

At twenty-eight, I considered myself a connoisseur of beautiful women. Never had to work to secure a woman's affection and I'd been told plenty that my good looks were a menace. Even had a hoard of women claim to love me over the years. Not once did I feel a woman was out of my league.

Until now.

The woman's body was to die for. I watched through the glass as she moved from her desk to a file cabinet and back. Her movements were quick, efficient, and laser-focused on her task. I hadn't expected *this* woman when I'd arrived. Yes, she was young. That could be easily determined by her unlined, dewy pale skin. However, I wasn't prepared for her to be gorgeous…magnificent, really. Her hair was the color of a roasting chestnut. Not quite brown or blond, but more a comingling of all the colors that made fall my favorite season.

As I watched her work, my body warmed and my skin felt unbearably tight, confined by the three-piece suit I'd donned. She wore a midlength skirt that barely kissed her knee. I'd heard them referred to as a pencil skirt, though I hadn't the slightest bloody idea why. A pencil was a thin, straight writing instrument. This woman was slight, yet curvy in all the places that counted, with the tiniest speck of a waist. Good God, the heels she had on were stiletto and sexy as hell, connected to tight, toned calves. I could imagine those "shag me shoes" around my waist, the spike digging straight into the tender skin of my arse as I worked her over.

Basically, she had the body of a *Playboy* model, her breasts undoubtedly large but covered demurely behind a fitted top that only showed a hint of pearlescent cleavage when she bent over to retrieve a document. Christ, the more I looked, the harder I got. It took Herculean effort to not stride in, set a hand to that body, and show her exactly what I'd like to do to her.

I pulled my mind out of the gutter and then straightened my back. I opened the door as she looked up, the perfect globes of her breasts straining against the material as she stared. Her lips were full and glistened like a wet ripened strawberry. Edible as they looked, that wasn't what drew me in. It was her eyes. They were green but almost yellow, catlike as they assessed me. A color I'd not ever seen, and I've dated a lot of women, stared into the eyes of many women as I shagged them into oblivion. Nothing in my past came close to these.

She stood, and I almost cursed the loss of seeing directly down her shirt to her perfect tits, until she took it up a notch and smiled. A genuine "how do you do, nice to meet you, I'm a good person who actually gives a shite about other people" kind of smile. It made me feel vulnerable and a kick off my game. One thing I found out being an attorney in New York was you didn't often meet a genuine person. She may be the one in the eight million that lived here. I endeavored to find out for sure.

"Hello, welcome to Jensen Construction. I'm Cami. Mr. Walker, right?" She held out her hand. I grasped it with both of mine, turned it over, and kissed her wrist. She gasped and tensed when my lips touched her.

"Aren't you just the most precious thing?" I placed one last kiss on her pale wrist. Her skin was so delicate I could see the lifeblood of her veins, the blue such a contrast to her white skin. Something carnal, animalistic in me twitched at the sight.

Cami tilted her head as I let her hand go. Her eyes narrowed. "I've never had anyone kiss my wrist before. Is that a cultural thing?" Such an innocent. I almost felt poorly for how much I wanted to dirty her up.

"No." My eyes took in every inch of her spectacular body from the tips of her four-inch heels to the top of her flowing locks. "One look at you, and I knew I needed to have my lips on you." Her mouth opened, and she bit her bottom full lip, sending a hot jolt of lust straight to my groin.

"Okay. Well then." She moved behind her desk, putting distance between us. She held one hand to her chest, her breathing heavier than when I'd come in. Smugly, I'd hoped it was me who made her heart beat faster. "Mr. Jensen isn't back from his appointment yet. Have a seat."

Instead of sitting in the chairs along the walls, clearly the waiting area, I leaned a hip against her desk. Her cat-eyes scanned my body. She wasn't running away. That was a good sign. Maybe she liked what she saw.

"Tell me something, Cami?"

"Yes, Mr. Walker?" Her voice was breathy like it was earlier on the phone. It tweaked my senses pleasurably. I could tell she was unnerved and I enjoyed it immensely.

"Nate."

"Excuse me?"

"Call me Nate. I want to hear my name come from those beautiful lips."

A rosy hue crept up her neck and pinked her cheeks. She was nervous yet still hadn't bolted. "Um, okay, Nate," she said, uncertainty lacing her words.

"Better." I grinned and she sat. I took that as an opportunity, walked around to the other side of her desk to invade her space further by sitting on the edge of her desk, close enough to touch her. The need to be next to her was ridiculous. It was as if an invisible tether pulled me toward her. "Now, tell me something that nobody knows about you."

"Huh?" Her russet-colored eyebrows furrowed. "Like what?"

"That's for you to decide. I find it's easier to get to know someone if you start with something that nobody knows." She looked down and bit her lip again, possibly to avoid eye contact. Either way I needed her gaze on me. If I couldn't have her whole body wrapped around me, I'd settle for the eyes.

"Eyes on me, Cami." With one finger, I tilted her chin to face me. She visibly trembled at my touch. Made me feel powerful. Driven to see it again, and often. "When you speak to me, I'd like to see your beautiful eyes. They're bewitching."

"You're making me nervous," she admitted.

"That was not my intent, love. I apologize." I leaned back but didn't leave the edge of her desk, still wanting to be near her. "Though I must admit, I'm intrigued by you. So, tell me something about yourself that nobody here"—I held my palms up and out to the side gesturing around the office—"knows about you?" Even though this was my game, and one of the ways I usually sucked a woman into my charm, I was wholly unprepared for her reply.

Cami worried her lip again, and then closed her eyes. "I used to be a gymnast."

I groaned and swiped my fingers through my hair a few times. "Are you trying to kill me?" Visions of her long, curvy body bending this way and that…naked…sweating. It was too much. I was hard as steel.

Her shocked expression told me she was not being coy or forward as I'd thought. She really was as sweet as I'd pegged her over the phone. "No. Why would you say that?"

"Because I'm trying really hard to keep my hands to myself, and when you tell me something like that…it's almost impossible."

CHAPTER TWO

"Mr. Walker…" I pushed back on the rolling chair. I needed distance from this man. In his presence, I didn't feel like myself. He put me in a jittery, skin-tingling place I wasn't used to.

"Nate."

I took a calming breath. "Nate. You're extremely forward."

His lips twitched into a slow grin, a panty-melting, lip-biting, nails digging into the tender flesh of my palm type grin.

"True. When I see something I want"—his light eyes scanned my shape, undressing me—"I take it."

"Excuse me." I stood quickly and moved farther away from the desk and him, needing the distance. Nate stayed put, calmly leaning against the wooden surface. The dark gray pinstriped suit was elegant, and fitted to perfection on his long frame. It hinted at a tight body beneath, fully concealed in the three-piece designer label. "You know, you've got a lot of nerve. You don't even know me." I clenched my hands into fists to prevent him from noticing them shaking, desperately trying not to let him see just how much he affected me.

Slowly, like an animal stalking his prey, he rounded the desk moving toward me. I took one step backward and then fought it, feeling ridiculous. It was broad daylight. He wasn't going to hurt me. Nate reached out and traced an index finger down the side of my cheek. Gooseflesh rose along my arms, and I closed my eyes.

"I want to know you better. Have dinner with me?"

For about ten seconds, I stared at his beautiful face. Dark hair swept back in a sexy style, though I could tell he'd spent time running his fingers through it. Lightly tanned skin, shaped eyebrows the color of coffee perfectly matched his thick head of hair, mustache, and goatee. His lips were full and pouty. I couldn't think of another term. He had a sculpted jaw, and his facial hair was trimmed intricately. It made me want to kiss the lips surrounded by that halo of dark hair. It also made me curious as to how it would feel to have that hair scrape along my neck as he kissed me or between my breasts…*my thighs.*

I shook my head, realizing I was daydreaming two feet from a beautiful male specimen who had asked me out on a date. A date. A real one.

"Why?" I asked, shocked that this striking man wanted to spend time with me. He smiled, prepared to answer. I stopped him with an arm out, palm up. The synapses in my brain connected, providing intelligent information previously muddled by the strong presence in front of me. "Doesn't matter." I shook my head. "No, sorry. I'm not able to have dinner with you. Thank you for asking."

"Tomorrow perhaps?" he continued in that sexy British accent.

It just wasn't possible. I shook my head once more. "I appreciate the gesture, Mr. Walker, but I'm very busy. Thanks anyway."

"I don't understand, love?" Nate put his hand on my

shoulder. The warmth of his palm seeped into my skin. I leaned into it for a second, once again taken with his nearness.

"You don't have to understand. It's just the way it is." I slid his hand off my shoulder, wishing it could be different. That I was different. My life…different.

Hank strode into the office a huge smile on his face. Each time he visited with the OB-GYN, he came back in the best mood.

"How's she doing?" I asked happily, needing to change the subject and avoid Nathaniel's advancement. Nate turned, and Hank grabbed the man's hand for a friendly shake.

"Perfect! Of course I was right on the dot about how much my baby has grown. Twenty-six weeks"—he held out his big palms in a circle—"and a nicely shaped head of lettuce. My baby girl is growing, heartbeat is extremely strong. Aspen is as happy as a clam."

"Why's that?" I laughed. Hearing about the doctor's visits from a man's perspective was entertaining. I didn't have that with Tanner's biological father and thoroughly enjoyed Hank's thoughts on the subject.

"Yes, mate, do tell," Nate added.

I was surprised Nate cared. He didn't seem the type to be interested in another man's growing family or the details along with it. He was confident, a bit overly so. A man used to getting what he wanted. He looked at me, and one brow rose in question. Just that motion was incredibly cool and sexy as hell.

Hank shrugged and smiled. "She didn't gain weight this round, so she said we're celebrating tonight!"

Both Nate and I laughed. His manly chuckle sent

shivers skittering along my spine to settle warmly at the sensitive dip at my lower back.

"Figure I'll take her to dinner and be sneaky about fattening 'er up a bit." He put his fingers to his lips in a shushing motion. "But don't tell her I said that. I want to make sure my baby girl and wife are getting everything they need. And *the book* said she was supposed to gain a couple pounds this time around."

"Mr. Jensen, it's fine if she doesn't gain. Pregnant women fluctuate. Look it up." Hank's eyes focused on me as he scratched his hand along his five o'clock shadow.

"You know I will. Now, Nate, partner. Thanks for coming. Cami, sweetie, do you have everything ready on that issue?" Nate's eyes squinted when Hank called me sweetie. It didn't bother me. From him, it was a term of endearment, not demeaning in the least. If I didn't understand where Hank's heart was, I'd correct him.

"Yes, sir, right here." I handed them both the packets. "Do you need me to take notes?"

"Naw, go on home. I'm heading out right after Nate and I here clear up this little issue with some bad product shipped to the Howzer job last week. Bastard's trying to get me to pay for poor product that crumpled under pressure."

I smiled and nodded, pulling together my things. Hank marched into his office, still mumbling about the company that sent busted materials on an important job. It had set the build back three weeks, which was why Nate was here in the first place. They needed to discuss suing them for lost dollars.

"Just a moment, mate," Nate said to Hank.

I pulled my things together quickly, grabbed my purse

out of the drawer, and threw the strap over my shoulder. I made it to the elevator before he caught up with me. I pressed the down button repeatedly, hoping the doors would open. No such luck.

"Hey, Cami, wait up." Nate closed a large hand around the crook of my elbow. I turned and looked into his blue eyes. He was so handsome. In different circumstances, I'd love to stare into those eyes all day. Nate licked his lips and tilted his head to the side. "Lunch, tomorrow. My treat."

"I can't..."

"You can, and you will. I'll be here at twelve sharp."

I shook my head no, but he backed up with that sexy grin plastered across his unbearably gorgeous face.

"Nate...really, it's not a good idea."

"It's a brilliant idea. Best I've had in a long time. Tomorrow, precious." He turned on his heel and opened the glass doors, firmly cutting off any protest I may have made.

Shoot!

What was I going to do?

I'd made it home in record time. Though I wouldn't be able to tell you how I got there, as my mind completely focused on a certain sexy British lawyer who was determined to steamroll me into getting his way. Jin, my roommate and best friend, was making stir-fry for dinner when I arrived. She wore a tiny coral-colored slip dress, so short it looked like a T-shirt on her petite frame. Just like our children, we were exact opposites. I'd regularly felt like an amazon at five-ten standing next to her barely five-foot-two and size-zero frame. Her olive skin tone was a lovely compliment to her dark eyes and thick, shiny black hair that just skimmed the edge of her ass. I always joked with her that she was a dead ringer for Lucy Liu's character in Charlie's Angels. She said she wished she looked like Cameron Diaz's character. Jin was Korean and completely obsessed with everything American.

Like me, Jin didn't really have any family. Together, we were our own little family. Jin watched the boys during the day so I could work for Jensen Construction, and then on the nights where I had my shift down at Gems. Jin introduced me to the gentleman's club back when we met. Now she worked four nights a week and was their most popular stripper. Men liked sexy little Asians, but I held my own and did okay. At least I thought so.

"Hi, honey, I'm home," I said while giving Jin's cheek a friendly kiss.

"Perfect timing. Dinner's just about done. Can you get the boys?" she asked while loading plates with steaming veggies and chicken over a bed of jasmine rice.

I made my way into the boys' bedroom. My little man was sitting on the floor busily pushing his race car along the race track imprinted into the room's area rug. His light brown hair fell in unruly waves around his head. Zachery, Jin's son, was lying next to him coloring. His long jet-black hair matched his mother's and touched the coloring book as he drew. Even though Jin loved American culture, she didn't cut his hair, letting it grow long and thick. I constantly teased her that he looked like a little girl when his hair was down, but she didn't care.

My heart filled with joy as I watched the boys play. The two were inseparable. If Tanner was in the kitchen, Zach was sure to be near. If Zach was in the room, Tanner would choose to play there. They just enjoyed each other's company, and for boys four and five years old respectively, you'd think they'd fight or have jealousy issues. These two didn't. It gave me hope that they'd be close friends throughout their lives, just like I was with Jin.

"How're my guys doing?"

"Mommy!" and "Auntie!" were screamed simultaneously as the boys clamored at each hip. I crouched down and hugged them both, relishing in their fresh, just-bathed scent.

"Zach, your mommy needs you to wash up and get to the table for dinner." He ran out of the room and to the bathroom.

I ruffled Tanner's hair, and he grinned. His father's big blue eyes shining happily as he put his hands around my neck. I cherished the small moments of time I had alone with my son each day. I lived for it. "Did you like work, Mommy?" he asked with his sweet little Mickey Mouse, high-pitched voice.

"Very much, baby. Thank you for asking. Did you have fun with Jin and Zach today?"

He nodded enthusiastically. "I built you something today!" He ran to his small dresser and opened his "treasure box." No one was allowed to go in it. I respected his need to have something that was his alone. Everyone needed boundaries, and I encouraged him. He put both his hands together almost as if he was praying. Then he came to me, put them right in front of my face, and slowly opened them.

In his tiny palms was a beaded bracelet. It was all mismatched colors of red, green, yellow, blue, and purple. "It's a rainbow for you to wear. So you can always have a rainbow. I built it for my mommy. Do you like it?"

I pushed back the tears from spilling and hugged him tight. "I love it so much. So much, Tan Man. Thank you."

"Will you wear it to work tomorrow?" His innocent eyes stared into mine. He bounced with excitement. I couldn't say no even though I didn't want to wear it to work. Someone could say something, notice it. His eyebrows knit together as he waited for my reply. "You don't like it?"

"Baby, I do. It's just that work is…" His lip trembled, and it broke me. "Of course I'll wear it to work." I slipped it on my wrist, and he looked at it happily. "Fits perfectly. My very own rainbow. I love it."

"I love you, Mommy."

"I'll always love you more, Tan Man. I always love you more."

★ ★ ★

For the first time in what seemed like years, I was looking forward to a date. Not just a quick meal and a shag. Today was an actual 'get to know you' type of outing. The last time I'd given the dating pool a shot was when I'd taken out business tycoon and billionaire Aspen Reynolds, now Aspen Jensen. I'd hounded her for a date, thinking I could bed the pretty blonde with little effort, and found that in the end, I was attracted to her cunning intellect, business mind, and genuine kindness. I couldn't add her as one of the many notches on my bedpost. No, she was a classy bird, and when I'd kissed her at the end of the evening, we both laughed. She had come to the same conclusion. We were never going to be more than friends. A love connection just wasn't there. And that was that.

Since Collier and I'd entered the States, I'd done

nothing but take a woman out with the sole purpose of taking her home for a quick fuck. It's been my routine for the past five years, and recently I realized I'm bloody tired of it. The more I spend time around the Jensens, and my brother and his girlfriend, London, along with new friends Dean and Oliver, the more I realized how completely alone I was.

Yesterday when I met the reticent receptionist, I hadn't planned on feeling an instant connection. It was as if the air that surrounded her was calm, cool, and inviting, like a tropical breeze on a deserted island. Being near her not only ramped up my libido to embarrassing proportions, but I felt a sense of rightness in her presence. My lifestyle had been nothing but hard and fast negotiations, quick settlements, and meeting client after client. It got worse when my brother and business partner, Collier, almost died a few months ago. In his absence, I'd had to take on the brunt of our caseload at Stone, Walker, & Associates. Collier was now back full-time in the office and happier than ever. He'd moved in his girlfriend, London Kelley, the sister to our client and friend Aspen Jensen. Collier being back gave me the extra time I needed to pursue my own interests. Right now, all I was focused on was a tall brown-haired beauty.

I left the office in a rush, ready to pick up Cami for our date. Hank Jensen's receptionist. Christ on a cross, the world was too small sometimes.

When I arrived, she wasn't at her desk. I glanced at the clock, and it read eleven fifty. I was early. And then I heard it. Her laughter. Cami had opened the door to Hank's office and was smiling widely. Her shoulders shook in laughter at what I could only surmise was Hank on the other side of the door. I was not prepared for how insanely beautiful she was as she stood tall and graceful against the doorjamb. Her skirt today was a couple inches shorter than yesterday and had a flirty ruffle at the bottom. It hugged her thighs in a sexy, yet professional, way. The blouse she wore was silk and slid along the curve of her breasts, giving me quite the side view. They were large, but it was obvious she tried to downplay them. I respected that about her.

"Thanks, Mr. Jensen. I'm going to take lunch in a few minutes. Did you need anything before I leave?" She still hadn't noticed me.

"Hank!" I heard my mate roar, clearly annoyed that she called him Mr. Jensen. I watched as she leaned her long frame against the door, presenting me her backside. She wore those sexy-as-sin stiletto shoes again. They were black and tall. My gaze slid from the tip of one spike along her dainty-looking ankle up her shapely calf, and then had to muffle a groan when that same leg came up and caressed the other one the way I wanted to. It was easy to imagine those long legs wrapped around my body, those shag-me spikes digging into the tender skin of my arse as I impaled her against the nearest wall.

My prick hardened painfully in my trousers. Feeling something for a woman I had just met was incredibly unusual. Not being able to control my body's impulses made me feel like a randy teenager. I couldn't quite wrap my head around what was different about her, but I was determined to find out.

Cami turned around and gasped, her gaze meeting mine. "You came?" Her tone held a sense of wonder.

I stood and tucked my hands into my pockets making

sure to give myself a bit of extra room in the groin. This one frightened easily, and I didn't want to scare the poor thing off by presenting her with a stiffy.

"I said I would." Her gaze scanned my form, taking in the dark suit I wore. She opened her mouth, and then closed it. A hand came up to her chest. I wondered if her heartbeat quickened because I affected her. I hoped so. "Are you ready to go?"

"Well, I really hadn't thought you would come." Cami looked away and down. "Sometimes men say things, but never follow through and I—"

"I'm not like those men, precious." Her gaze shot to mine as I moved to stand only a couple feet away. "I always follow through." I touched the strands of a loose lock of silky hair. She had it pulled back, and one stubborn lock that was shorter than the rest fell freely to dangle along her curved chin. I leaned really close, but not enough to touch her. She stiffened as I let my breath billow along her ear. Her scent was unusual. A mix of watermelon and baby lotion. Did she smell like that *everywhere?* Delicious.

I took a step forward letting the heat of my body encroach on her space. She sighed and tilted her head, offering the long white column of her neck. It would be so easy to take that offering. Instead, I moved slowly as to not startle her, and leaned my cheek against hers. "I follow through in all things. I never leave a woman wanting," I whispered, dragging my cheek against hers in the lightest of caresses.

As I pulled away, I noticed her eyes were closed. She took a breath and licked her lips. I had to bite mine to stifle the urge to steal a taste of her berry-red mouth.

"Shall we?" I asked, tucking her hand into the crook of my arm.

She looked reticent, but instead of pushing back, she lifted her shoulders and rounded them back letting out a long breath. "Let me just grab my purse."

I tugged her toward the exit. "You won't need it."

She stopped. "I have to have my phone on me at all times just in case…" She looked wildly behind us as if scoping out her escape.

"In case of what, precious? You have to call for help?" With one quick turn of my hips, I pressed her form against the glass with the force of my body alone. She moaned, and her eyes widened when I centered my erection against her belly. I wanted her to know exactly what she was doing to me. I set both hands on either side of her head, caging her like a wild animal. "I assure you. These hands are used only for pleasure." I showed them to her and then slid one palm from the line of her chin down her neck to settle at the hollow where neck and shoulder connected. I wanted to peel back the layers of her shirt, sink my teeth into her pale skin, and mark her there.

"I just… I'd feel more comfortable having my purse and phone." She sounded breathy and strained.

I caressed the side of her face. She held my gaze then looked away. Direct eye contact made her uncomfortable. "Eyes, Cami." Those catlike orbs focused on me. "Get your purse. I'm famished." Taking a couple steps back, she scurried around me and pulled a tiny purse from her desk drawer. It couldn't possibly have held more than a phone and wallet. I was used to women who carried around a duffle bag full of God only knew what.

"Ready?" I asked with a grin.

Again, she looked down and walked toward me. When she reached my side, I used one finger to tip her chin up. It irked me that she felt compelled to look down. "You're so beautiful. I feel remiss in not saying so earlier." A lovely blush stole across her face, and a small smile split her red lips.

"Thank you."

I cupped the side of her neck and petted her pretty cheek. "I think I'll tell you every day that you're beautiful just so I can see that blush paint your pale skin." She took a deep breath and closed her eyes.

"Let's go, precious."

CHAPTER THREE

We walked silently side by side down the long city block. I was nervous going out to lunch with a man like Nate. Truth be told, any man would scare me. It had been so long. As if he sensed my hesitance and insecurity, his hand grasped mine. He tilted his head to the side and watched me. Maybe to see if I'd pull away? I wouldn't. Couldn't. It was the single connection I needed to feel calm and more at peace with going on my first date in…well, my first date ever.

I looked at the busy patrons as we walked hand-in-hand down the city block toward The Place. Nate's warm palm against mine felt nice, right somehow, and the silence surrounding us completely comfortable. Neither of us felt the need to fill the space with inane conversation. When he mentioned he was taking me to one of the hottest eateries in town, I had to control my desire to squeal. The Place, as it was simply named, was a hip, trendy restaurant that masqueraded as affordable but was really anything but. I'd never been able to afford it, and I didn't think the general population could either. It was where the elite of New York City enjoyed lunch.

Once, Hank sent me to the restaurant to pick up lunch for him and his wife. The workers fawned all over the fact I was picking up lunch for *the* Aspen Reynolds. Of course, I knew her as Mrs. Jensen by then. The chatty steward made a point to gush on and on about how lovely she was. I agreed with him, of course. Hank's wife was insanely beautiful and undeniably smart. None of that mattered to me. When she introduced herself as Hank's fiancée back when I started work at Jensen Construction, she was kind and down to earth. Nothing like the obscenely rich socialite people claimed her to be in those horrid magazines.

It was humbling to know that even when you had more money than could possibly be spent, you still were compelled to wear a mask. Aspen Reynolds—not Jensen—was all business, powerful, able to cut you down to size if you so much as crossed her. I knew Aspen Jensen, the polite, loving, intelligent wife of my equally charming and down-to-earth boss, Hank Jensen. People were just people. We all had our problems and roles we were expected to play in life. I liked Aspen even more when I realized that she shared her true self with me. She didn't feel compelled to put on an act. Unfortunately, I wish could offer the same in return. There was a side to my life I hid and wasn't planning on revealing. Ever.

Nate led me to a seat near an open window. This section of the restaurant had an indoor-outdoor feel. Technically we sat inside, but our table butted up against a huge window that opened out onto a garden where others were happily enjoying their meal. The sun's rays sprinkled through the trees, and the sounds of the city were drowned out by the piped in music. It felt incredibly serene for the busy lunch hour.

"This okay, love?" Nate asked, and helped push my chair in.

"It's wonderful, thank you."

When the waiter arrived, Nate ordered water and

something he called a "charcuterie" plate as he handed the waiter the menus we hadn't opened. I was disappointed for a moment. I was looking forward to poring over the menu until he added, "I wanted to get right down to getting to know you." It was really sweet and fit the alpha male side he'd presented yesterday and today.

"There really isn't much to know." I shrugged and placed my hands demurely in my lap. I'd never been to such an expensive place. I wanted desperately to fit in. Sometimes I thought I failed miserably. My clothes were secondhand, and my dwindling pitiful bank account could attest to my lack of success.

"Start at the beginning." His blue eyes sparkled. I found it hard to look away. "Tell me about your name. Where did Cami come from? It's rather uncommon. Did your mum and dad have a reason for it?"

"I don't know." His eyebrows knit together. Trying to change the subject of why I didn't know where my own name originated from, I went another direction. "It's actually short for Camille. That's my birth name."

"Camille is lovely. I rather like Camille. Unique. Just like the woman." Nate winked, and I felt myself flush with heat.

"Thank you."

"And your mum and dad? Where are they now? Here in the city?" he asked with a twinkle in his lovely green-blue eyes. I loved how he used the word "mum" instead of "mom," but really didn't want to get into the specifics of the fact I didn't have one.

Avoiding my past was going to be harder than I thought. Not that there was anything of great interest or importance.

I was a nobody. He'd figure that out and move on to the next hot ticket. Which would be better for me. Easier. I wasn't the kind of girl you took home to your family.

"I don't know my parents. I grew up in foster care. I was placed in one home or another as far back as I can remember."

"Does that mean you don't have any siblings?" His tone was kind and made me want to share with him.

I shrugged. "I guess it's possible. Sometimes I lie awake at night and think about the fact that I may not be alone. I could have a brother or sister somewhere." He smiled, and put his chin into his palm while leaning against the table.

"Siblings aren't all they're cracked up to be, you know?" His smile showed an adorable dimple on one cheek almost hidden by the dark swath of hair from his goatee and mustache. My heart sped up as I studied his face. Men like him graced the covers of magazines and dated perfect model types whose biggest worry was whether their handbag matched their outfit. I was not that girl. Yet, here he sat at a table with me. *For how long?* Once he knew about Tanner and about my other job, he'd be gone as fast as my first love. Tyler—the man who screwed me over in more ways than one.

"You sound like you speak from experience."

He nodded. "I do. You've met my brother, Collier Stone."

"That's right! The little mix-up." I looked down at my hands, regretting the accusatory way I'd spoken to him yesterday.

Nate's finger tipped my chin up. "Eyes, precious. I like to watch your eye color change as I speak to you. It's mesmerizing." Once more, my face heated. "You're so lovely when you blush," he whispered over the table.

The waiter took that moment to return with a variety of nibbles that ended up being an array of meats, cheese, and fruit. "I hope my choice is okay," Nate said. There was enough to feed an army but in dainty little plates with multicolored dips that I assumed were mustard or honey. "Shall I explain them to you?" Nate had obviously ordered this before.

I shook my head and smiled at him. "I like surprises. There are so few in life." I picked up a slice of salami, added a square of white cheese, dipped it lightly into the first saucer, and then took a bite. Sharp cheese coupled with the tang of the mustard and salt from the meat mingled with each other to provide a scrumptious pairing. I licked my fingers and nodded. "You should try that combination. Here, let me make you one." I danced in my seat a bit, excited at finding a good mix on my first try.

As I put the trio together, it dawned on me that Nate wasn't speaking. I looked up and found him watching me intently. His eyes blazed with a heat so hot I could almost feel it across the table. "What?" I asked, sounding more breathy than I intended. The man just did something to me.

"I like watching you. You're incredibly beautiful, Camille." He said my name in a way I'd never heard before—soft, sensual, and filled with desire. I took a deep breath, licked my lips, and then held out the offering to him. Instead of taking it, he leaned forward and took the morsel into his mouth letting his lips graze the tips of my fingers. The bolt that rippled through me at that miniscule touch shifted up my arm spreading through every limb, awakening something that I thought was long gone. "You were right. Meat, cheese, and you…bloody delicious."

My skin burned. "So, tell me more about your brother?"

"Brother and sisters," he corrected and my eyes widened. Wow. That's a lot of family. "One half-brother, Collier, who you've met." I nodded, remembering keenly the blond godlike man that handled a lot of our legal needs. Collier Stone was another stunning man. Long, lean, with a perfect structure. He had blond layered hair, chocolate-brown eyes, and was deeply in love with Aspen's sister, London Kelley. "My sisters are Emma and Ella. Emma works for Collier and me as the office administrator. Ella is married and lives back home in London with her husband and son."

"You must miss her terribly. I know if I had a sibling, I'd want to be near them always."

"Would you?"

I nodded emphatically. "Of course. I find that people with large families take those people for granted. I don't have any family to speak of except my s—" I stopped instantly, realizing my mistake.

"Except your what?"

"Um, my roommate, Jin."

"Tell me about this roommate Jin. What does he do?" Nate's shoulders tightened and chest seemed to broaden.

"Jin is a she, and she's my best friend." Nate visibly relaxed. "She does this and that. Anyway, tell me about why you came to the States."

Nate slowly took a bite of a pear and leaned back. His suit coat flared out, his dress shirt stretched across his body. I could just barely see the ridges of taut muscles through the fine fabric, but it was enough to spark my libido. With great effort, I bit back a groan that bubbled up. I wished I could see more of his body. His gaze shot to mine catching me looking my fill. Immediately, I looked down and away.

"Eyes." His demand had me lifting my gaze instantly. "Don't ever be embarrassed about looking at me, Camille. I enjoy your eyes on me. Especially if you like what you see." He grinned. "Do you, Camille?" His voice was low, gravely, as if he gargled with a box of rocks. "Do you like what you see?" he asked boldly.

I was transfixed. His gaze, the way he looked at me literally held me captive. Taking what he wanted, he owned my vision. I nodded and then whispered, "Yes. What I can see of it."

His hand held mine over the table. He turned it over and brushed his thumb across the silky skin at my wrist sending shivers of excitement in every direction. "Would you like to see more of it?"

I closed my eyes and imagined him naked, hovering over me, so close to entering me…the loneliness in my life disappearing. A moist sensation tickled my palm. When I opened my eyes again, his lips pressed into the center of my hand. He kissed along the soft patch of skin where my thumb and hand met and bit down. A hot poker of lust speared though my arm down my chest to settle hotly between my legs.

With no concern for who was around or what we were doing in the middle of a busy restaurant, he licked my wrist. I couldn't help the moan that slipped out. He looked up, eyelids at half-mast. Clearly he was as taken with me as I him. Slowly, without a care in the world, he trailed his warm tongue along the sensitive skin from my wrist to the inside of my elbow where he paid extra attention, kissing me there in small baby-sized pecks of skin.

A daze. There was no other word to describe the floating, pleasurable place he put me in. And as quickly as the feeling of lust and deep desire entered my consciousness, it was gone the moment his lips left my skin.

"What's wrong?" Confused, I sat up more fully.

"Nothing, precious. I just don't want to share your desire with anyone else. That look on your face." He groaned and adjusted his pants. "I plan to be the only man to see you let go." His long fingers twirled around, making a gesture at the busy restaurant. As I looked, a few patrons' eyes quickly shifted away. Apparently we'd given quite the show.

"Oh my God, what am I doing?" My hands flew to my face as the realization hit me at how easily he put me into a sensually induced coma, right in the middle of a packed eatery.

★ ★ ★

Christ! Cami was so responsive. Not Cami… *Camille*. The name rolled off my tongue like a purr. When I put my lips and tongue to her skin, her entire body relaxed. The rigidity left her shoulders, her back arched as she flowed toward my touch. It was unexpected bliss, knowing the effect I had on the lovely brunette. Those catlike eyes of hers shone bright green with the deepest flecks of yellow-gold when desire overtook her. I wanted to see that look in her eyes all the time, caress the need prickling in the air around her body, and sate it.

Women never had a strong effect on my senses. Usually, I saw an attractive bird, went after her, and bedded her.

Simple as that. Standard laws of attraction. Man sees pretty girl, man's body reacts to pretty girl, man wants to shag pretty girl.

With Camille, I wanted more. Much more. A primal urge to own every piece of her was strong. So strong that my cock was at full mast just having tasted the satiny skin of her inner arm. That fruity smell, along with hints of baby lotion, was strongest at the sensitive crook of her elbow. A carnivorous hunger came over me when I reached that spot and took in her lovely fragrance. Every fiber of my being wanted to mark her. Sink my teeth and suck that delicate skin until a purple bruise bloomed in all its glory, indicating my ownership. The need to have any man within a twenty-mile radius know this woman was unavailable grew stronger the more I stared at my precious Camille.

I pulled her pale hands away from her face. "Camille, relax. You're with me. Don't worry what others think. I could give a rat's arse what any stranger thinks." She peeked those catlike eyes through her fingers before she released them in her lap. "Eat, my dear. Food's getting cold."

Her eyebrows narrowed. "It's already cold," she said.

I laughed out loud. "Bollocks, we waited too long!" She bestowed one of those heart-melting smiles on me. The woman was a knockout but paid no mind to it, swaying the odds of making her mine to tip positively in my favor. "So, how was it growing up in the foster system?"

The smile left her lips. She wiped her mouth with her napkin, and set down the bite of fruit she'd been nibbling on. Her face turned pensive, and her posture slumped. "That bad?"

"You really want to know?" The way she asked the

question, her voice inflecting uncertainty, jangled my nerves. What had been done to her?

"I wouldn't have asked, love, if I didn't want to know." She took a deep breath and sipped her water. Her lips pinched tight, and one hand locked into a fist, the knuckles turning bright white. I put my hand over hers to soothe it until she released the lock. I laced our fingers together and pressed our palms against one another. Electricity. The moment our palms touched, electricity zipped through every nerve ending.

"I'd been in the system as long as I could remember. There's no information about where I came from, who my parents were, or what happened to them. Though, I've never been in the financial position to take much time or effort to look." Something about the way she said "financial situation" spoke to me. A receptionist working in New York City couldn't make enough to live on, even with a roommate. It was a base position, entry level. I'm sure Hank paid her appropriately, but in a city this large, she had to be struggling.

"Continue," I urged. Her green eyes swirled with sadness as she sighed.

"Well, some of the places were okay, especially when I was little. I learned really quickly to do as I was told, when I was told to do it, and move as quietly as possible." I didn't like where she was going. "I had one home that was really good to me, but my foster mother lost her dad and ended up having to move her mother in to take care of her. The room she got was mine, so I was sent away. I really miss them. I was nine. That was the best year of my life." She looked out the window a beat, lost in her memories.

The best year of her life was when she was nine years old? She had to be in her early twenties which meant her best year was over a decade ago. Sadness for her pooled in my heart making me want to pull her into a tight hug, protect her from all the negative things that could harm her.

I took a deep breath to cage my declining mood. "What about your teen years?"

She pulled her hand away and crossed her arms over her chest. Those beautiful green eyes turned dark, smoky with anger.

"I was in a few homes during those years. I went to three different high schools. I had to keep moving around."

"Why so often?" When she looked at me, I was floored by the heartache I saw in her features. A huge wall lifted in front of her. I clasped both of her hands across the table. "Camille, tell me. Let me in."

Her eyebrow rose in defiance. "Once the schools figured out I was being mistreated by the foster parent, social services would come in and pull me from the home. I'd get evaluated for abuse and moved to the next home. This happened three times in a row."

"Christ, Camille. What type of abuse? They didn't..." I couldn't even stomach saying it. Thinking it alone was like a poison to my soul bringing a violent emotion I wasn't prepared for. A hatred so thick and strong it ran through my veins and filled them with the need to fight. A powerful sense to maim and harm anyone at the mere suggestion that someone could hurt this woman consumed my current thoughts.

"No. I wasn't sexually abused. Not really. One of the teenage boys tried to get at me once, but one of the other foster kids pulled him off me. I got a really bad beating that night by the foster mom for 'lying' about her son touching me. She pulled down my pants and whooped me with a belt in front of her son. She didn't realize he was stroking himself while she did it."

"Fucking cocksucking wankers…"

She smiled and squeezed my hands. "Let's not talk about this. My childhood wasn't the best, but I survived. I'm alive, and I'd rather spend my time enjoying lunch with you than talking about the past. There's no sense in hashing out something that won't ever change." For such a young woman, she was incredibly wise. "How about you tell me something about yourself. What do you love?"

"Aside from my work and my family?"

"Of course, silly. Work is something you do for a living. Family is something you're born loving. What else are you passionate about?"

I steepled my fingers and watched her eat. Camille was incredible. She just shared something unbelievably private and painful, yet she was not dwelling on it. "I love to swim. I try to swim just about every night."

The harshness in her features loosened up with the change in conversation. "Really? Where? Like at a gym?"

Damn, she was sweet. So sweet I wanted to take a bite out of her. "No, there's a pool in my building."

"What do you like about it?"

"The freedom, the sense of balance I get after I've pushed my body to the limit doing laps. Floating on the surface after is a very calming experience. You? What do you do when you're not at work?"

Her eyes went wide, and she lost the grip of her water

glass. It crashed down to the table. She barely caught it after spilling water across her lap. She jumped back, but a salad plate-sized wet circle bloomed across her skirt. I threw my napkin on her lap and helped to pat it dry. Once I'd sopped up most the water, I looked up into her eyes.

"Thank you," she whispered, her lips a breath away from mine. I knew in that moment I could kiss her, and she'd allow it. Welcome it even. Instead, I backed away and took the gentleman's route. There's was plenty of time for that. Now was for wooing.

"So, you were going to tell me what you do outside of work." My voice was husky and deep when I reiterated my question. Again her body stiffened. She didn't like sharing information about her daily life. Somehow, I think she shared the information about her past to avoid speaking about her present.

She swept that errant lock of deep brown hair back around her ear. "I'm taking online classes."

That surprised me. "Really, like Uni classes?"

"Uni?" she asked.

I laughed. "University. Sorry, love."

"No, it's fine. I like your accent. It's…" She looked down and away.

"Eyes, Camille." She lifted those beautiful greens back up, and they were now a mossy green, darker around the edges. "It's what?"

"It's sexy," she whispered so quietly I almost didn't hear her.

"You think so?" I cocked a brow for effect, loving that she found something about me attractive.

"Yeah." She nodded, and that pretty pale skin of hers

turned a rosy pink.

"I'm glad." I grinned, and she blushed. So lovely. "What are you studying?"

She shook her head as if clearing her thoughts. I *so* had the bird in the palm of my hand. I preferred to have her arse in my hand, though. She reacted to me. Responded beautifully. I could tell she tried not to, but it was useless. There was a connection between us, and I'd be damned if I was going to let her deny it.

"I'm taking courses to get my bachelor's degree so I can teach."

That was it. She was too good to be true. A sodding teacher? Perfection and innocence wrapped in a gorgeous package. Everything I should never be allowed to have but desperately wanted. "Such a noble profession. Teaching our youth. What grade level?"

It was enchanting, seeing her eyes light up. "Grammar school. Anything between first and sixth grade would be ideal. I think I do really well with the little ones."

"I'll bet you do." I clasped her other hand and noticed the multicolored beaded bracelet. "What little love made this adornment?" I touched a few of the colored beads. She didn't say anything. When I looked up she seemed frightened. Her face was devoid of color. I looked around the restaurant. Nothing seemed out of order. "What's the matter? Did something scare you?"

"Uh, no, I think we need to go. I need to get back to work." She pulled her hands from mine and stood. "I'm going to use the restroom if you don't mind."

"Certainly."

Camille rushed to the loo as if there were angry dogs

nipping at her heels. What happened? We'd certainly gone over some rather unsavory parts of her past, but she seemed fine after that. It wasn't until I mentioned the bracelet that she became skittish. For heaven's sake, why?

After paying the bill, I met her in the foyer. I clasped her around the hip and led her through the door. Instead of letting go, I kept my hand there. It was refreshing walking with a woman who was so tall. In her heels, she was close to six foot, nearing my six-foot-three height. Our strides synced, and there wasn't any awkward fumbling or bumping into each other. It just worked.

When we reached the lift at the AIR Bright building, I could tell whatever bothered her had dissipated. Her steps had been lighter on the latter half of our walk. I thanked God and the Queen Mum for the fact that the lift was empty as we stepped on. The second the doors closed, I backed her against the wall. She gasped and clung to my shoulders.

"What are you doing?" Her eyes were wild, her breath instantly labored.

"This," I said as I slanted my lips over hers. The kiss was soft yet hard at the same time. Her mouth molded to mine. The fingers at my shoulders tightened as I put my hand on her waist, tugging her closer. I brought my other hand to her neck and tilted her head exactly where I wanted it. I teased the seam of her lips with my tongue. She opened, and I dived in. Soft and gentle was no longer an option. Once I tasted the crisp perfection of her mouth, I wanted to drown in it and smother her goodness over my entire body. I pushed against her, sealing her to my form as I plunged into the heaven of her kiss. For a timid thing, she kissed like a vixen, gripping my back and holding me firm.

One of her hands plunged into my hair, making me wild for her. I thrust my erection against her softness, and she moaned loudly. I pulled away, needing air but not wanting to leave the perfection of her mouth. We breathed in each other's air as our foreheads rested against the other. Thoughts, feelings, needs filled the air in the tiny space.

Ding!

The sliding doors opened, signaling our arrival. Camille straightened immediately and pushed on my chest. Instead of backing up, I brought her with me.

"You're not getting away so quickly. Have dinner with me?"

"I can't." She pushed around me. "I have to go to work. Thank you for lunch."

"This isn't over," I said, holding the doors of the lift open.

"No?" Her hand was over her lips where my mouth had just been.

"This was only the beginning, precious. I'll be in touch." With that promise, I let the doors close and pressed the button to the lobby. Looks like I'd be chasing sweet Camille a bit more. It had been a long time since I had been given a solid challenge. Camille was worth it.

CHAPTER FOUR

The apartment was quiet while I prepared for work. It wasn't easy working on a Thursday night when you had to work for Jensen Construction bright and early Friday morning. Regardless of how little sleep I got, it's what I had to do to pay my portion of the bills. I wasn't eligible for medical coverage or a raise until I'd been at Jensen Construction for six months. At least I only had to work at Gems two nights a week, unless I was called for special bookings.

Hadn't had one of those in a while. Which was heaven and hell wrapped into one solid yin and yang ball of frustration. Hell because I didn't like to be stuck in one private room dancing for only a small group men. Something about it felt more tawdry and elicit. Dirty even. The men's attention focused solely on me, my nakedness. What they imagined doing to me made me more uncomfortable than dancing on stage in front of a large crowd. Unfortunately, those private room bookings came with a much larger payout. The girls that worked the private rooms received thirty percent of the fee and anything you earned by way of tips. Plus, there was a bodyguard available at the ready to take care of any overzealous patrons—which was needed. Often. I guess heaven wasn't perfect either, but the payout sure did help pay the rent.

I slid up the thigh highs and clipped the emerald-green garters to the black nylons. Jin's entrance couldn't have been timed better.

"Can you tighten the corset?" I asked as she set down her book. *Gone With the Wind*. I rolled my eyes. "Hopeless romantic," I said and then lost the words as she squeezed the corset, cutting off all breath. "Jesus, that's tight."

"But looks amazing." Her eyes were as dark as night when they skimmed over my form. "Why the green and black?"

"St. Patrick's day. Apparently it's 'Luck of the Irish' night." I grinned and propped the tiny little Leprechaun hat onto my head and pinned it to the hair I piled at the crown, allowing perfect curlicues to slip out strategically.

"Well, you look beautiful. Then again, 'Justice' always is the highlight of Gems."

I rolled my eyes at her use of my stage name. I chose Justice because it was an oxymoron. There wasn't any justice in having to strip for money.

"Says the perfect size…oh wait, what's that? Oh yeah, the perfect size zero!" I grinned as she pinched my hip. I swatted at her hands.

"So, are you going to tell me about him yet?" Jin leaned back onto her bed, her elbows holding her up. Her long black hair spread like a curtain of glossy ribbon across her pastel sheets.

"Who?"

"The 'who' you went out to lunch with the other day."

"What? How did you know?" I stared at her smiling face through the mirror.

"I'm psychic. Duh!" She rolled her eyes and sat up, crossing her legs. I narrowed my gaze and waited a moment. "Fine. I called to see if you were available at lunch. Rosie, that other office chick, said you had a lunch date."

Damn Rosie. She was such a busybody. I needed to be careful around her if I was going to keep my private life private. Sighing deeply, I knew I wasn't going to get out of here until I spilled something about my date to Jin. Besides, I wanted to talk about it. Needed to. The thoughts of Nate, of his kiss, burned and sizzled throughout my day, making it almost impossible to concentrate on work.

"His name is Nate. He's a lawyer. British."

"And…" she pressed. I layered on another pound of mascara. "Well, is he hot?"

I slumped down on my bed across from hers and clasped my heated cheeks. "So hot, Jin. I've never met anyone like him. He's incredibly sexy. He's forceful and confident." I looked into space, remembering the way he pressed me into the elevator wall and kissed me like I was the only woman in the world he wanted to kiss…ever.

"Forceful?" Jin's eyes narrowed into points. "What do you mean by that?"

"No, no. Don't get the wrong impression. He's just… I don't know. He fills the space in a room. Larger than life. His presence demands attention."

Jin's eyes sparkled and a coy grin slid across her lips. "You have a crush on this guy? I'll be damned. I didn't think it would ever happen!"

"Oh, shut up! I do not have a crush. He's just a hot guy that I'm going to see at work sometimes. Just because he took me to lunch and kissed me once doesn't really—"

"He kissed you!" Jin jumped up and landed like an elephant on my tiny bed, making us both bounce. Though certain parts of me bounced more than others and almost bounced right out of the top of the tight corset. "Oh my God, you have to tell me everything. How did it happen? When? Where?"

I took a deep breath and then told Jin everything that we discussed at lunch including the freak-out when he mentioned Tanner's bracelet.

"Why did you freak? Does he not like kids?"

"I don't know. It never came up."

"Wait a minute. You told him about Tan Man, right?"

I shook my head, shame coating my mood.

"Cam…" her tone warned. "You can't hide a child from a man you're interested in."

I stood quickly, and fiddled with my hair. "I don't know what's between us. I'm not hiding anything." Big. Fat. Lie. Probably one of the first I had ever told my best friend. "I will tell him. *If* we see each other again. Which we probably won't."

Jin's lips pinched together, and she pointed a finger at me. "Did he ask you out again or say he wanted to see you again?"

I shrugged and grabbed my purse. "I have to go."

"He did!" She stood and looked me in the eye.

"He might have asked me to dinner, which I declined. Then he said that things were not over between us." Jin whooped and jumped into the air.

"I knew it. You're dating a lawyer. What are the odds of *that*?"

Yeah, great. Jin was alluding to the fact that my ex was a rich lawyer, too. "I doubt I'll see him again."

"You are so clueless about men, Cam. They don't take you to lunch, kiss you up against the wall in an elevator at work, and then ask you out and all of a sudden dissolve into thin air. You'll be hearing from him. Of this I'm certain." She clucked her tongue and snapped her fingers.

"I'm not sure. I hope you're right. There's something about him, Jin. Something that draws me. It's like I want to be closer to him."

Jin swung her hips and tipped her head. "Yeah, and it's called lust, girlie. Pretty soon, sweet Cami's five-year dry spell is going to end. Girl, you're finally going to get laid!" She smacked me on the ass and helped me shuffle toward the door on my four-inch stiletto heels.

On the way to Gems, I started to worry. Jin might be right. If I continued to see Nate, we'd likely end up in the bedroom but what then? I hadn't been with a man in five long years. Even then I didn't know what the hell I was doing. I took my cues from Tyler. Not once did I so much as orgasm when we had sex. At least I didn't recall ever having one. Based on the information I had read, seen in movies, and talked over with Jin, I was pretty certain I'd remember an all-over euphoria that lasted a few seconds to long minutes. Above and on top of that, I surely had never had multiples of them. Maybe I couldn't orgasm when a man touched me?

The more I thought about Nate and becoming physical with him, the more frightened I was. Thoughts of Tyler years ago flashed across my memory.

"No, Cami! You're doing it wrong. Don't bite my fucking dick…suck it! Put your lips around the head and suck." I tried my best, frantically taking his cock into my mouth and pretending it was an ice-cream cone, but it wasn't working. Apparently, I did

everything wrong. Tears formed in my eyes.

"Oh Christ, Cami. Don't cry. Just, hold your mouth open."
I did what he said. "Now close it around my dick." I followed his
direction. "Now suck."

He gripped his hand into my hair so tightly pain shot down
my spine, but I didn't move my mouth. "That's it. Now I'm just
going to fuck your mouth, and you're going to take it. Got it?" I
nodded as he plunged deep into my mouth. The muscles around the
back of my throat constricted, and tears formed and then slid down
the sides of my cheek to drip off my chin.

I didn't care. Even if I had to gag and choke, I was determined
not to stop. To please him, make my man happy, I could suffer
through anything.

He fucked my throat so hard that time, I couldn't speak
the next day. Even though I'd given it my all, Tyler wasn't
happy. He never was. From then on out, he'd tell me to
open my mouth, hold onto his pant leg, and wait while
he shoved his cock into me. Usually, he'd pull out right
at the end and blast his cum all over my face and tell me
how perfect I looked covered in his spunk. The memory
sent chills through my body, and I clasped the heavy coat
closer to my scantily clad form. Once the cab I splurged on
dropped me at Gems, I hustled in.

Gems was a gentleman's club, not one of those seedy
strip bars. The women were all beautiful and healthy. The
owners tested for drugs and alcohol use during shifts to
ensure their dancers weren't drunk. Gems wanted to be
known for being a high-class establishment. The employees,
especially the dancers, were not allowed to drink, smoke,
take drugs, or even eat on the premises. They didn't want

their girls drunk, sloppy, or high as a kite while entertaining extremely rich businessmen. You had to have some serious cash to be a member of Gems.

The place was actually quite beautiful. The stage was set in a perfect square with a riser that brought each woman up from the floor. There were different props, pulleys, and hanging mechanisms a dancer could use. I stuck with the standard pole routines. Prior to being hired years ago, I was a talented gymnast, so the transition to being flexible on an upright pole instead of a balance beam, bars, or a vault was relatively easy. Didn't take long for Jin to teach me the standard moves and for me to expand on them. The main floor, where I typically danced, served as the normal strip show. Men gathered around the stage, and women danced for tips and a little more than minimum wage.

I was on in five minutes. Rushing through the catacomb of dark hallways under the first floor, I threw my stuff into my locker and checked my image in the mirror. After pinching my cheeks and glossing my lips one more time, I turned to head on stage.

"Good luck out there, Justice," one of the girls said as we traded places on the stairs of the main stage. She'd just left her routine and was clutching her clothing in one hand. She had cat ears and a bow tie on but nothing else. I had a robe I left at the edge of the stage. I put it on right after performances. Some strippers were modest when not on stage. I was one of them.

"Thanks, Kitty!" I waved and then made my way onto the dark stage. Tiny pinpricks of light in the glossy black stage led the way to the pole.

"Luck of the Irish, my ass," I mumbled as I positioned

said ass with my cheeks pressed up against the pole. As the lights rose, so did my arms. I clasped the metal bar over my head, arched my back to delectably display my corseted breasts as the light went up. Catcalls and male howls filled the air around me.

"Justice! Justice!" Several patrons howled my stage name as they caught a glimpse of my body. Smoke swirled at my feet, and I used the strength of one arm to lean out, grasped the pole by the hand, and did a perfect spin. Brilliant swirls of colored lights gleamed in my peripheral in a burst of rainbow delight. Midair, I swung my legs up, gripped the pole with my thighs, and let my entire body dangle upside down prettily against the pole. My arms came out and I held myself upside down.

Delicately, I trailed down the pole and then, with a flick of the wrists and thighs, swung back around. All the blood rushed from my head to blur the patrons. That's the way I liked it. No faces. No judgment. I preferred when the lights were so bright I couldn't see how many there were, who was watching, or what they were doing to themselves. I just did my routine with as much gusto as I could muster and somehow it worked. Night after night, I earned great tips and smacks on the ass from the owners.

Toward the end of my routine, I slid the zip slowly down the bodice of my corset and briefly caught the gaze of a patron just off to the right. He seemed familiar, but it was too dark to tell. The DJ played the music that led up to the big reveal. "Looks like we've caught the leprechaun folks, now let's enjoy that gold at the end of the rainbow." His smarmy words screeched loudly over the big speakers. I held my breath. The cigar stench was thick in the air. It was a miracle I didn't vomit all over the stage.

I knew what these men saw when they looked at me. Nothing but a pretty package of flesh to fantasize about. I hated that this was my life but pressed those thoughts deep down so I could get through the night. Realizing Tanner could one day find out what I'd done to support us forced huge armfuls of guilt pouring down my throat, clogging my chest. The men roared in excitement as I zipped the corset all the way down, holding the ends together to build the anticipation a bit longer.

"Justice, baby. Don't be shy. Show the men those gold coins," the DJ spoke. There was a man standing just out of sight at the corner of the stage, his face in shadow. I opened the corset and revealed my size D breasts to the crowd. I had pasted gold coins over the pink tips of my nipples. The man in shadow moved closer, just his face now outside the light as I cupped the large globes offering them to him, swaying my hips along with the music. He held out what looked like a hundred-dollar bill but could easily have been a one. From the looks of his crisp dark suit, I knew he had money to burn. I sauntered over, giving all the men around the stage a good show. Bills floated to the stage like raindrops. When I got close enough for the man to put the hundred in my G-string, his face entered the light, and my world imploded.

Tyler.

★ ★ ★

Every speck of my skin tingled as swirls of cool water sluiced along my body. The movement soothed me, sliding along my back, ribs, and thighs, down to my toes. Every stroke pushed me closer to my goal. Once I reached the other side,

I sank, flipped like a fish, and pressed hard off the plaster wall, rocketing through the shallow end. Nothing gave me such peace, serenity, and connection with my inner self like swimming did. Today I needed it.

Thoughts of a tall, curvy brunette with a jaded upbringing kept spilling into my head, convoluting my thought processes as I tried to defend my client this afternoon. Thank God my brother, Collier, had been there to back me up. He stepped right in like the gentleman he was. Fucking wanker. Now I owed him one.

Thinking back to lunch, I remembered how green Camille's eyes became when she spoke of becoming a teacher. She must love children to want a job where you were surrounded by twenty or thirty of the little rug rats in close quarters each day. I liked kids. What I knew of them. Really hadn't had much exposure to children over the last few years.

Sucking in a bout of air, I plunged my head back into the water face down and let my arms lead me to the edge. As I was about to push off, a hand tapped my head, throwing me back.

"I've been calling your name for the last few minutes, mate!" Collier stood alongside the pool, still wearing his suit from court. He pulled the button of his suit jacket at the waist, letting the sides open. He ruffled a hand through his hair.

As a modern man, I could honestly say that my brother was a good-looking bloke. In the looks department, the most we had in common were the Armani suits we wore. Collier was blond and brown-eyed like our mother. I was the dark horse who took after my father. Dark hair, tanned skin I didn't have to maintain, and light eyes. The exact opposite of my elder bro.

"Hey, Colly. How goes it?" I slicked back my wet hair.

Collier pulled up a sun lounger and sat, hands clasped between his knees. "You tell me? What happened in court today? You were doing a bodge job defending our client until I stepped in."

I yanked myself out of the water and grabbed the towel next to him, taking that precious few moments to compile my thoughts. Once I dried off a bit, I wrapped it around my hips and sat.

"So?"

"I don't know. My mind was somewhere else, I guess." Purposely avoiding his eyes, I slid my T-shirt over my damp torso. A couple of women on the other side of the pool had watched me swim. One of them frowned as I covered up. I shook my head and smiled, not really able to avoid flirting with them. It was part of my nature. You didn't just turn that off after one day of being with someone incredible. For Camille, I think I could give it a try.

"Your mind was somewhere else? You half-wit, that was a two hundred thousand dollar commission we could have lost had I not stepped in. Our client was clearly wronged, and you almost gave it away. You've always been able to set aside your shite. So what has your trousers in a twist? And where were you at lunch? We were supposed to go over our notes before court."

I stood up and paced a bit trying to unleash the nervous energy. "I was on a date."

Collier's voice was tight. "You blew off our lunch meeting for a piece of arse?"

In two steps, I was in front of my brother, the lapels of his suit coat clutched in a death grip. "Camille's not like that. Don't you ever talk about her that way. Got it!" I growled through my teeth and then shoved him. He caught himself on the lounger and then stood. Pacing in a circle I came back, realizing how much of a daft bastard I was. When I turned around to apologize, Collier had the biggest shite-eating grin on his face.

"What?"

"You're smitten with a bird."

"Am not!" I defended, but my heart wasn't in it. Camille's sweet face and innocent smile ran through my vision.

"You are. You're arse over tit for a girl. Bloody hell." Collier smacked his knee, tipped his head back, and laughed. "I never thought I would see the day where the great ladies' man would fall for a woman. We must celebrate. Where is this lovely bird?"

"Her name is Camille, and it's not what you think."

"Isn't it?" Collier retorted.

"No, it's not." I knew my face fell into a scowl.

"And why not?" His gaze narrowed.

"Because I've just found her, okay. She's Hank's secretary." His eyebrows rose at that information. "I took her out today, but she frightens easily. She's sweet this one. I'm not sure how to handle sweet. The women I'm used to know what they are getting in to." Miserable, I sat and put my head in my hands to rub my temples.

"Do you plan to treat her like your usual fare?"

"Bollocks, no! I said she's different." Collier nodded and waited. "There's just an innocence about her though.

I'm drawn to her. Today, when I kissed her…bloody hell, it was amazing."

"You've already kissed her? She couldn't be that innocent." He grinned.

"I couldn't help myself. When I'm near this woman, Colly…shite. I just need to touch her. Be closer to her. Smell her, taste her. Christ." I pulled on my wet hair until the roots tingled with pain.

Collier smiled and then clapped me on the back. "So what are you going to do about it?"

"I have to get her to go out with me again. I'm thinking flowers to start. What do you think?"

After a chuckle, he responded, "I think that could be a good start. I've met Cami. She seems shy and timid but smart as a whip. My suggestion would be to go easy on her. Don't go in with your normal egomaniac charm because it won't work."

"Yeah, you're right. How the hell did you get so wise in the ways of women?"

"London owns my arse, and I have no complaints." He looked down at his hands. "I think I'm going to marry her if she'll have me."

"Yeah? You think she'd say no?" Instantly, I felt worry and dread prickle at the back of my neck. His nervous energy proved he was unsettled about something. Collier's ex did a number on him a few years ago, cheating and running off with some hotel entrepreneur. London was the first woman he'd given his heart to since. They seemed good together, but love was fickle. Something I had never experienced myself.

"I don't think she would. I'm just not sure she cares

about marriage after what she went through losing her husband so tragically and so young."

"You guys are past all that rubbish though, right?"

"We are, but it's still there under the surface. I know she loves me, but it's still pretty new. I just want to make her mine legally. She may have other opinions on that." Collier grinned and winked.

"Whatever you decide, I'm here for you. Be happy to stand up alongside any pending nuptials."

"Thanks, mate. Now, remember what I said about Cami. Be kind and gentle."

I nodded as we walked toward the exit. "Kind and gentle…what the fuck does that even mean?"

"I don't know. I read it off a Hallmark card once."

CHAPTER FIVE

Pea soup. That's what the thick gelatinous mush previously known as my brain felt like as I sat at my computer staring blankly at the white screen. I needed to type a few letters for Mr. Jensen, but all I could think about was last night. The nauseating experience of seeing Tyler and allowing him to slide a crisp hundred-dollar bill into my G-string still soured my gut even twelve hours later. Dodging my worst nightmare after he caught me on stage was an epic performance. One of my best.

Once I realized who he was, I instantly went into fight or flight mode. Like the perfect little birdie, I chose flight. Before his gaze ever touched mine, I pirouetted on one heel and did a perfect back handspring off the stage and out of sight. The men in the club had gone absolutely wild, the cheering and applauding at my exit was something I'd now be known for. When the husband and wife duo who owned the club found me backstage shaking like an eighty-year-old woman, they thought it was from the adrenaline and paid it no mind. Thank God for small favors. The last thing I wanted to do was explain. My goal, while the bosses spilled their excitement in a glorious rush of accolades and booze-breath, was to get the hell out of the club as fast as my spiked heels would take me.

A ping from my computer noted that I received an e-mail and broke me from my reverie at the same time the door opened. A pair of scrawny legs, worn-out red Vans, and a giant bouquet of yellow sunflowers mixed with white daisies completely covered any view of the person delivering them.

"Delivery for Ms. Johnston," a pubescent voice rang out behind the array of sunshine and happiness.

I stood and grabbed the mosaic vase made up of tiny multicolored squares in myriad pearlescent hues. "Thank you," I said, setting down the flowers. They were quite possibly the most beautiful arrangement I had ever seen. The yellow sunflowers, my favorite, split open with a wide center that reminded me of a perfect sunny day. I couldn't help smiling.

The young man's eyes widened as he scanned my form. Then he quickly looked away from my chest, shuffled his feet, and presented me with a clipboard. I thanked him. He had a hat on backward, and his hair was sticking out in all directions beneath it. He couldn't have been older than eighteen. This was probably his first job. I sympathized with the kid. At almost twenty-three, this was my first *real* job, aside from waiting tables or dancing on them.

"Thanks, uh, yeah…okay. Bye then." His voice cracked as he made a quick exit.

I gave a small wave, dismissing the nervous delivery boy, and looked at the incredible display. These were for me? Had to be a mistake. I'd never been sent flowers before. I spotted the small green envelope and pulled the card from the luscious golden petals and thick leaves.

Camille,
These reminded me of you. As lovely and warm as the sun.

Have dinner with me.
Nate

I placed the little card back into the envelope and stuffed it into my purse as the phone rang.

"Jensen Construction, Cami speaking. How may I help you?"

"Go out with me," a familiar voice pulsated through the receiver. A ridiculous wide smile split my face as I collapsed into my office chair.

"The flowers are beautiful. You didn't have to do that."

"How else was I going to get your attention?" I could hear his smile and his British accent made me salivate.

"Nate, you don't even know me—"

"I want to know you better." His voice a deep rumble that slid across my nerves making me tingle everywhere. "Have dinner with me. Tonight?"

I thought about my schedule this evening. Another night at the club, and then I was off for the week. Unless I was called in for a special booking. "I can't. I have to work."

"Hank doesn't make you work that late." A hint of frustration tinged his words.

"No, my *other* job."

"Which is?"

"Look, Nate. I just…I can't. I'm sorry." I blew out a deep breath wanting to accept his invitation but knowing it wasn't possible. Men like him shouldn't date women like me. There was a natural order to things. When he found out that I was a single mother and stripped to make extra cash, he'd toss me aside like yesterday's garbage.

"Camille…"

"Nate, thank you for the flowers and lunch yesterday. It was…the best date I've ever had." *The only date I've ever had.* "I have to get back to work. Have a wonderful day. Goodbye." I hung up so fast it was as if the receiver was coated in acid. Then I stared at it. Dared it to ring again.

While I stared, waiting for it to strike back, a warm hand settled on my shoulder. I jumped up and screamed like a little girl. A much deeper girlie scream matched my own.

"Jesus, Cami! You almost scared the gay right out of me!" Oliver held a hand to his chest. He stood back and leaned against the wall. His labored breathing matched my own. I laughed catching onto to what he'd said. *Scare the gay right out of him?*

"Ollie, honey, it's not possible to scare the gay out of you." I turned and found Aspen Jensen standing with her arms crossed above her baby bump. Her perfect suit and blouse accentuated her womanly glow. I didn't remember ever looking so pretty while pregnant with Tanner. Most days, I barely rolled out of bed, threw my hair into a ponytail, and shoved my body into the Pepto-pink waitress getup. This woman made being pregnant look like a Miss America pageant.

"Mrs. Jensen, Oliver, hello. How are you?" I settled back into my chair. The flowers stood like a huge banner display on the edge of my desk stating, "Someone likes me!" Oliver zeroed right in on them. Probably because they were the only thing remotely personal on top of the hard oak surface. It was easy to avoid personal questions if you didn't display anything personal in your work space.

"Who sent the flowers?" Oliver touched the petals of a daisy. He looked around the bouquet, obviously searching for the card I'd stashed at the bottom of my purse.

"A friend. What are you two doing here? Mr. Jensen is out for the afternoon."

"Ollie, you said we had lunch today?" Aspen frowned, dug into her purse, and then pulled out her phone. Oliver's eyes narrowed as he pulled out some electronic contraption from his breast coat pocket. It looked like a cross between an iPhone and an e-reader. I'd never used either. I couldn't afford them. I had a pay as you go phone and only two people, Jin and the teenaged neighbor we hired to babysit, had the number. Oliver pressed a few buttons and concentrated on the glowing screen.

"I confirmed lunch with Hank on Monday evening," Oliver validated his reply.

I waved a finger at him. "Ah, but you didn't speak to me." I checked Hank's calendar just to be safe. "Mr. Jensen is not the best at inputting his personal appointments." I glanced at Aspen and she nodded. "Usually, he tells me, and I make sure he doesn't miss anything important. He's currently at the city building getting permits approved. He won't be back for at least two hours."

Oliver's lips pinched into a pout. Aspen hugged him to her side. "It's okay. I know you were looking forward to your daily bitch session. I'm sure we can make time for dinner or breakfast tomorrow."

"Fine, but that hot cowboy's ass is mine!" He pointed to Aspen accusingly. "You haven't allowed me any time with him, and we have a lot to go over before my baby girl arrives. We haven't even agreed on a nanny!"

Aspen's placating smile widened as she winked at me. "That's because Hank doesn't want a nanny. He thinks maybe his mom will come for the first couple months after the baby's born and help out." Oliver looked at Aspen, eyes wide, mouth agape.

"We cannot have 'maybes' with our baby. Jesus Christ on a stick! When I get my hands on his fine ass, he's going to get a licking that keeps on ticking…and it's not going to be in a good way!"

That was it. I couldn't hold it back. I cracked up laughing at their comedic show. Tears pricked my eyes, and I staunched the flow with a Kleenex.

Oliver's eyes narrowed at me, and then he put his hands on his hips. "Well. I was promised a lunch date. So, you're coming with us. Get your things, little miss Someone-Sent-Me-Flowers-But-I'm-Being-All-Secretive. Let's go…scoot. Every second you drag ass, Aspen loses another million."

My mouth dropped open, and I jumped to grab my things. Rosie was back from lunch and would catch the phones and visitors. I really had no reason not go with them. "Really?" I asked.

Aspen smiled and held open the door for us. "Not really. Maybe a thousand or two…" Her voice trailed off as we walked onto her personal elevator. Perk of owning a building. You had your own elevator that opened only to specific persons. I'd only seen Aspen, Hank, Oliver, and Dean—Oliver's significant other—use it. The lift was very high tech. She pressed her finger on the display and said "One" into the quiet of the space. The doors shut, and it went down.

"Since we don't have to go to that healthy, green-seaweed, tree-hugging restaurant to please your caveman, what does my baby girl want?" He patted Aspen's belly. She rolled her eyes and shoved his hand away.

"You and Hank are ridiculous. I would like to have Thai food at that greasy place around the corner. Tasty Thai." She looked at me, and I nodded. I could go Thai any time, and I wasn't picky. "And I don't want to hear one damn word about it! And if you tell Hank, I'll tell Dean about that firemen's calendar you're googly-eyed over. I bet he'd wonder why you keep the page on October even though it's March!"

Oliver visibly shivered and leaned into me as we exited the elevator. "She's really hormonal lately. Hank has been trying to force feed her all this healthy crap when all she wants to eat is a burger." He snickered and Aspen stopped on a dime.

"Stuff it! Come on, Cami. Let's go." She grabbed my arm and locked hers within mine. "All right. Get my mind off this giant bowling ball pressing heavily on my bladder. Who were the flowers from?"

I chuckled. Aspen was the first woman besides Jin who ever initiated "girl talk" with me.

"Hey, don't leave me out. I'm not the shitty pickle on the side of the plate that no one wants to eat." Oliver hooked onto my other arm. I sighed, realizing there was absolutely no way of getting out of this.

"It's really not a big deal." I shook my head. "Nathaniel Walker sent them to me."

Both of them stopped while I propelled forward, which yanked me back. It was like a game of slingshot with me as the rubber band. "Sexy-assed Brit? Has the face of my candy man, David Gandy?" Oliver confirmed.

I shrugged. "I don't know who that is."

Oliver looked stricken and pulled out his electronic whatever thingy and frantically typed. "I'm hungry, come on. Talk while we walk," Aspen pulled us along to the Thai place.

"He came to the office for a meeting with Mr. Jensen the other night."

Aspen nodded.

"Then he just told me he was having lunch with me. I didn't think he was really serious, but the next day he showed up right on time. We went to The Place and had lunch."

"Really? And then today he sent you flowers?"

"Yes."

"Interesting." Her lips twisted and she bit her bottom one. "He likes you. A lot."

Oliver nodded and then leaned over to show me a picture of what he called "Gandy Candy." It was an image of a stunningly beautiful, half-dressed male model walking a runway in his boxers. My cheeks felt hot, and I looked away, nodding at the similarities between my Nate and Oliver's model crush. *My Nate?*

"Girl, he has you in his sights. Did he ask you out again?" Oliver asked.

That's the part I didn't really want to get into. They would want to know why I said no. I couldn't tell them.

"He did, but I haven't decided yet if I'm going." I chose the noncommittal route to leave me with less to explain.

"Was he a shitty kisser? It's okay, you can tell me." Oliver frowned.

"No! He was an amazing kiss…"

Oliver's eyes went wide, and his smile grew even wider.

Aspen laughed and covered her smile with her hand.

And now they knew we'd kissed. Dammit!

"So, you've already kissed." I shook my head, trying to make him stop. "Oh no, honey, you're spilling your guts. There's no going back. And you said it was amazing. Right, Aspen?"

She nodded.

My shoulders sagged as Aspen led us into the restaurant and out to the street side where wrought iron bistro-looking tables sat.

"Look, can we talk about something else?" I pleaded with my eyes.

Oliver rolled his. "Fine. Whatever, let's order, eat a little, and then we'll continue with the third degree." He reached over to Aspen's belly and rubbed it again.

She had to be tired of all the touching. This time she allowed it, placed a hand over Oliver's, and smiled at him.

"Let's talk about my baby!" Oliver offered, and Aspen scowled and then pushed his hand off her belly again.

★ ★ ★

Ask and ye shall receive. I believe that's the quote. Who gives a blimey fuck. The woman who had destroyed all my thoughts, controlled every speck of time in my brain, was sitting at a bistro table not far from where I stood. I gestured to my colleague and best mate.

"I'm in the mood for Thai, and I see a couple mates of mine."

Ty flicked his glasses down and scanned the view across the street. "The blonde and brunette with the suit?"

"Yeah, come on. I'll introduce you to Aspen Reynolds."

"The Aspen Reynolds. As in AIR Bright owner, Bright Magazine owner, pretty much owner of the stock market?"

I grinned and gestured to cross. "That's the one."

"They call her the 'Octopussy' at the stock exchange because she has her hands in so many pies. And the 'pussy' part." He made a gesture of a pyramid with both hands and licked his lips. "I hear she looks like a fucking model, and every man on the exchange wants a piece."

I stopped in my tracks to stare in horror. A cab squealed past me, ruffling my suit coat with the near close call. Ty pulled me out of the way in the nick of time. Bugger!

"Shite. Don't ever let her husband hear you say anything like that. He's a big guy, Southerner, and old-fashioned. He'd beat the living hell out of you."

"Duly noted. I think I can hold my own with the ladies and their husbands." Ty waggled his eyes with a disgusting grin.

It was times like these that I wondered how we'd been friends the past few years. Sure, we both treated women like something to get our jollies off on, but at least I respected them enough to not talk about them after. And...I never dated married women. He dated them even when he was married himself. It was the exact reason why he was divorced and paying a hefty alimony payment every month.

As we walked closer to the restaurant, I could hear Camille's lilting laughter. Christ, it did things to me. Sent me from grumpy to glorious in a few seconds. Aspen looked up and recognized me. I waved, and she stood, her pregnant belly protruding proudly.

"Wow, Aspen. You've gotten even more beautiful since the last time I saw you."

"Smooth, real smooth, Nate. Come join us. I believe we know someone else in common." She winked and nodded her head toward Camille. I grinned, looking over at my beautiful girl. Only she wasn't looking at me. Her eyes were on my colleague, Ty. The wide-eyed deer in the headlights look she had across her face shook me to my core. Did they know each other?

"Camille, lovely to see you." She shook her head and then closed her eyes, blinking a couple times. "Are you okay, precious?" Without a second thought, I hopped over the small iron fence, and crouched down to clasp her hands. They were clammy and cold. "What's the matter?"

She looked at me, her eyes frightened. It was the same look she'd given me in the restaurant on our date. As quickly as the look came, she shook her head, looked over my shoulder at Ty, winced, then blew out a breath. "I, uh, I'm fine. Sorry."

I pulled up a chair and handed her the glass of water in front of her. "Here, love, take this." She took a sip, but her gaze wasn't focused on me, the glass, or our friends. It was locked on Ty. Jealousy roared up my spine and out each limb, tightening, clawing at my senses, forcing out the beast in me.

"Have a seat?" Aspen gestured to the open space between me and her.

"Thank you. I'm Tyler Thornton, a friend of Nate's."

We both sat, and Camille looked the other way, focusing on anything but me and my friend. I slid my hand into hers, and she held it in a vise grip. Something was wrong. The tightness of her jaw, the ramrod straight spine said this was not the place to discuss it. With long strokes, I soothed her hand until she loosened her grip. The waiter arrived, and Ty and I ordered. Camille sat silent.

"So, Camille, this is my best mate, Tyler Thornton." She looked at Ty, something akin to hurt slashed across her gaze. She took a deep breath and held out her hand. It visibly shook until Tyler extended his own and clasped it.

"I believe we've met. Though it's been a few years, hasn't it, sweetness?" Ty's endearment, tone, and the way he held her hand as she tried to pull it away spoke volumes. My inner beast drew its claws. I tightened my hand into a fist.

"Yes, it has." She looked away.

"So, Cami, I see you're no longer a waitress." His blue eyes undressed her, scanning her form from tip to toe. She wore the standard black pencil skirt and a fitted green shirt that brought out her eyes. It took every ounce of respect for my friendship with him not to react like a Neanderthal, thump my chest, swing her over my shoulder, and carry her off to my bedroom where I could stake my claim officially.

"Ty," I warned. "This is a friend of mine. A *very…* close friend." I slid an arm around her shoulders insinuating possession. I was pleasantly surprised when she snuggled into my side. It was the first time she'd willingly pressed closer to me. It felt beyond right. It was downright perfect.

"Just making polite conversation," he said, glancing at my hold on Camille. I wanted to smash the corresponding smirk of his face with my fist.

The conversation changed. Ty dominated the discussion, ranting on about a couple of companies Aspen was looking into purchasing. Normally I would have paid close attention. As Aspen's lawyer, I made sure she made sound legal decisions. Entering into a possible business venture typically called for my expertise. Unfortunately, I was in no shape to participate. My focus was diverted to a stunning brunette currently acting strangely.

Camille pushed her food around her plate. Sometimes she'd look up, gaze at Ty, and bite her lip so hard I worried blood would appear. I wanted to sooth that ache, kiss away the pain she inflicted on her perfect pout. There was something between her and Ty, and I needed to find out what.

In the middle of Ty's description of a new company he was championing, Camille stood up as if the building caught fire. "I have to go." Her voice was thick with emotion and cracked on the last word. She riffled through her purse and pulled out her wallet.

"Oh no, honey, this is a business lunch." Aspen waved her off. Camille nodded, putting away her wallet.

"I'm sorry." She looked into my eyes. Fear, sadness, and regret all warred for top billing in her gaze. Then she shot a glance at Ty and winced.

He leaned back and with the most smarmy expression possible said, "It was *really* good seeing you again, sweetness. Maybe we can catch up sometime."

"I can't take this," Camille blurted and ran out of the restaurant. I moved to chase after her.

"No!" Oliver stopped me with a hand on my chest. "Something stinks about this." Oliver pointed between Ty and me. "I'm going to check on her. Make sure Aspen gets back to the office safely. Got it?"

"Yes, but I—"

"No buts. Take care of my girls." He pointed to Aspen, kissed her cheek then patted her belly. Aspen cringed, clearly annoyed with her personal assistant. "I'll see you at the office after I find out what the hell set a fire under our girl's ass."

"That ass is sweet. I can attest to that." Ty held his hands about a foot apart and thrust his hips.

"Cocksucking wanker!" I pulled back my hand, ready to pummel the bloody bastard. A huge arm grabbed my bicep, preventing me from hitting my mark... Ty's smirking mug. A body-builder type patted me on the back.

"You gonna start a fight with a pregnant woman at your table?" The beefy stranger gestured to Aspen. I looked at her surprised face. Her hands covered her round bump protectively.

"Sorry. Thanks, mate."

"Respect!" The testosterone-filled man fist pumped me. I'll never understand the fist pump. Or was it bump?

"What the fuck, man! You were going to hit me?" Ty yelled. He fluffed his suit coat and buttoned it at the waist.

"Don't ever talk about my woman like that!" I growled, making my intent very clear.

"Your woman! Now she's *your* woman? Just a half hour ago she was your friend." Ty flicked the shoulders of his suit coat and ruffled a hand through his brown hair. "I've already had her, and it wasn't worth the effort. You can have my sloppy seconds."

"I'm going to murder you," I gritted through my teeth.

Aspen put a hand on my chest and then Ty's. She looked at Ty and then back to me. "Enough. Tyler, it was... well, not exactly pleasant meeting you. I think it's time for you to go." He frowned as she added, "Nate, walk me back to AIR Bright."

I stood seething as I watched my best friend walk

out confidently into the city streets. Women everywhere checked him out as he went, and now I knew he'd had my woman. My precious Camille. Christ!

CHAPTER SIX

Tears raced down my cheeks as I stood in the elevator at AIR Bright. I'd give anything to avoid going back to work, but I needed this job. The money I made working for Jensen Construction was fair, but not enough for us to live on alone. At least not yet. I was low man on the totem pole, only a receptionist. That wage did not pay my half of the rent, daycare on the days Jin couldn't watch Tanner, or food and medical coverage living in New York City. It was just enough to take me off government assistance. Hence, the reason I still worked at Gems. I hoped I'd get a good raise and more responsibility along with medical coverage when I had my six month review. When that happened, I would quit Gems for good.

"Cami! Hold the door!" Oliver's voice echoed off the walls in the building's lobby. Instead of holding the doors, I hit the "Close" button repeatedly, mashing my thumb into the round disk. I should have known one of them would come after me. At least it wasn't Nate.

The doors closed before Oliver reached them, and I let out a sigh of relief. I stood silently in the corner as it stopped a few times to let people get on and off before reaching Jensen Construction's floor. It was just enough time to calm myself using the meditative breathing tactic I learned during Lamaze class when I was pregnant with Tanner. After seeing Tyler, incredibly attractive, his suit fitting like it was tailored to highlight his long, lean body to perfection, yet still the worst possible jerk, almost sent me into a full-blown anxiety attack. When the doors opened, I was shocked to see Oliver leaning against the opposite wall, feet crossed at the ankle, hands in the pockets of his designer suit.

"How did you…?"

Oliver grinned his pristine metro-sexual features adding to his mirth. "Private elevator. Benefit of being BFF with the building owner."

I passed him entering the office. With practiced ease, I slid into my desk chair, put away my purse in the bottom drawer, adjusted my hands over my desk and looked at Oliver.

He sat his hip on my desk, tapped his fingers against the surface, and scrutinized my face. "So, you just going to sit there and pretend you didn't just run out of lunch as if your hair was on fire?"

"I apologize. I wasn't feeling much like myself. I'll apologize to Mrs. Jensen, too."

"Mrs. Jensen? You're serious? You're worried about my girl?"

My lip shook. I held in my emotions. "Yes." It came out in a whisper, but I meant it to sound strong and confident.

"You really are as sweet as a gumdrop on Sunday morning in the sticks." He took a deep breath. "What in the world had you in such a tizzy?"

I shrugged.

"Oh, no." He pointed his finger and swung it into a circle in front of my face. "You are not getting out of this convo. We were having a good time, 'bout to get our Tasty Thai on, then sexy Brit shows up with equally steamy Tyler, and you freak out. Batshit crazy." He pinched his lips and then continued his rant. "And I'm not leaving here until you tell me why!"

My mouth opened and closed. I didn't know where to even start. Thoughts of Nate and Tyler were spinning a vortex of regret and fear through my mind, blurring the edges of my vision with unwelcomed tears. Regret that I'd ever been with Tyler and the unwelcome realization that he hadn't changed one bit in the last five years. Worse was the fear that dug into my heart like an icepick. He'd tell Nate about our past. It made me feel dirty, as disgusting as bugs crawling all over my skin.

Oliver took one look at my face, grabbed my hand, pulled me out of my chair, and yanked me into a hug. I didn't know how to react. I hadn't been hugged by anyone other than Jin in years. The tears returned and slid down my cheeks wetting his designer suit as I gripped his back. He stroked my hair, pushed me away from his body holding each bicep. "Sweetie, you can trust me. Whatever it is. I've got your back."

"I had a relationship with Tyler. Years ago."

"Honey, I think everyone at the table gathered that." He moved his hands up and down my arms. It felt nice, calming. Normal even. I'd never had a male friend. Hell, I didn't have any real friends besides Jin. I had mutual acquaintances at the diner and at Gems with the other girls.

"Was it a bad breakup?" I was grateful he spoke. I had no idea how to start. Thank God Hank was still out and he wasn't seeing this.

"Yeah, Oliver. It was real bad."

His eyes narrowed. "Did he hurt you?"

"Not in the way you think. He didn't hit me, though he wasn't a gentleman." He nodded and waited patiently. I looked around the office. Everything was quiet. People were still at lunch. "If I tell you, you have to promise me…"

Oliver gripped my hands tightly. "Cami…not a word. I'll breathe not a word."

"Even Mrs. Jensen?" He looked down, guilt covering his serene face. Then he took a deep breath and nodded. "Tyler and I have a history. We were only together for a short time. I got pregnant."

Oliver's eyes widened the size of silver dollars.

"He told me to get rid of it and gave me ten thousand dollars to make the problem go away."

Oliver gasped. "That two-bit, skanky shark, preying on a sweet young thing. You must have been so scared."

I nodded. "Without going into details, I found out he'd been cheating on his wife with me. Got me pregnant and wanted me to get rid of it. He gave me money and pushed me out the door."

"Sweetie, I'm so sorry you had to do that, go through that. I can't imagine having to have an abortion and do it all alone." He wiped the tears from my eyes. I shook my head.

"You don't understand…" My voice cracked, and I swallowed the giant lump that had been built with years of fear and loathing of Tanner's father.

"What don't I understand?" His soft brown eyes filled with sympathy and indignation. Oliver was a gentle soul. A genuine human being with a huge heart. I could see why everyone loved him. It was hard not to.

"I didn't do it," I whispered and sucked in a sob.

"Didn't do what?" His face held confusion as he studied

me and held my hands.

"I didn't have an abortion."

Oliver's mouth dropped open, his brows raised in high triangles. "I have a son." He blinked as if he'd just woken up. "Tanner. He's four."

"Holy Mother of God. Fuckin' hell. I did not expect that."

I pulled away from him and crossed my arms, hugging myself.

"Does he know?"

I shook my head.

"Does Nate know?"

Again, head shake.

"Does anyone know, Cami?"

"It's nobody's business!" I fired back.

"You've been raising a child…that rich skanky shark's child, for four years alone! In New York Motherfucking City?"

"Yes," I spat. "Keep your voice down. It's nobody's business but mine. I didn't plan on ever seeing him again. He made it clear he wanted nothing to do with me. Called me a whore and claimed the baby wasn't his! I was eighteen years old; I had no idea what to do. I took the money. I've been raising my boy alone ever since."

Oliver shook his head back and forth. "This is too much, Cami. You should be getting support from that bastard. How are you able to live?"

"That. Is. Not. Your. Concern," I bit out each word slowly. I hoped he'd hear me and feel the words deep down to his shiny wing-tipped shoes.

He took a deep breath just as the door opened and

Hank strode in. "Hey, buddy, how goes it?"

Oliver put up a hand to Hank without even looking at him. "Hold up, cowboy. Cami, this isn't finished."

"Oh, but it is. And I expect you to keep your word," I reminded him, plastering on the biggest, fakest smile I could muster.

His eyes narrowed, and then his gaze turned gentle. What I saw next didn't make me happy. As a matter of fact, it angered me. Pity. He looked at me quietly with a heaping dose of pity smeared across his pointed, perfect features. That was the one thing I never wanted to see on anyone's face. I worked hard. Really hard to provide for myself and Tanner.

I glared at Oliver, and finally he said, "I promise." He turned on a heel and threw his hands in the air. "Nannies! You"—he pointed at Hank—"and me need to talk about our baby. We cannot be living off of 'maybe' your mama will come to NYC and take care of our girl. Unacceptable."

Hank's eyes narrowed, and the smile on his face turned into a smirk. Oh boy. "You spend a lot of time thinking 'bout this? You seem to keep forgettin' that this is *my* daughter with Aspen."

"And I keep telling your sexy fine ass that Aspen was mine first. Therefore, her daughter is my daughter by proxy! Now, can we please get on to the important stuff? I have a list of prospective nannies to go over with you." He pulled out his high-tech device from his breast pocket and tapped the screen a few times. "Work history, super-secret spy type personal investigations I had done on each one of them. I'm ready to go through them with you. Now's as good a time as any?"

Hank's hands pulled into fists, and he took a deep

breath. "Buddy…"

"Of course you got time. This is our baby girl we're talking about. Come now." Oliver grabbed Hank's bicep and tugged him toward his office. "Damn, Hank, you've been hitting that gym hard. I'll bet my Pen loves that."

Hank shook his head but followed Oliver into his office and shut the door.

Finally, I sat in my seat, pulled out my compact from my desk drawer and refreshed my powder, covering the redness from the crying spell.

A sick, gut-wrenching feeling swept through me. What if Oliver didn't keep my secret? Aspen would tell Hank, and the entire crew would find out about Tanner. It's not that I was embarrassed of my boy. He was the perfect angel child. I adored him. He was intelligent way beyond his four years. His brown hair and blue eyes were his father's, making him gorgeous. Everyone who had seen me with him said so. But the circumstances were not something to be proud of. I held a great deal of shame about finding out I was pregnant at eighteen and being a mistress to a married man. To top it off, I'd accepted ten grand and disappeared.

I should have been smarter and made sure Tyler used protection, but I was young, dumb, and thought I was in love. Now, almost twenty-three and a single mother, what would Nate think? I'm certain a man like him wouldn't want to be shackled to a woman with a child. He'd want a perfect woman. One that wasn't damaged goods with baggage, living in a tiny apartment barely above poverty level, with a roommate, who bared it all for cash twice a week. Now that he knew I've had a relationship with his best friend, he was not going to want anything to do with me.

★ ★ ★

My Camille, the sweet precious innocent woman whose taste I couldn't and didn't want to get off my tongue, had shagged my best mate. It wasn't enough to know they'd bonked. I needed details. Thoughts of their bodies merging inspired wicked nausea to rise up my throat. The only way to rid myself of it was to confirm the truth.

After a few beats of tapping my knuckles against the desk and staring out at the landscape, I'd had it. I couldn't take it anymore. I pulled out my phone and brought up the messages program.

To: Tyler Thornton
From: Nate Walker
How long ago did you see Camille?

Not even seconds later a reply popped up.

To: Nate Walker
From: Tyler Thornton
Her name is Camille?

Fucking tosser. I gripped the phone so tight I worried it would crack. Another text pinged.

To: Nate Walker
From: Tyler Thornton
Relax, it was years ago. Popped her cherry. I broke her in real good. You're free to have a go of her.

"Motherfucking piece of rubbish! I'll fucking kill you!" I roared at the phone and then swung my arm back to lob it against the glass windows of my office. He took my sweet Camille's virginity! Christ, this couldn't be any worse.

Collier ran in, hollering, "Whoa, whoa! Brother mine. What has you in such a snit?" His brown eyes focused on mine and held. "Deep breaths." After a few breaths, I calmed and sank down into the leather chair. "What is it?"

"You know Ty?"

Collier rolled his eyes, opened his jacket at the waist, and sat with one ankle on top of his knee. Cool as a cucumber. Blondish-brown hair fell in layers over his head, framing inquisitive brown eyes. Reminded me of Mum, instantly relaxing my ire if only briefly.

"Yeah, I know your best mate. Bugger that he is." He scowled. Collier had never liked Tyler Thornton. Always said he was a wanker. Now I believed him.

"He shagged Camille." I said the words and swallowed the sour taste it brought to my mouth.

"Holy shite. Really? I'm sorry, mate. I thought she was single?"

I shook my head. "Happened ages ago. Years. Still he's stuck his prick in *my* woman."

"Your woman?" Collier questioned, shock and doubt written across his face.

"Yeah. I thought maybe…"

Collier leaned forward, putting his elbows on his knees. "And now what? You found out that she's had relations with him years ago and you don't want her anymore?"

"No…maybe, Christ! I don't know."

"That's cold, brother. Just the other day you were ready

to woo this girl. Now because she's had a bad shag years ago, you're moving on?"

"No, I don't want to, but what choice do I have? Fucking Ty has been with her. How the hell am I going to be with her, knowing my best mate's been in my woman?" I turned to look at the view of the city through my office window. The sun was setting over the horizon. Skyscrapers cut into the hues of color like knives stuck in the ground and pointing at the sky.

"Easy. If she means something, you get over it. I did."

I spun around. "What do you mean? You have London."

"Yes, I do." His head tilted to the side. "But her best mate, Tripp." I nodded. "He had her first. Many times over. At first, I was a jealous tyrant. Now he's one of my best mates. I'd do anything for the guy." I had totally forgotten that Tripp and London had a physical relationship prior to her and Collier coming together.

"And what made it okay?" I couldn't believe my own ears. I sounded like a right knob.

"Besides the fact that I fell in love with her?" He studied his hands for a bit. "I talked to her. Had words with Tripp. We came to an understanding. What they had was physical and during a time both were very wounded. They'd used one another and, in turn, became great friends. They love each other but are not *in love* with one another. That made all the difference in the world." I clasped my hands into a prayer pose, elbows on the desks surface, really taking in what Collier had to say. "At the end of the day, I wanted her more. The stuff with Tripp…that was the past. We decided to leave it there."

"Has it worked for you?"

"It has." His gaze held mine. "You like this girl?"

I nodded.

"You like her enough to want more than a quick shag?"

I nodded again, unable to speak.

"Then find out what happened in the past, and once you do, you leave it there. In the past. Then move on."

Jesus, my brother was smart, always able to put things into perspective. Over the years, I had been with a lot of women but never more than once or twice. I hadn't even been with Camille, and I wanted her for more than just one night. I wanted her for a lot longer than that. Maybe even forever. Physically, I needed to feel her curvy, lengthy body under mine. I wanted to worship her…for hours. She's all I could think about. But more than that, I enjoyed being with her. I wanted to laugh with her. Learn more about who she was, what made her tick, what made her smile, laugh, cry. Everything. She was the first woman in my entire life that I wanted to put forth an effort.

"Thank you, Colly."

Collier's lips split into a snarky grin. "Any time. You gonna call the bird?"

"Until she answers." And I meant that bone deep. "And if she doesn't…well, then I'm going to pay her a visit first thing Monday morning."

"Good man! London and I are taking holiday for the weekend." I watched him stand and adjust his suit jacket. "I'm going to head out. Go home, grab our bags, and whisk my woman away for a long weekend. I've cleared my schedule through Tuesday. I'll be back in the office on Wednesday. Let's try to do dinner soon, yeah?"

"Sounds good. I'll cook. Invite the gang?"

"Perfect. Hope you make headway with your girl. I want you to be happy, mate."

"I think she just may be the answer."

"Yeah?" He put a hand to the door handle.

"She's special, Colly."

He put a finger to his lips and then his chin. "So are you. Don't let her get away over a prick like Ty. He's not worth it, but I have a funny feeling she might be."

"I think you're right."

"Good luck, mate!" Collier said as he walked out the door.

Luck. With a beautiful woman who has a tendency to run when things get interesting? I'm going to need a lot more than luck.

I picked up the phone and dialed.

"Spark Investigations. You've got Spark."

"Hello, Jonny. Need to call in that favor you owe me."

"You got it, Walker. Name?"

"Camille Johnston."

"What do you need? Short story or long?"

"I want it all, but as soon as you have it, send me the essentials."

"This personal?"

"None of your business. Be discreet. This one means something to me."

"I'll have you the short in a couple hours. The long in a few days."

"Perfect."

Two hours later, I received the e-mail I'd been waiting for.

To: Nate Walker
From: Jonny Spark (Spark Investigations)
Camille Christine Johnston
Age: 22
Birthday: July 3rd
Address: 2020 Beach St. Apt# 35, Bronx, NY 10472
Employment: Jensen Construction and Gems
Roommate: Jin Sang - Female - age 25

I read through the rest of the e-mail showing her phone number, length of time at her apartment, the high school she graduated from, and so forth. My eyes settled on her employment. I was trying to recall what "Gems" was. I was pretty sure it was a bar, which would make sense if it was a job she had after her work at Jensen Construction. The area she lived in wasn't bad but not the Ritz either. It was also a solid thirty to forty minute drive from work. She didn't have a car registered to her name. That's all the information Jonny sent for now, which was more than enough. Medical and any familial contacts would come later. I had her number and address. The rest would come. Maybe I'd read it, maybe not. I felt like a bit of right arsehole for investigating her, but she left me with no real choice.

Camille liked me. I knew that much from our phone conversations and lunch date. Not to mention the mouthwatering kisses we'd shared in the lift. Mostly, I knew it from the way she pressed her body into mine at lunch today when she seemed scared and uncomfortable. Women didn't get that close and look to be sheltered by a man's arms that they weren't into. Whatever had happened between her and Ty was a long time ago, but he still had a negative effect on her. One way or another, I was going to find out why.

CHAPTER SEVEN

The weekend passed in a blur. Both Jin and I were called into Gems. She was contracted for a private booking, which made it necessary for me to cover her shift on the floor.

We had our teenaged neighbor Leah watch the boys. That girl was a godsend, but she didn't come cheap. To get a sixteen-year-old to give up her Saturday night, you had to make it worthwhile. Jin and I halved the bill, but still it came close to forty bucks a piece.

It was a long evening. The only reason Leah's mama let her stay so late was because they lived across the breezeway, letting her mother check on her within seconds. It gave Jin and me an extra level of comfort, knowing Leah had her mother so close in the event of an emergency.

Sunday was hectic. The boys bounced off the walls. Due to the busy week and evenings spent working, they hadn't had enough one-on-one time with either of us. Basically, we had two forty-something pound children all over us like white on rice. Both grappled for an ounce of attention, and for two mothers who hadn't come home until three in the morning, a seven a.m. wake up call from two little boys was rough. As usual, we had to grin and bear it.

I made pancakes while Jin put on the cartoons. We spent the day watching Disney movies and dozing in between playing snack courier every thirty minutes to our little ones. It was impressive how much a four- and five-year-old boy could put away in snacks. It was as if their bellies were endless pits of nothingness.

On Monday mornings, Mr. Jensen liked to treat everyone to their first cup of coffee at the office. I stumbled off the elevator and into Jensen Construction arms loaded with Starbucks. With great effort, I eased the two containers holding four steaming Styrofoam cups onto my desk feeling a great sense of achievement that I didn't spill a drop. All those shifts waitressing at the diner taught me a thing or two, and I never got an order wrong. The office loved that about me.

"Good morning, love." The voice I'd heard in my dreams every night this weekend smoothed over my senses, sending my heart to a heavy pitter-patter. I twirled and leaned against the desk.

There he stood, inclined against the wall. All kinds of tall, dark, handsome, and British, looking spectacular in a pitch-black suit with a slate-blue tie that matched his eyes. Good-looking didn't even come close to Nathaniel Walker. He exuded confidence and sex appeal. So much so that I waved my hand against my face to cool the blush I knew was coloring me crimson.

"What are you doing here?" I asked, dumbstruck and breathless. Seeing him standing there blew me away like a dandelion's flowerets escaping in the wind on the breath of a wish.

"Isn't it obvious?" His smirk added the tiniest dimple barely hidden by his goatee.

"Not to me, it isn't."

"Let me be a little less obtuse then." He took a few steps toward me, and I took a couple backward. Those pouty lips twitched in, what I could only surmise, was humor. Instead of caging me in like I expected, he stopped at the huge bouquet of flowers he'd sent. Long fingers toyed with one of the daisies. "I want to take you out to dinner. You're going to say yes."

"Nate I ca—"

"Yes, you can and you will. There's something between you and me, and I want to find out what. The only way to do so is to spend time together…alone." He emphasized the last word in a decidedly sultry tone.

"I'm surprised you still want to go out with me. After lunch…"

"It seems you have a past with my best mate, Ty." I winced and tried hard to swallow the bile that rose at the mere mention of that horrible man's name. "I can see it on your face, and though it makes me feel as though I've gone raving mad, I can't deny there's something between us. Do you not feel it?"

I could have ended things right there by agreeing that I "did not" in fact feel anything for this beautiful man. Unfortunately, I was never any good at lying. My heart screamed lies at my brain, my brain yelled at my voice, and my voice spit out the truth and nothing but the truth, so help me God. Dammit!

"Of course I feel it!" I put my fingers over my lips, wishing I had more control over myself.

A huge smile split Nate's face, and at that moment, I would have said anything to see him alight with such joy.

"Brilliant! I'll pick you up Friday evening."

"Nate, no, I can't Friday. Um…how about Sunday?"

"Sunday is hardly the time for a proper dinner and

night out. I want to take you on the town, precious." God, that sounded so good. His term of endearment soothed along my nerves putting them at rest. It didn't change that what he wanted was utterly impossible. I worked at Gems on Fridays. Saturdays, I watched the boys so Jin could work. Sunday was the only weekend night I had available.

"I have other obligations I cannot change. If you want to go out, it will have to be Sunday."

His eyes twinkled as he stepped close to me. I inhaled deeply when I felt the warmth of his body, enjoying the manly goodness of his cologne. He smelled divine. Unlike all of the strong and overpowering perfume-soaked gentleman that frequented Gems. Sometimes I had to wipe Vicks VapoRub under my nose to avoid gagging as I danced. Nate's scent was distinct and unique—a mix of sweet, citrus, and man. If I could bottle it and wear it all day, people would think I was a drug addict for randomly sniffing myself all day long.

Nate trailed a finger down the side of my cheek. I gasped and his thumb slid across my bottom lip, petting it sweetly. "I'll take what I can get, but I want the entire day starting with brunch. Eleven work?"

His gaze traced every curve and feature of my face. Those blue eyes went from light to dark. He licked his lips, and I had to grit my teeth not to moan. I felt like Pavlov's dog. He got near me, rang *my* bell, and I salivated, ready to eat *him* whole. I'd never desired a man like I desired Nathaniel Walker.

His nose rubbed lightly against mine. It was probably the sweetest gesture I'd ever received from a man. "So what do you say?"

There was only one thing I could say with his presence

surrounding me, body warm near mine, breath against my face enticing me, seducing me without even trying. "Okay," I whispered.

He brought his hand up so both framed my face, thumbs caressing my cheeks. His eyes searched mine. I hoped he liked what he saw because I could drown in those murky blues of his forever. "I'm going to do something highly inappropriate."

"You are?" The words were only a murmur. He heard them and nodded. His head moved slowly toward mine, putting me in a trancelike state. Nothing but he and I existed in that moment.

Nate licked his lips and my knees shook. "I can't avoid this. It's too much." I could taste his minty breath. I blinked slowly, allowing his words to sink in as he caressed the apple of my cheeks with his thumbs. "I'm going to kiss you now."

"At work?"

He nodded. "Yes, at work."

"Okay."

"Okay." He smiled, closed his eyes and then his lips were on mine. So warm, just barely moist. He rubbed his lips along mine, not forcing or pushing, just pressing against them. He alternated from top lip to bottom, which he then sucked into his mouth, licked along the plump tissue and released. The kiss was over before I really had a chance to participate. It was heavenly, and I wanted more. So much more.

His hands came to my hips and pulled me flat against him. I could feel the steely ridge of an erection. The fact that I turned him on made me feel powerful, womanly, sexy. The heat from his body seared me from my chest to my pelvis as he leaned in toward my ear.

"You're delicious. I can't wait to taste the rest of you." His bold statement was accentuated by his tongue swirling then nipping the edge of my ear down my neck. Gooseflesh coated my limbs, and I clasped onto his shoulders, moaning under my breath at those lust-soaked words. It had been a long time since a man paid me any attention. "Christ, you're responsive."

He rubbed his prickly goatee against the tender skin of my neck, and I thought I might have an orgasm just from the anticipation of feeling that beautiful mouth and chin drag along other parts of my body. It was incredibly easy to imagine.

"Nate, please…"

"Please what, precious?" He nipped at the skin where my neck and shoulder met. Liquid heat shot down my body and settled between my thighs.

"Please stop," I half-moaned.

Abruptly, Nate pulled away, his eyes fierce, hands firmly holding my biceps at arm's length. "What?"

"This is my workplace." My voice was deep and husky. One side of his mouth twitched into a crooked smile. His face relaxed.

"Are you saying I'm turning you on?" An eyebrow rose to a perfect point. I could feel my body heat and flush along the skin of my face, neck and chest. "Christ, I love seeing you turn pink for me." I shook my head and let my hair fall into my face. He planted two fingers under my chin and lifted until my gaze met his. "I understand." Quicker than I could respond, he cupped both sides of my cheeks once more and laid a quick kiss on my mouth.

Fate took that moment to intervene. As Nate pulled away, leaving me stunned stupid, a deep chuckle filled the air. I closed my eyes and hoped it wasn't who I thought it was. Nate turned his head, smiled a very cat that ate the canary grin, and gripped me by the shoulders hauling me against his side.

"Morning, mate," Nate said to Mr. Jensen.

"I see that it is just that. Mornin', sweetie. Everything peachy?"

God, take me now. I nodded and tried my best to wrestle out of Nate's arms. He was having none of it. He squeezed me tighter, molding me to his side.

"Pick up my fancy coffee?" Mr. Jensen asked, his Southern drawl strong and amused

"Yes, absolutely, Mr. Jensen." I turned and scooted away from Nate. I pulled out Hank's pure black Sumatra blend coffee and handed it to him.

"How's Aspen? Did she tell you we had a bite together late last week?" Nate asked.

"She did." Hank's gaze shifted to me as his head tilted to the side, assessing me. I hated when people scrutinized me. Ignoring both men, I pulled up the start program and logged in, bringing up his schedule for the day.

"My wife is doing just great. Glowin' and taking great care of our daughter to be," he said.

"Brilliant! Love to hear things are so well. I just came by to wish my girl here a great morning." Nate nodded to me and I could sense a blush flutter along my cheeks.

"Your girl?" Hank had no qualms about zeroing right in on the comment. This couldn't possibly get any worse. My personal life was spilling into my professional life like a pancake coated in too much syrup, too thick and sickeningly sweet, the kind you couldn't stomach. I didn't know how to deal with this change in my world.

"If she'll have me..." Nate's words smoothed the jagged edges of my heart like calamine over poison ivy filling the wounds with a healing balm. I couldn't help but smile through my nerves.

"Mr. Walker was just leaving. Right?" I prayed he'd take the hint.

Nate looked at his watch. "I should shove off. Due in court within the hour. May I see your phone, Camille?"

Without thinking, I pulled my pay-as-you-go flip phone out of my purse. His eyes narrowed and flipped it front to back as if it came from outer space. He pressed buttons, his eyes hyper-focused on the task. Then all of a sudden a sweet chiming sound filled the room. He pulled out his own phone from his breast coat pocket and hit a button.

"Now I have your number." He grinned. *Sneaky.* "Until Sunday then. Expect a ring from me this evening."

I opened my mouth but didn't know how to deny him in front of my boss. With a wink and a smile, Nate turned and held out his hand to Hank. "Good seeing you, mate."

"You as well, partner."

Without even a glance back, Nate took his long, lengthy muscled body out the door and out of the office.

"So, you and Nate, eh?" Hank waggled his eyebrows. I rolled my eyes and shook my head.

★ ★ ★

Today by far was the best day I'd had in what seemed like

forever. Starting my morning off with the sweet taste of my Camille's lips left me feeling like a million bucks. And I knew exactly what a million dollars felt like…abso-fucking-lutely brilliant!

Court went smashing and consisted of putting a daft bastard away for embezzlement, getting another client out of tax trouble, and settling a battle against a suppler who'd sent faulty equipment to the Jensen job. Overall, I jumped tall buildings in a single bound. I was on top of the world and there was only one reason.

Camille Johnston.

I could hardly wait to get home. I pulled my 2014 BMW 7 Series into the carport, took the elevator to my floor, tossed my keys and money clip into the ceramic bowl by the door with little concern, and settled into my flat. I changed into loose cotton pajama bottoms, poured three fingers of an eighteen-year-old Macallan, and stared out over the cityscape. The caramel honeyed notes from the scotch slid along my taste buds warming me from the inside out. It was lovely at this time of night. All the lights of the cars trailed one another in a game of follow the leader. The copious numbers of yellow cabs weaved through sleek sports utility vehicles like little ducks waddling after one another.

The itch to ring Camille was strong laced with a heaviness I wasn't familiar with. Women were always a means to an end. My career and the success of my career had always been forefront in my mind. Watching Collier fall for a woman, do everything to make her happy, and fail taught me a great lesson. Women can hurt you in more ways than one.

When Collier suggested five years ago that we take a

leap across the pond to the States, I jumped at the chance. I was twenty-three and working myself to the bone alongside my elder brother. We built something magnificent, and it had been successful beyond our wildest dreams.

We were both multimillionaires with great flats. Our mum and dad's house has been paid off. We owned a stick of apartments in a swanky building in New York, and business was booming.

Only now things were different between Collier and me.

A few months ago, I watched Collier almost die. Then I watched him find love again. This time he fell for a woman who was more afraid of love than a cat was of water. He changed because of her in the best possible way.

I missed that it was no longer me and my brother fighting battles and kicking arse. We still worked together, ran our empire as a solid unit, but it wasn't the same. He wasn't, and I wasn't. The past year, I no longer looked forward to going out at the end of a dastardly work week to find a willing bird to bed. It was very hollow and unsavory in the light of day, and I was tired of it.

And now, there was *Camille*.

I thought of our time together, though all too brief. The woman's pointed small nose, high cheekbones, pink kissable lips, and emerald eyes completed a stunning face that was surrounded by a halo of golden brown hair. The combination did things to me. Sod all, the woman could bring me to my knees to worship at her feet, all to capture one of her sweet smiles. That tiny dip of her lips, and I was a goner. Lost forever.

It surprised me that this woman, Hank's receptionist,

had such control, a control she didn't know she had. When I wasn't with her, I thought about her. Today was one of those days where I sorted it out by just showing up at her work. My Camille had quick feet that preferred running to standing still in my presence. Today though, she proved just how taken she was with me. I ate up every second.

I remembered her lowered gaze, that pink little tongue licking her lips, her gasps, and during our kiss, the little sound she made at the back of her throat. It was a combination of a moan and a growl. I'd go to great lengths to hear that sound again and again. I planned on doing just that this weekend. Sunday.

Bollocks. Why a Sunday? It didn't make sense, but I'd do whatever it took to spend the day with her. I sat down in the high back chair facing the city and dialed her number.

After four rings, I thought for sure I'd be leaving a message but a small little voice answered. "Hello?"

I pulled the phone away from my hand and checked the display. No, it said "Precious Camille" in bright white font on the screen.

"Hello, who is this?" I asked softly.

"Tanner," a soft whisper answered.

"Tanner, my name is Nate."

"Hiya, Nate! You talk funny." The little voice giggled in a way that could only be conveyed by a child's innocence.

"You think so? How old are you?"

"Four," was practically screamed into my ear, piercing my close to thirty-year-old eardrum painfully.

"Wow, that's a big boy. Can you tell me, Tanner, is there an adult there?"

"Yep," was all I got. Nice and direct. I liked this kid.

"And what are their names, sport?"

"Mommy and Auntie."

Ah, now I get it. This must be her roommate's child. Funny, she never brought up the fact that her roommate had a son. We had so much to learn about each other. I looked forward to digging into every facet that was my sweet innocent girl.

"Tan Man, who are you calling?" I could hear the lovely lilting voice of my Camille in the background.

"I didn't call. I swear. He called me!" His little voice sounded downright indignant. I chucked in response.

After a rustling noise, a winded Camille spoke. "Who is this?"

"Good evening, precious."

The phone went completely silent. I had to check that it was still connected. Then I heard what sounded like movement a door opening and closing loudly.

"Um, hi, Nate," Camille finally said.

"Is this a bad time?"

"No, not exactly."

I carried on without bother. "I just spoke to a lovely little boy. How is it that you didn't mention your roommate had a child?"

I heard Camille take a deep breath. "Uh…well, it's complicated, Nate." Camille's life just kept getting more interesting, opening up like peeling layer after layer from an onion.

"How can a child be complicated?"

"It just is. Anyway, how was your day?" She changed the subject. Camille was an expert at that, but I didn't mind. I just wanted to talk to her. Let her voice carry over the length of my day, releasing the tension. If I were a prissy chap, I'd consider a long soak in the tub whilst I spoke with the beautiful woman. But I wasn't, and I wouldn't. I preferred to gaze at the busy streets of New York, and sip my whiskey.

"Not as good as my morning," I said, innuendo heavy between the words.

She giggled. My Camille let out a laugh and a giggle, and it was heavenly. Everything about her entertained and enthralled me. "Mine too," she said softly.

"I'm counting the days until I get to do it again."

"Kiss me?" she asked.

"Yes. And more…" I let the rest of what I was thinking sink in.

"You scare me, Nate." Her voice trembled, and I didn't care for it. The last thing I wanted was for her to be afraid of me.

"Because I think you're a beautiful woman? One whom I enjoy kissing and want to kiss other parts of her?"

"Yes, all of those things. I'm not very experienced," she admitted on a sigh.

What did that mean? "Experienced? Explain that to me. Not experienced sexually or with men?"

"Both, either. I mean…"

"Doesn't matter, love." I cut her off. I would not stand for her thinking down about herself. "I'll pick you up Sunday, we'll have a lovely brunch, and take it from there. Sound good?"

Before she could answer, a loud banging noise rang through the phone. "Mommy. Auntie!" I heard.

"Uh yeah. Perfect. I have to go." She hung up before I could say good day.

Even with the abruptness of her ringing off, I smiled wider than I think I ever had before. I shot back the remainder of my drink. The whiskey burned a fiery trail down my throat to settle warmly in my gut. In less than a week I'd see my sweet Camille again.

Before she rang off, I could have sworn I heard two different little voices calling her. Was that possible? I shook my head. That would mean there were two children living with her and one of them called her "Mommy." Camille didn't have children. She was far too young and that was something I'd have found out immediately from her or my private investigator.

That reminded me—I hadn't received the full report on Camille from Jonny Spark yet. I'd have to check in to make sure he was paying up on that favor.

CHAPTER EIGHT

Throughout the week, I received daily texts and a nightly call from Nate. He figured out quickly that it was best to call around nine, though he didn't know it was because that's when the boys were sound asleep. It was getting harder every day to keep Tanner a secret from him. At this point, I didn't even know where to start or how to broach the conversation. After two weeks of purposely avoiding any topic remotely related to children, I felt stuck. So much so that now I feared admitting the truth would be a huge issue. Something that could potentially make him lose interest in me.

Daily, I was at war with the fact that I wasn't sure whether or not I wanted Nate to move on. I enjoyed the time we'd spent together, looked forward to our date this afternoon, but I still didn't believe he could fit into my day to day life. Wealthy, stunningly handsome attorneys didn't up and change their lifestyles for a receptionist, single mother who stripped part-time. They just didn't. Jin thought I was crazy to worry. She talked me off of the cliff multiple times when confessing how I didn't see this thing between Nate and me going anywhere. She encouraged me to give it time, but also to tell him about Tanner. For some reason, I just couldn't get the words out. It was as if I'd open my mouth to tell him, and it would fill with cotton, the words not able to push through the dense, fibrous material, choking off every syllable.

Having a man call and text me regularly made me feel desired and wanted. The feeling was foreign to me, and I was afraid if he knew the truth it would end. Maybe that was selfish, but I wasn't ready to lose him. He made me feel beautiful. Unlike Tyler and the gentleman at the club, he treated me with respect. Those men looked at me as if I was a piece of meat. And for all intents and purposes, that's what I was. I shook my hips suggestively, bared my breasts, and took their cash without remorse, and I planned to do it again and again to provide my son with the life he deserved.

Thinking of the life Tanner deserved, on top of the daily text and calls from Nate I looked forward to, I received several more from my new friend Oliver. He was bound and determined to get me to sue Tyler for child support. Oliver was convinced I would be living the high life with the amount of money and back child support Tyler would owe, even taking into consideration the ten thousand he gave me to "get rid of it." He didn't understand. I didn't want anything from Tyler. I'd done just fine on my own, and Tanner didn't need to know who that man is or what kind of person he came from. If I sued for support, Tyler could turn around and sue for custody, and claim I disappeared with his child. I had read a lot about the subject, and I *would* up and disappear if that despicable excuse for a human being was given access to my child.

With a deep sigh, I slipped the gauzy maxi dress over my shoulders and down my length. It was kelly green and matched my eyes. I added a crocheted thick belt around the waist to accentuate my curves and stepped into my favorite pair of well-worn wedge sandals. With a chunky necklace, gold earrings, and bangles, I was ready for my date with Nate. He didn't share where he was taking me, and I didn't ask, preferring to be surprised. Regardless of where we went, the dress would be appropriate for just about anything. I grabbed a long cardigan that went well with the outfit and made my way to the living room.

Jin was sitting on the floor with the boys around a game of Chutes and Ladders. "You look great!" She hopped up and hugged me.

"Thanks, I'm going to wait on the steps for him. Are you sure you're fine with watching them through the evening? This is supposed to your day off, too, and I've got you watching Tan Man."

Jin rolled her eyes and shook her head. Tendrils of black hair swung from side to side. She belonged in a Pantene shampoo advertisement. I coveted those shiny ebony locks. No matter what I did, my hair would always be a dull brown with a little bit of body. At least I could rock the beachy look, mostly because it didn't take any effort other than a few spritzes of gel here and there and a crunch of the hands.

"Relax, Cam. I'm not doing anything. Besides, you'd do it for me." She knows I would and I have. She's had her share of one-night stands, but she always came home even if it was the middle of the night.

Quickly, I hugged her and headed toward the door. I was startled by a loud knock. Bone-crushing fear skittered down my spine. Jin's eyes widened.

"Looks like your secret is about to be revealed," she whispered. I looked at her with the biggest puppy dog expression. She stomped her foot and went over to the boys. "Guys, can you come with me for a second?"

"But…but…I'm about to go down the big ladder!" Zach griped.

"And you will in a moment." The knock at the door got louder. I pressed my hand against the cool wooden surface willing Jin and the boys to hurry.

"Just a minute!" I called through the door. When Jin had the boys out of sight, I opened the door quickly.

"Hey you," I said, breathless, trying desperately to control the jittery nerves skating along the surface of my body.

Without words, I was pulled by strong hands that plunged into my hair at the nape and Nate's warm lips were on mine. For long moments, he moved my head from side to side then slipped his tongue into my mouth, holding me in place against him. The kiss was wet, hot, and had my temperature to scalding in seconds. I gripped the back of his neck and kissed him like I'd never get another chance. He tasted of mint and man. Delicious. Behind me the door closed, breaking us out of our trance.

"Sorry. When you opened that door and stood there with your eyes shining like shamrocks in the sun…I just couldn't contain myself. I had to kiss you."

"No complaints here," I said still in his arms. He kissed me one more time, pulled away and laced his fingers with mine. I loved when he held my hand.

"So who slammed the door on us?" he grinned.

"That would be Jin. She probably didn't want to see us, you know…" I looked down knowing my cheeks would be stained pink.

"I'd like to meet her." Nate tugged my arm as I was trying to pull him toward the stairs.

"Not right now. She worked late last night and is probably still in her pajamas."

"Oh yeah? What does she do, work at a pub?"

"Yeah, something like that. Come on, I'm starving!"

"Then I must feed you, my love." The words "my" and "love" ran together from his lips, filling me with hope for a future I didn't think I could have.

Instead of a fancy brunch like I expected, we ended up at the famous Carnegie Deli on 55th and 7th Avenue. The sandwiches were literally the size of my head, piled sky-high with meat. It wasn't possible to eat a whole one in a sitting, so we agreed to share a turkey and Swiss. Seating was limited in the bustling tourist location, but I didn't care. We actually ended up squeezed between a family from Minnesota and a couple speaking what I assumed was Russian. The male from Minnesota thumped his chest, made a growling sound, and plowed through his entire pastrami on rye, washing it down with at least three beers. It was downright impressive. Through our lunch Nate and I took bets on whether or not the man could finish it. I won the bet and Nate quickly handed me over a crisp one-hundred-dollar bill.

"What is this? We bet a dollar!" I screeched loud enough for the tables on either side of us to pay closer attention.

"Oh, I thought it was a hundred." Nate squinted and tilted his head to the side, his gaze focused intently on mine.

I shook my head dramatically, realizing he had no intention of taking the money back. "No way. I could never afford to bet that much. Take it back!" I felt swathed in heat as my emotions ran wild.

He shook his head and shrugged. "A bet's a bet, love. I thought it was for a hundred."

As nice as it would be to have an extra hundred dollars that I didn't have to shake my moneymaker for, there was no way I'd take it from him. The idea alone soured my gut, making the turkey-and-Swiss sit like a lead brick.

"Take it or I go home now!" I knew I was being irrational. Nate's features went from happy to aloof, then straight to confused. Once the crazy train left, there was no stopping it. I finished, "Don't ever hand me a hundred-dollar bill again."

That visual was too close to home. Nate made me feel like a lady. As if I was special. Not some cheap stripper who twirled her goodies for cash. I never wanted him to think of me that way. I never wanted him to find out about my side job. I crossed my arms defensively and looked out the window.

I will not cry. I will not cry. I will not cry.

"Hey, hey, precious. Blimey. What's the matter? I'll take the money back." He pulled the bill from the table and placed it in his pocket. "Okay. No worries?"

"Thank you," I whispered and looked down at my half-eaten sandwich. Technically, it was half of a half, but I was still stuffed to the brim.

Nate lifted my chin, his eyes dark with concern. I smiled for his benefit and he gave me one in return. "There's my precious girl." I could feel my cheeks heat as he petted my bottom lip. "So beautiful."

After Nate settled the bill, he clasped my hand and we walked the streets of New York. Something as simple as holding this man's hand made me feel important, special somehow. It was still early when I realized he'd walked us to the theatre district. My mood had improved over the twenty-minute walk.

"Are we seeing a show?" I inquired with a happiness I didn't even try to hide.

He grinned. "Would you like that?"

"Very much! I've never been to a Broadway play. I've never been to any play!" I looked at all the theatre signs surrounded with big flashing bulbs. Even in the daylight, it seemed brighter and more exciting than any other part of the city. When I caught Nate's gaze, he looked at me with sadness.

"What is it?" I clasped both his hands, and he pulled me into a tight hug. New Yorkers rushed by us, grumbling their annoyance at our position in the center of the sidewalk.

Nate held me close, a hand braced on my lower back and the other clasped at my nape, keeping me pressed firmly to him. He whispered in my ear, so low I could barely hear him, "I want to show you everything, Camille. Give you the world. Experience life with you."

I gasped and pulled back. "Nate?"

"It's true. Your innocence, your love of life, of every new thing…it's intoxicating. I want to drink it whole. Bathe in it. Remove my clothes and swim naked in it. Letting the goodness wash away all that came before the moment you entered my life."

Instead of a reply, I kissed him. Slow, deep, in the middle of the New York City street. The bells, whistles, horns, city noise all disappeared as I entered the world of love. I was falling in love with him.

★ ★ ★

Christ! It wasn't possible to feel this much so quickly. Or

was it? All I knew was that having my sweet Camille's lips on mine, holding her within the security of my arms, I was happy. Not happy as in, "Yeah, I'm happy my team won the game" or "So happy you got that deposition in on time without any errors." No, this was all over, from the soles of my shoes to the very tip-top of my hair, "I'm never going to have anything better than this woman right here," kind of happy.

The feeling was so new to me that I held onto my woman tighter, never wanting to let her go. Instead of pulling away, she clung to me, nails digging into the skin of my back as I plastered her against me. Finally, I pulled back, gave her a small peck on the lips, gripped her hand, and walked toward the theatre.

"Okay, we have a few choices. We can go sweet with Mamma Mia!" She shrugged. "We can go tough with Rocky." I punched the air playfully and watched her nose crinkle, immediately knocking that off the list. "Or, we can go sexy with Chicago." I waggled my eyebrows. She gave a coy smile. "Chicago it is!" I said with a laugh. Her eyes lit with excitement, and she did the cutest thing I had ever seen. She jumped up into the air and spun around, her green dress flowing around her in a cloud of color. My God the woman was ethereal.

"I take it you like that idea?"

She hugged me tight and kissed my cheek. "I'm so excited!"

If she had that response to everything we did, I would go a long way toward planning outings as often as our schedules allowed. I wanted nothing more than to see that smile adorn her beautiful face and those emerald eyes alight with glee. Knowing I put that look there made me feel like a king.

We got our tickets, sat at the bar, and had a couple cocktails prior to the show. We were early, but she didn't mind. Camille was perfectly content to sit and talk with me the entire hour before the show started. My girl wasn't high maintenance and went with the flow. I was beginning to believe she was the perfect woman.

We held hands, and I made a point to touch her throughout the show. Nothing overt or unsavory, just a sweep of my thumb along her bare neck, a tickle to the knee, a kiss to the ball of her shoulder. It was refreshing to be giddy and enjoy a show with a woman. No pretenses, no ulterior motive, just being myself while out with the world's most beautiful woman. And she was just that. Beautiful. In all the ways that mattered most. Camille was kind, laughed a lot, sweet and innocent in so many things. I felt a roaring sense of protectiveness coupled with an overwhelming desire to expose her to all the wonderful things she'd never experienced.

When the cast took their bows, I watched her profile. Her smile was the biggest I had seen yet. She clapped so loud and hard I worried she'd bruise herself.

"What did you think?" I asked as we made our way out of the theatre.

"What did I think?" She grabbed her skirt with one hand, my hand in the other, and swung them both, almost skipping down the street. "It was incredible. Amazing. Wonderful. Sad. Exciting. Sexy. Oh, just everything!" she beamed. She was happy, alight with joy. I wanted to capture this moment. With great stealth, I pulled out my phone, tugged on her hand, aimed, and when she turned around, I clicked. Her multicolored waves were flowing around her face, her cheeks were a rosy red, lips a bit swollen from the kiss I'd stolen in the dark at the end of the show, and her eyes were shining. She was a goddess.

"Not fair! My phone doesn't have a camera," she pouted.

"What? All phones have cameras!" I scoffed.

She shook her head. "Not mine. Mine is just for calls and text. No frills, but it works just fine." She patted her purse as if petting the head of her most trusted furry friend.

"Where to now?" she asked as I put my arm in the air at the edge of the street. Before too long, a yellow duckling pulled to the edge of the street. We entered the taxi, and I held her near.

"My flat. I'm going to cook for you," I whispered and then nuzzled the side of her cheek, trailing my nose along the fine column of her neck. Her scent was strongest here and I adored it.

"You're taking me to your house?" Her tone clearly expressed trepidation.

"Precious, nothing that you don't want to happen will happen. I assure you."

She took a deep breath. "No, I trust you." She turned her head and her eyes captured mine. The green around her irises were as dark as the sun, setting over the city landscape. "I want you to cook for me…and possibly more." The last part was a whisper. I heard every word. My prick tightened in my jeans, and I moved to adjust.

I took a deep breath and stared into her eyes. "I will cook for you. You will eat, drink, and if it feels right…we'll consider more."

She smiled and leaned in for a kiss. I let her control this kiss, forcing myself not to burrow my hand into her hair and crush her to me. I wanted her to know that I valued her trust and that even though I wanted to shag her more than I wanted my next meal, I'd wait for her to be ready. When it happened, everything would change. I could only hope it changed for the better.

Her lips held mine, and her little tongue shot out and licked my bottom lip. I opened my mouth in a groan. She took advantage, tentatively dipping in for a taste. She was delicious. Tasted of almond and cherries from the mixed amaretto she drank earlier. It made me so thirsty I wanted to drink from the well that was her kiss all night long. Camille deepened the kiss, moving closer to my body until she was practically sitting in my lap. I didn't mind. The more of her touching me the better. Her tongue danced along mine, a sensuous tango with little flicks and nips of her teeth to accentuate her desire.

We were so busy making out in the back of the cab, I didn't realize the carriage had stopped moving.

"Hey, love birds! We're here. Whad-da-ya say you pay up and move your sexy time to your own space, eh?" the cab driver scolded us in a thick, New York accent.

Camille's cheeks pinked instantly. She held her hand over her lips and got out of the cab. I paid the man, tipping extra, and ushered my girl into the building.

"You live downtown?" She surveyed the area. "We're so close to AIR Bright!"

I smiled. "Living in the city has its conveniences. One being Stone, Walker, & Associates is just down the street. I walk to work unless it's raining or I have clients to meet."

"I have to take a train to work. I enjoy it though. Gives me some quiet time I'm not used to having."

"Oh yeah? Why's that? Because your roommate and her son are loud?"

"Sort of. I'm looking forward to finding out what you're cooking for me." She nudged my shoulder with her own, catapulting me into moving.

We rode the elevator up to my floor making small talk. I opened the door to my flat and took her jumper and hung it on the coat tree. When I turned around, she had entered the main living area and was spinning in a slow circle, her mouth open, a wondrous look plastered across her lovely face.

"Wow, this is amazing." The last word came out sounding like two words "Auh-Mazing." Something about her loving my home sent my heart thudding in my chest like a bass drum.

"I'm glad you approve. I'll give you the tour." I held her hand and showed her the spare rooms, the den, my home gym, each of the three bathrooms, and the wine closet. I brought her to the master bedroom. Instead of entering, I opened the door and let her look in. I didn't want her to feel I brought her here to get her into bed. I genuinely wanted her to feel comfortable in my space and enjoy a home cooked meal with me.

Once she oohed and aahed over each room, I brought her to the kitchen to one of my high back stools at the bar. "Fancy some wine?"

"Yes, please."

I served us both wine and then got right to work on

the chicken marsala I had planned to woo her with.

"So who designed your place?" she asked.

"Actually, I did. But I'm having my brother's girlfriend, London Kelley, redo the entire thing. You know London." She nodded. "I'm looking for something a bit more sophisticated."

"Really?" Her jaw hung and her eyes widened. "It's so magnificent. If I lived in a home like this, I'd never want to leave."

"Thank you. I think it needs a woman's touch, and since a woman has never lived here, it feels too bachelor pad." I poured the pasta into the boiling water and took a sip of wine.

"So you've never lived with a woman?" She must have regretted asking. She gasped after the words escaped her pink lips.

I laughed. "Never met a woman I wanted to share a living space with. Until now maybe." I crooked an eyebrow in her direction. Her eyes widened and her face paled. "Relax, love. I'm not asking you to move in with me." Her entire body visibly relaxed, which I found adorable. "I can't help saying though that I enjoy seeing you sitting in my home, drinking a glass of wine, me preparing a meal for you."

Camille lowered her eyes but her smile gave away her pleasure. "I like being here. It feels comfortable. I worried that it wouldn't."

"Why's that?"

"I told you before. I don't have much experience… with, um, men. I haven't dated really in the last few years."

The word "years" struck a chord. Tyler had said he

dated Camille years ago. She just confirmed that she hadn't dated in years.

"When was the last time you were on a date?" I did my best to soften my gaze and leaned over the counter to get closer to her.

She took a deep breath, blowing a few wisps of hair from her brow. "Can we talk about something else?"

I shook my head. "No, precious, we can't. How long?"

She pinched her lips, looked away, and then finally spoke, "Five years."

"You haven't been with a man in five years? How long ago were you with Ty?"

Camille's shoulders tightened. She lifted her glass to take a sip, and then responded through her glass. "Five years," were her muffled words.

"Ty was the last man you were with?" I jolted as she bit her lip, clenched her hands into fists, and nodded. Christ. Fuck all!

"I told you I wasn't very experienced." Her voice was so low I could barely hear her.

"Camille, is Ty the only man you've ever been with?" My tone was clearly shocked, because for fuck's sake, I *was* shocked. I couldn't imagine such a beautiful woman only having been touched by one man. And of course the fucking sod was none other than my best mate.

"Is it really that big of a deal?" she asked, pulling a long lock of hair into both of her hands and rubbing it delicately between her fingers.

I placed my hands on the granite counter and took a cleansing breath. Was it really that bad? Yes. It was womanizer Ty who'd taken her virginity so carelessly. I knew that based solely on his vulgar reply to my text last week. Regarding the inexperience, no, that was a blessing. She was practically untouched. Heat built at the base of my spine spreading heavily to my balls and cock. Throughout the afternoon, I was trying to keep it together but just the thought of being with such an innocent had me hard as the countertop.

I glanced at the lovely Camille. She worried her lips with her teeth and held her hands so tight her knuckles had turned white.

I weaved a path around the bar, slid my hands to her waist along her thighs to push her knees wide apart. She gasped as I pressed in between her open legs, caging my body exactly where I wanted to be. Her skirt was safely guarding her modesty, but this close, I was able to fully gauge her feelings.

"It's not a big deal. I'm sorry I asked. That was uncalled for. You tense up when I mention Ty's name." Again her shoulders tightened. I cupped each side of her neck, rubbed the area where her shoulders met, and massaged the tension until she was a wet noodle in my arms.

She groaned and tilted her head back. I took that as an offering of her delectable neck. I placed long slow kisses from the tip of her chin down the underside along the front of her neck to the hollow between her clavicles. There I dipped my tongue and swirled it, tasting her. Her hands slowly became more inquisitive, her nails dragging along the bare skin of my forearms, driving me insane with lust. My sweet Camille had no idea what she was doing to me. If we didn't stop soon, I'd have her laid out bare on my kitchen counter. She deserved better than that. So much better. Camille deserved to be worshiped, and I planned on doing just that.

CHAPTER NINE

Nate pulled away and slid his hands along my arms from the ball of my shoulder down to my fingertips. Chills raced along the skin he caressed. With a sweetness that could only be seen in his eyes and the tilt of his head, he brought my hands to his lips and proceeded to kiss every finger.

With a deep breath and a calming sigh, I answered him. "It's really okay that you asked. I put it out there. I'm embarrassed that *he* was the man I gave myself to, but it was a very brief relationship. It only lasted a little longer than a month and ended poorly. He's not a good man. Not like you are." I held his hands, and repeated his motion kissing each of his knuckles instead.

When I looked up, I was surprised to see a glacial, icy glare. "What do you mean he's not a good man, Camille? Did he hurt you?" he said through clenched teeth.

"Nate, it was a long time ago. I barely remember. Right now, I want to focus on us, you and me. Tonight." At that moment, a buzzer went off. For a few long moments, Nate ignored the blaring alarm. "You're going to burn our dinner, and then how are you going to woo me with your cooking prowess?"

His features softened and a coy grin melted the anger from his face. "You'd be surprised at my abilities, precious. Cooking is but one of my specialties." He waggled his brows and placed a sweet kiss to my wrist, and then moved from between my legs to manage the rest of the dinner duties. Instantly, I missed having him there. His warmth had seeped into my skin and straight through to my soul. Who knew that dominant alpha, type-A personality Nathaniel Walker would end up being a gentleman? That was a most pleasant surprise.

I was certain that his aggressive, confident nature would flow into his relationships, but he was treating me like a lady, being the perfect…well, the perfect man. Not pushing or taking advantage as he had when we first met. It would be all too easy for him to steamroll his way into my panties. I almost wished he would push a little harder. I wanted to let go, be with him in all ways. He'd had me on a slow burn since the moment we spoke on the phone two weeks ago. Watching him cook, move around his kitchen, all tight muscles and strong arms had my body tingling in places it hadn't in so long. Every time Nate put his fingertips to my skin, it electrified, sparked, turned on something that had long sat dormant.

We ate his home-cooked chicken marsala paired with the most scrumptious caprese salad I'd ever had at the bar in his kitchen. He asked about my online schooling and whether I enjoyed working for Hank. I explained that I was holding out hope that at my six-month review, I'd get a raise and full medical benefits. He frowned at that information. Probably something he'd never had to worry about. What I didn't share was that if a raise and benefits occurred, I'd be able to afford to quit stripping at Gems, which was the ultimate goal. It would also give me more time in the evenings to work on my studies, allowing me to get through my coursework more quickly. As was my new habit, I made sure to change the subject back to him, so he couldn't barrage me with questions about things I wasn't prepared to answer.

Nate told me more about his family and how happy he was that his brother, Collier, had found his soul mate in London, Hank's sister-in-law. He shared the experience they had a few months prior when Collier almost died the night of Hank and Aspen's wedding in a nasty car accident. Then after medical tests, found out that her best friend Tripp, who I hadn't met yet, was a match and gave him a kidney.

"That is wild! I can't believe that. And you say Collier and Tripp weren't close?"

Nate shook his head. "Quite the opposite actually. The two men barely tolerated one another," he laughed.

"And he still donated his kidney to him?"

Nate nodded and took a bite of his pasta and chicken with a huge grin on his face. I loved that smile. It could make any dark day brighter. "Wow. I can't imagine what that must have been like for London. And now they're the best of friends?"

"Yeah. It all worked out aces!" Nate stood, went to the fridge, and pulled out some fresh pears. He set them on the cutting board and started slicing.

I got up from my chair and moved around the counter. "Can I help?" My arm brushed his and he smiled. He sliced a piece of pear and held it up to my lips.

"I was going to make a pear dish that would rock your world." His eyebrows rose as he focused intently on my mouth. He brought the pear close to my lips. I licked them and watched his jaw tic. "Open." His words slithered down my spine and settled between my thighs.

Grabbing his wrist, I pushed his hand down. He dropped the slice of pear. "I'm not hungry for food."

He placed his hands at my hips and brought his pelvis hard against mine. I could feel the distinct outline of an erection along my stomach. "What are you in the mood for, my love?" I closed my eyes and let those words give me courage.

"More," I whispered.

His fingers tightened, digging into the flesh at my hips.

"Open your eyes, precious." I did, and what I saw made my knees weak. His light eyes were almost black. His hands came up to cup each side of my neck, thumbs sliding along my cheekbones. "Are you sure?"

"I want to be with you, Nate." My words sounded shaky but heartfelt.

"Christ." His lips crushed mine, his tongue seeking entrance. I gave it to him, then took my own drink of his kiss. He tasted like the rich wine we'd consumed, and I wanted so much more of it. In a debonairly smooth move, Nate bent me low, hooked an arm around both of my knees, and lifted me off the floor without breaking our lip lock.

He carried me through his home until he stopped and set me on my feet. The bed frame pressed into the back of my legs. His lips moved down my neck, gliding along the column. His fingers searched my back and then wandered along my rib cage. "Blimey! Where in the hell is it?" He pulled back breathing erratically.

I yanked at my belt, and let it fall to the floor. "It doesn't have any zippers. It goes over the head, silly." I laughed.

With a flourish, he tugged the end of my dress and whipped it over my head. The green fabric floated delicately to the floor. He took a step back, his gaze roaming over every inch of my skin. "Camille, Christ. I had no idea…" His words were lost as he inhaled, his nostrils flaring. Fear consumed me as worry filled the space between us. He stood silently taking in every speck of my bared body. Uncertainty slithered through my mind, not confident he liked what he saw. Every second seemed like an eternity until finally he growled, "You're so bloody perfect." Then…he pounced.

All the air left my chest as he captured me. A willing participant to his desire, his lust, his everything. Those long fingers slid along the curve of my hip, up each bump in my spine, until lastly he curled a hand in the hair at my nape pulling me closer. I could feel his words against my bottom lip as it trembled. "You're going to own it," he whispered a gravelly tone that I felt pierce my heart.

"Own what?" I closed my eyes, preferring to let his voice set the mood.

"Everything, anything." His words spun through my mind like a merry-go-round, delightful at first, then dizzying. He nipped my lips, sharp little bites expressing his need. His hunger was strong and matched my own. I could feel the current of desire running through him in my fingertips digging into his shoulder blades. "As long as I get it in return," he finished. I tilted my head back trying to understand and put some space in the haze of need surrounding us.

"What do you want?" I asked as he soaked the skin of my neck with shallow kisses, dragging his teeth along the sensitive skin. "Anything…please, Nate," I begged, not knowing what I was begging for. What I needed. I just needed something and knew beyond a shadow of a doubt that he'd be the one to give it to me. "Anything you want from me…it's yours."

He growled low in his throat, and I knew my words broke through the haze. The corresponding kiss lifted me to the heavens, to where my deepest darkest dreams lay, waiting for someone to come along and make me believe again. Someone to help make my dreams come true.

"I want it all, precious." He cupped my neck and used his thumb to bring my chin down so that our gazes locked. "Your body."

I shivered.

"Your heart."

I lost the ability to swallow.

"Your soul."

I stopped breathing.

Then he captured my lips. Light, sound, feel, and touch collided in a supernova of need. I ripped at his clothes. His shirt was gone in a millisecond. The pants were shoved down in a torrent of activity, our hands working as one solid unit. I hadn't even a moment to view his body before he was on top of me, my thighs cradling his waist.

Nate kissed me the way every woman dreamed of being kissed. Slow and chaste, then hard and deep. His tongue searched and found, taking what he wanted. I gave freely.

He pulled back and I chased his mouth, craning my neck to suck that luscious bottom lip, nibbling the flesh. A groan spilled deep from his throat.

Long fingers trailed up each rib until his hands were there. Right *there*, squeezing and molding the mounds of my breasts. He unclasped my bra, and slid each cup aside. Nate moved back onto his haunches, caging me with a muscular thigh at each hip. I gripped each thigh and then scratched my nails along the rough solid muscle. He inhaled, his jaw clenched tight, his gaze eating up every inch.

Nate's hands caressed each breast then focused a finger on the tender peaks. He lifted his thumbs to his mouth and licked the digits before bringing them down to my breasts once more, circling each nipple in maddening spirals. Ribbons of pleasure ripped down my chest and settled heavily between my thighs, soaking my panties. I arched and closed my eyes, not able to watch him touch me. It was too much.

"Years since you've been touched…" He pinched each nipple lightly, incrementally adding pressure. A low-pitched mewl escaped my dry lips. I wetted them and sucked in quick breaths as he alternated between petting, twisting, and plucking at both peaks simultaneously. Pleasure shot through me, and I dug my nails deep into his thighs. "That's it, precious. I want you wild for me. I'm going to make you come just from playing with your perfect tits."

Oh my God. The things he said, the words he used intensified my desire for him to embarrassing proportions. Wetness coated the thin fabric of my underwear. My hips undulated, moving up and down, all around, driven by an incessant throbbing in my clit, seeking the sweet pressure he was denying me.

"I love watching you fall apart in my arms," he said as he added pressure to each nipple. The small pinch of pain coalesced into extreme pleasure. I closed my eyes tight, focused on the feeling of his fingers, single-handedly plucking me into oblivion. He was going to get his wish. I was going to soar into the clouds. The pressure built low in my spine. He shifted his hips and rubbed his erection against my clit, once, twice. I shook uncontrollably. My nails dug firmly into the thick muscle of his thighs.

"You're stunning, Camille." A wet sensation brought me from the precipice of orgasm until I looked down and watched his tongue come out to flick at one reddened erect peak. My nipples were so hard and tight they looked like pencil erasers. I moaned at the sight, never having felt this turned on in my life. His light eyes shone brightly as he watched my face. I could barely keep my eyes open, but I had to watch. I needed to see him bring me over the edge. One of his dark brows crooked into a point as the flat of his tongue swirled in circles around a glistening tip.

It was too much. His eyes on me, body holding me flush against his golden skin. I tipped my head back, arched into him as the heavy ache between my legs grew, splintered, ready to blow. "Eyes, Camille."

My eyes opened and held his. He put his lips to the oversensitive tip, and with a sexy grin, laid his mouth over it, and sucked. Hard. That's all it took. I crashed into nirvana. Long drawing pulls from the tortured flesh sent ropes of pleasure directly to the aching space between my thighs. His hands grasped mine and held them above my head as a tingling, burning sensation, ripped through my limbs, trying to find a way for this extraordinary ball of energy to exit. He was relentless in his pursuit of my orgasm. Nipping, sucking, not letting up. Pleasure soared, swelled higher. Just when I thought I'd come down from the top, couldn't withstand one more spike of pleasure, he switched breasts. I felt like I was going to explode. My body gyrated in thin air as he held me in place.

He wasn't going to let me come down. I was convinced I would die from extreme joy when finally one of his hands plunged into my soaked panties, found the hard kernel of my clit with two fingers, and massaged the tight knot.

I screamed out in agony, in pleasure, lost to the heaven that was his touch as a stronger, harder orgasm ripped through me. His mouth covered mine in a heated kiss, swallowing my cries. It was as if my body was possessed. My legs spread wide, accepting what he gave greedily. His hand jerked and tugged at my cleft, wringing every last tremor. Finally, his fingers slowed allowing me to come down from my second mind-bending release.

"God, precious. I'm going to eat you alive. I have to. I can't stop." Nate's eyes were wild and completely black with lust.

Before I could respond, he crawled down my body, kissing my nipples and giving them a little suck. I moaned with the pleasure-pain, the peaks too sensitive for more attention but still reacting to his sweet torture. He didn't play long, continuing down my body, nibbling each rib, licking into my navel. "Your scent. Bloody hell. Gotta have it."

"What? Nate, what are you talking about?"

"Your taste on my tongue." When the words hit my lust-riddled brain, I panicked. My thighs snapped together just after he pulled off my panties.

★ ★ ★

"Open, precious." I tapped each knee. She shook her head, her face unreadable.

I figured it was her, I'm-so-far-gone-out-of-my-mind-I-can't-take-anymore look. "Don't worry. I'm going to make it so good for you. I made you come sucking on your pretty tits, then by fingering that hard clit. Now I'm going to do it by licking your wet pussy."

She bit her lip so hard the skin around it turned red. She shook her head again.

"Oh, yes, and then, baby, I'm going to make you come so hard around my prick you'll pass out screaming my name."

"Jesus, Nate." Her tone warned.

"Come on, open up." I tugged at her knees. She didn't let go. "Precious." I looked at her face. Something had changed. Gone was the lust-filled gleam of moments ago. Excitement and lust no longer clouded her pretty features. What remained scared the hell out of me. It was the same frightened look she'd worn when she spotted Ty at lunch. "What's wrong?"

"I…um. I've never done that…" Her voice trailed off.

"What?" The pleasure haze was softening, and her words slowly seeped through but didn't make sense. How was that even possible?

"Tyler never did that." She pointed to the general vicinity of her sex and then turned her head to the side, breaking eye contact. I wouldn't have it. I needed her eyes. They said so much more than she was able to verbalize.

I pulled her chin back, cupped her cheek, and slid my naked body down alongside hers. She relaxed slightly when I brought an arm around her middle. With slow movements, I trailed just the tips of my fingers along her belly, traced the circle of her tiny navel, and spread my fingers wide across her ribcage. It was hard for me to see her spread out, naked, my own veritable feast, and still be able to put the brakes on.

"You're telling me that daft bastard never had his mouth on you?"

Camille curled her head into my chest and hugged me. She shook her head. "It took a long time to realize it was never about me. Years, in fact. It was always about him getting off. You gave me the first orgasms I've ever had with a man," she mumbled into my chest.

That arsehole. Piece of shite motherfucker.

He used my sweet Camille to get his jollies and never once gave her an ounce of real pleasure. It was blasphemous. Unthinkable. I'd never use a woman like that. Particularly one so young and impressionable. Christ. She'd been eighteen and a virgin. It was going to take a lot for my relationship with Tyler to survive this, if it could at all.

I tilted her head back from her hiding place along my chest. Her eyes were watery, but I wouldn't allow tears to fall. She would not be embarrassed by this. Hell, the fact that she was even more inexperienced set a primal thrum buzzing through my veins, setting off an allover body hum, the animal magnetism of a man who's about to stake his claim. "Precious, I'm not him. I'm never going to be him. I want to worship your beautiful body. Repeatedly." I cupped her hip to accentuate the point. "I want to give you pleasure. Everywhere." I kissed her soft lips. "Every way possible." Kiss. "And I'm going to. Starting now."

"Will you make love to me?" Her voice didn't hold the strength and confidence I wanted to hear when in bed with my girl for the first time. That would change now.

"Yes. A million times yes." I kissed her deep, letting our tongues sway and meld together. Soon she relaxed into my kiss and tugged on my hair, trying to get closer. Her excitement built. Rolling her onto her back, I nudged a knee in between hers and settled between her thighs. Home. This feeling, lying naked in the arms of *this* woman felt right. Perfect. "There will be time for other fun things later. I'm dying to be inside you."

"Please, Nate. I need you." Her voice cracked and something inside me broke along with it. The wall I'd built around my heart where the need and desire for another living being to share my world was obliterated with those three little words spoken from her lips. She needed me. Someone on this earth besides my family needed *me*. For the first time I admitted I needed *her* right back.

With extreme effort, I slowly opened the petals of her sex and centered my prick at her entrance. "Precious, you have me." I pressed deep into her willing body, one slow inch at a time. So deep, I couldn't go any farther. We were fused. Just one person. I closed my eyes and touched my lips to hers as she inhaled at the height of my body entering hers. "You have all of me."

"Nate…it's so…God, it's so good."

And it was. Having her lithe body wrapped around me, her tight pussy clenched like a fist around my cock was bliss. Nothing had ever been better, until she pulled her legs up to close them around my waist. Impossibly, my cock dipped in an inch farther. We both moaned, sharing one another's breath.

I couldn't stay still any longer. I had to move. Make her mine. Bring her to the precipice again. Watch her fall apart all around me. Holding one leg high on my hip, I pulled out and then slid home again. She gasped and pulled her other leg higher letting me in, opening her body fully for the taking. Long strokes in and out had her purring like a baby kitten. It was my own personal symphony, one I played over and over again until her gasps and moans grew loud. Sweat beaded on my forehead as I staved off my own release, wanting, needing to watch the crescendo when it hit.

"I love…so, oh God. Nate. Nate!" she cried out. I lifted her hips, palmed her arse, and rammed my cock home, grating along that magic spot deep within her. I watched her face as she opened her mouth, a wordless whisper escaped, like a powerful gust of wind roaring past my ear, wild and untamed.

One, two, three hard thrusts into her sexy body, and I leaned down, slipped my hands under her shoulders for leverage, and clung tight. The pressure built low in my back and spread out through my prick. Camille's lips were all over me. She kissed along my hair line, licked the sensitive skin along the thick tendon down my neck, and nibbled my earlobe. Sod all, she was perfect.

Bright pinpoints of light seared my vision as she kissed me. I felt the heavy weight of the boys going high and tight. One final thrust into her sweet cunt, and I growled into Camille's neck, biting down on the spot where her neck met her shoulder. Mine. She inhaled then and sighed as heavy spurts of my release poured into her body. I rubbed out the last vestiges of pleasure against her clit, crushing it with the weight of my pelvic bone. She gave a little "oh" as her pussy clenched around my cock one last time, milking every drop.

After, I stayed on top of her for long minutes, not wanting to leave the serenity of her embrace. I knew I was weighing her down, but she clung to me with all four limbs, not relaxing her hold. "Precious, loosen up." I laughed.

"Don't want too." She nuzzled my neck and nipped the skin there. I closed my eyes and enjoyed feeling her wrapped around me, our bodies flush against one another. The scent of our coupling permeated the air with a rich, musky aroma.

Finally, I felt her muscles slacken, and I pushed up. My hand caught something sharp as I balanced above her. Flitting around in the blanket my fingers grasped the offending item. I held it up focusing on the diabolical little square.

All air left my lungs as I stared at the unopened foil packet. Sliding out of her body, I watched with a sick fascination as my seed trickled out and coated her thighs. For a brief couple seconds, I enjoyed seeing my mark spilling out from between her legs. The alpha male in me wanted to howl at the moon that I'd staked my claim, laid my mark, filled her full. The intelligent thirty-year-old brain took over and scowled.

"Fuck!" I closed my eyes and took a deep breath. Camille popped to a seated position.

"What's the matter?" Her eyebrows knit together, and I hated to see the tension back on her brow. A scant few minutes ago she was languid, relaxed and coated in post-coital happiness.

"Tell me you're on the pill?"

Her eyes went as wide as saucers. She bit her lip and shook her head. All sound left the room. I think we were both afraid to breathe for fear it would tip the scales of fate negatively. We both just stared at the unopened condom packet. Tears built in her eyes, and one fell down the side of her cheek.

"Camille, don't…" I pulled her to me and tucked her head under my chin. "It's going to be okay."

"No, it's not. It will never be the same again."

"Precious, don't say that. Hey, hey, look at me." I pulled her chin around so that I could look into her eyes. "It will be okay."

Another tear slipped down each cheek. I wiped each one away quickly, hating them and the fact that I put them there. With a strength I wasn't sure I owned, I held her gaze and made sure not to flinch. "Whatever happens… we'll handle it together? Okay?" In that moment, I knew I needed to take the responsibility for our actions.

Finally, she nodded, and I snuggled her against my chest and laid back. We lay clutching one another until I felt her body relax, her breath soften. She slipped into sleep. Visions of baby boys and girls entered my thoughts. I tossed them aside like yesterday's rubbish. I could not go down that road now. Then, just as I started to fall asleep, the unearthly vision of Camille's lean body rounded, glowing and fertile with my child growing inside her was quite possibly the most splendid incantation of life's beauty I had ever seen.

Hours later, I awoke rested, ready to take on the day and handle our potential problem together. I rolled over and felt the space next to me. It was ice cold. There was no warmth from the body I had held, made love to, fallen asleep next to. She was gone. At some point in the wee hours of the morning, Camille had left me alone, naked in a bed that should have been for two.

CHAPTER TEN

It was wrong. I shouldn't have done it. Been beating myself up over it for the past several hours. The problem is that I'm not sorry I did it. Slipping out of that devastatingly handsome man's bed, his arms curled around my naked form, was the hardest thing I'd done in a long while. Yet, it still had to be done.

Getting attached to Nathaniel Walker was not smart, even after having spent the most glorious time with him. Our date was the stuff they made romantic movies about. A day filled with a lot of laughs, light playful touches, great food, good wine, and smiles a plenty. Then…there was the evening. God, the evening will provide me with a year of fulfilled fantasies…save for one; the one where prince charming sweeps the princess off her feet and they live happily ever after in his kingdom forever. But I needed to get real. I wasn't a princess, and New York City certainly was not a faraway kingdom.

Nate, though, he was a prince. A dirty-talking, smart-dressing, sexy as hell renegade modern-day prince. He was too good for the likes of me, especially after our slipup. If the world was against me, and so far it had seemed that way, I would likely be having Nate's child nine months from now. The mere thought soured and churned heavily in my gut. Not that I didn't love children—Tanner was my world. It's the thought of repeating history, starting all over alone…again, just when things were finally making sense. It was a living nightmare. I slammed my head onto the solid oak desk, wishing I had made better choices. I was almost twenty-four and potentially a single mother of two from two different fathers.

The theme song to the Jerry Springer show tinkled across my thoughts. I was a crummy statistic. Once Nate realized who I was, what my *real* life was like, he'd tuck tail and run. Oh, he definitely seemed like a responsible guy. He'd want to help. Pay child support. Maybe even want to see the child. Then again, he could turn out just like his best friend Tyler. The man who screwed me over all those years ago when almost the exact same thing had happened. I'd gotten pregnant immediately, and here I was living a sick, twisted version of déjà vu.

"Dammit all to hell in a hand basket!" Hank roared, entering the office, one hand on his disheveled, clearly irate wife, and the other tugging on a leash. Butch, Hank and Aspen's huge yellow Lab, bounced happily inside, yanking free of his master's hold and bounding over to me.

"Hey, Butchey, Butch, Butch. How's the big guy?" I shook the scruff around the dog's neck. A cloud of loose hair flew into the air and floated onto my black skirt. It didn't bother me. That's what lint brushes and sticky tape were for. "What are you doing here, huh, fella?" I looked at Butch but expected Hank to answer.

"Get Nate Walker on the phone…now! There's been an incident." Hank's words cut like a metal blade into granite.

I glanced at Aspen, who was picking grass and whisking dirt off her behind, a scowl dampening her pretty features. She looked like she'd been in a scuffle. Her hands came around her large pregnant belly and rubbed big circles around the entire circumference. Hank charged to his wife and placed a hand on her bump. "She movin'? What's going on in there?" His voice was harsh, very unlike his normal jovial timber when he talked to her. She put a pale hand to his cheek and the other over her belly.

"She's moving just fine. Feel her right here?" His body went still, and he focused all attention on his wife. After a few moments, he took a deep breath, got down on his knees, and laid his head against her bump.

"Thank God. You're okay, right, angel?" Why wouldn't Aspen be okay? What the heck happened? Aspen nodded and smiled, her grimace leaving her face as she watched her husband worship her. He kissed her belly and leaned his forehead against her stomach. "I don't hear you dialing, Cami. I need our lawyer right fuckin' now!"

"Hank, calm down. I'm fine. The baby's fine. Butch is fine."

I dialed Stone, Walker, & Associates, dreading calling Nate, but with no other choice. My pride or my job. No contest there. I dialed his direct line, hoping maybe he wouldn't be there and I'd have to talk to Collier Stone instead. I still had no idea what this was about, but I wasn't going to risk getting into trouble to find out. Hank's demeanor, the way he held his entire body stiff and on edge, brooked no argument.

If I was lucky, Nate would have answered, "Good morning, love," as I'd hoped to hear. Maybe even a flat "Nate Walker," but instead I was prepared for him to be angry at how I left. Unfortunately, luck had never been a lady named Cami. Anything he could have said would have been a step above what actually spewed like a verbal train wreck from the speaker phone.

"You have any idea how bloody maddening it is waking up in your bed *alone* when you expect to have the woman you spent all night shagging to be there, smiling, drowsy, and ready for another go? Why ever did you leave me naked and wanting, precious?"

Kill me now.

I risked a quick look at Hank, and then Aspen. Both their eyes were huge and round, mouths agape. *Fuck my life!*

"Um, Nate. I have you on speaker. Mr. Jensen asked me to call you." I closed my eyes and put my face in my hands. There was no way on God's green earth that my face wasn't hot pink or even dark fuchsia. I was probably close to being a bruised purple from holding my breath. I wondered if anyone ever died from holding their own breath? At this point, anything would be better than the mortification of my boss and his wife knowing I spent the evening having sex with their lawyer.

"On another note," Aspen jumped right in, saving the day. I wanted to bend over and worship at her feet, kiss her designer shoes, and thank her for the reprieve. She winked and started in, all business. "On our walk this morning through Central Park, we had a little trouble. You see this man…"

"This fuckin' dickwad tried to put his hands on my wife's belly," Hank hollered loud enough to shake the glass from the building next door.

"Oh no…" Nate chimed in.

Hank continued his rant. "Like her fuckin' pregnant belly is open season for any Tom, Dick, and Harry to grope.

You should have seen the rat bastard reach out with both hands to touch my fuckin' wife." Hank didn't usually cuss this much. Watching his face turn red, his jaw clenched so tight he could break rocks with his teeth, I knew he was too far gone to rein it in.

"Hank, mate, please tell me you didn't hit him?" Nate begged through the line.

What Nate couldn't see was Hank's giant grin. Went from ear-to-ear. "I didn't touch 'em…"

"Thank Christ for that!" Nate finished.

"My dog bit the slimy fucker!" Hank announced proudly. "Best fuckin' dog in the free world." He petted Butch's head and scratched behind his ears. The dog thumped his hind leg appreciatively.

"No, he didn't? Have you gone off your trolley?"

Aspen joined in. "Unfortunately, he has gone mad, Nate, but he's not kidding. We were taking Butch for a stroll through the park when we were stopped by a man. He seemed innocent enough—" Hank bristled, and Aspen laid a hand on his bicep. His shoulders softened. "Well, he made a move to touch my stomach with both hands. That's when things went downhill, I'm afraid."

"That's when things got down right interesting! My dog lunged at the baby belly groper and clamped onto his wrist pushing the fucker down. Took a good chunk out of 'em too. The worst part is that piece of shit grabbed my wife's hand and pulled her down with him. This fucker used a pregnant woman as a goddamned balancing stick! Throw the book at him I say!" Hank yelled, bringing his face close to the speaker phone to get his point across.

"Calm down, Hank. Remember, I'm fine. Baby's fine."

Aspen grabbed his hand and placed it on her stomach.

After a moment, he smiled, the tension once again leaving his body. It was as if his wife had some kind of magic salve or balm running through her system. All she had to do was be near and let him feel their child, and he turned to jelly.

"The dog bit your attacker? And I'm using the term *attacker* loosely, because I'm not certain you can claim that angle."

"Yes. Butch bit the man. The paramedics were called and he was taken to the hospital."

"Dandy. Have Oliver shoot me the information and I'll contact him. Maybe we can settle out of court. Though if he finds out who you are, Aspen..." His tone warned.

"I know, I know. Just make this go away like you always do."

"Fuck that! He tried to accost my wife, pushed a pregnant woman down, and *we* have to pay? Nuh-uh, no way. That bite is the least of his troubles. A small price to pay. He's lucky my wife needed tending to or his face would be smashed to smithereens!"

"Got it, Hank. I understand where you're coming from. Let me ask you this. Do you love your dog? Do you want to keep him?" Nate's voice was strained, and I wished I could place a gentle hand on him to soothe the tension.

"Of course, what kind of cockamamie question is that?"

"In cases where an animal attacks a person and draws blood, regardless of the circumstances, the dog will, at the very least, be quarantined. Then depending on whether or not the victim fights you, the courts more often than not side with the victim. In this case, the attacker didn't have a weapon, was taking a stroll in the park, and saw a beautiful pregnant woman whom he was enchanted by. He made a bad decision, but that didn't warrant what he's going to claim was a violent response. He was bit by what he's going to say is a wild, rabid beast of an animal. It burns me to say it, but this could go down the tube very quickly."

Hank lifted his arms in the air and spun around slowly.

"You following me, guys?" Nate asked.

"Yeah, we're processing the information." Aspen pulled her long blond hair over to one side, plucking more grass from the golden strands.

"This is fuckin' ridiculous." Hank burrowed his fingers in his already messy hair. He looked like he may have been doing that a lot this morning.

"That it may be, mate. The only trouble is, this sort of thing happens all the time. Our best bet is to pay the bugger off and call it a day. How would you like me to proceed?"

"Just do it," Aspen answered quickly.

"Darlin', no…"

"Hank, I don't want to hear it. I'm tired. I need to go change, deal with Ollie—who's going to freak out beyond words—and get to my meeting by ten. Nate, I trust you can handle this accordingly. Nothing happens to our dog."

"Damn straight. Best fuckin' dog ever," Hank mumbled as he walked his wife to the door. "Angel, really. You sure you don't want to call the doc? Get a quick checkup. It would make me feel better."

"I promise. If I feel so much as a strange twinge, I'll call. Okay?"

"You call me, and I go with you. No matter what I'm doin', where I'm at, I'm there."

She nodded, her eyes misting over before he kissed her, pulling her into his arms. His hands tunneled into her hair at the nape as he took control of the kiss. I looked away when it heated up. It reminded me too much of what I myself had, not twelve hours ago, but would never have again.

"Camille, pick up the phone." Oh no.

I ended speaker phone and held the receiver to my ear. "Hey," I whispered.

"This isn't over between us. We *will* talk later. Be prepared to have an answer as to why I woke alone, hard, and wishing my woman was by my side. You think about that," he said before abruptly hanging up.

His woman?

★ ★ ★

The longer the day wore on, the more brassed off I got. I know the condom slipup was scary. Hell, I was frightened, too, but it was something we needed to deal with together, as a couple. Yes, a couple. That's the way I thought of Camille. She was mine and I was hers regardless of what she thought. Christ, the woman was maddening, sneaking out of my bed in the wee hours of the morning after the best night of shagging in my life.

There was so much more I looked forward to showing her. Given the chance, I planned to take her every way possible, show her pleasure the likes she's never seen before and make it so good she'd never look at another man again.

Aside from how good the sex was, and it was off the charts, I'd never felt so connected to a woman before. For the first time in my life it felt like I'd made love to a woman. Not any woman. My sweet, Camille. She was everything good, kind and right in the world. I wanted her for my very own. There was no way she was going to run away from this. I knew once I had my prick buried deep inside her, those eyes would see straight through to my bloody soul, and it would only ever be her.

No more chasing birds in pubs and meaningless one-night stands. I finally had someone that I wanted to be with and was excited to learn more about. I enjoyed peeling the multiple layers of her personality. Not to mention her body. Christ! Her body deserved to be put up on a pedestal, painted to perfection, and hung in a museum so that all might experience a speck of her beauty. After that, she should be sculpted into the finest marble to last for eternity. But I wouldn't allow it. No man from here on out would set his gaze on what was mine. I'd go blooming mad.

My three hard rasps echoed in the breezeway outside of her apartment. As I was about to knock again, the door swung open and my girl stood there, long hair tumbling like a halo of colors around her shocked expression. Tiny bed shorts and a tight fitting camisole with little pink flowers imprinted in the fabric were all she wore. Her breasts rose and fell as her nipples tightened through the flimsy fabric. My dick hardened instantly. I could take her right here, right now and not be sorry. Not one sodding bit.

"What are you doing here?"

I looked down at my time piece. "It's later. Time we talked, don't you think? Nine o'clock has always seemed to work for you by phone."

"Yeah, *by phone*!" She looked over her shoulder then back at me. "Um, now's not a good time."

A growl reached my throat, but I pressed it down.

"Now's perfect." I pushed on her abdomen, forcing her to take a step back and inserted myself into her home. She closed the door with a long sigh.

Camille's shoulders stiffened, and she stood straighter. She was so cute when she thought she had control of the situation. "Really, you need to go. My roommate is getting ready for work, and, uh, you shouldn't be here."

"Of course I should be here. My girlfriend lives here. It's high time I see her place and meet her roommate."

Her mouth dropped open then she set her hands on her hips. "Your girlfriend?" she asked, eyes wide as the tires on my luxury sedan. Her voice shook life a leaf in a windstorm.

I tugged her into my arms. Her fingers dug into the lapels of my suit jacket as she buried her head into my chest. I closed my eyes, enjoying the sensation of having her exactly where she should be, in my arms.

"Precious, we need to talk. I wasn't going to wait around for my girl to find reasons to run away."

"You don't understand," she mumbled into my chest. I gripped her chin and held it with my thumb forcing her to look at me.

"What don't I understand?"

"I'm not who you think I am?" Her eyes misted.

"You're exactly who I think you are. You're the woman I want in my life and in my bed. There really isn't anything more to chin wag about."

"Nate—"

I cut her off by eating her words with my lips, teeth, and tongue. Her hands came around my neck, her luscious body slammed against my hard one as I deepened the kiss. That little mewl sound that made me insane with lust formed low in her throat and spilled into my mouth. My prick was at half-mast at the sight of her in her bed clothes. But now, with her sexy half-naked body pressed against mine, there was one place it needed to be. Deep inside Camille. I palmed her arse and tugged one leg over my hip to grind the rock hard erection into her sex. She moaned.

"Eewww gross. Mommy, why is that man sticking his tongue in your mouth!" A tiny high-pitched Mickey Mouse voice startled us both. Camille jumped out of my arms and threw her hands to her swollen lips. Her face was off-color, and she had that frightened look in her eyes again. The one I detested with every breath I took.

The little boy's words hit the synapses of my lust-riddled brain and fired at all ends. Sparks, lightning, and that buzzing sound you get when something blows your mind tore through my mind. Reason took over. I leaned to the side, grasped the sofa's arm, and planted my arse on it, feeling shaky and unbalanced. "Mommy?" I asked in disbelief, fear, and a shock so deep I couldn't feel the floor.

Camille nodded, turned around, and addressed the little boy. "Tanner, baby, why are you awake?"

"I heard knocking. If I saw Leah, you'd be having to work, and I'd be sad, Mommy." The brown-haired little boy with giant blue eyes shook his head. His lip quivered.

"Honey, Mommy's not leaving tonight. I don't have to work until later in the week."

"Who's the man?" He pointed a little finger at me. The other hand clutched a giant fluorescent-green stuffed lizard almost his size.

"That's Nate." Camille took a deep breath and placed both hands on the boy's shoulders. "Nate, this is my son,

Tanner."

"Oh Nate!" The little boy ran over and threw himself at my knees in a hug. "Auntie Jin says you're hot and nice and rich. You don't feel hot." He palmed my legs. "You smell nice. Kinda like oranges. I love oranges!" He turned on a socked foot—the other one was bare—and looked at Camille. "What's rich mean? Is that like when pirates steal gold, Mommy?"

"No, baby. No," Camille addressed his nonstop questions.

Fast as lightening, he turned to me once more. "Do you have lots of gold coins? Can I have one? I'd keep it berry safe and keep it in my treasure box!" he squealed.

I didn't know where to start. This child, *Camille's child,* was beautiful and bouncing with joy and happiness. His blue eyes bored into mine, waiting for a response.

"Well? You have gold?" He stuck out his little hand innocently.

"Tanner!" Camille scolded. I held up a hand to stop her from coming over, fascinated by this full of life young boy.

"Tell you what. The next time I see you, I will have a real gold coin for you." His little eyes lit up like a firecracker.

"You promise!" he screamed.

I put a hand up to my ear to stave off his piercing squeal. "Yes, sport, I promise. Now tell me, how old are you?"

"Five!"

"You are not five, Tanner, don't lie," Camille warned.

The little boy rolled his eyes. "Okay, so I'm kinda four, but I'm gonna be five! We just cele-a-bated my birfday!" His words were jumbled, but I could tell he was smart. Really bright for a four-year-old.

"That was your half-birthday we celebrated, Tan Man.

Remember…ice-cream on half-birthdays, cake on real birthdays."

His little lips pinched together, and he put a hand to his head. "I forgotted. But I'm gonna be five soon!" he yelped with glee. Camille sighed.

When I thought the situation couldn't get any stranger, a petite Asian woman entered the room wearing nothing but sexy lingerie and a silk robe open at the waist. My eyes took in the blue-and-black corset, stockings, and shag-me heels before I could look away. What the fuck was going on here?

The woman hadn't noticed me. She was looking at her outfit and pulling her long black hair back. "Cam, how does this look for toni…" Her words trailed off as she lifted her head and our eyes met. She twirled around, clasping the edges of her robe, frantically tying them shut. "Oh my God, oh my God."

"That was quite an entrance." I chuckled, trying to lighten whatever had just happened.

"Cam didn't tell me we had a visitor," she said through a clenched jaw. She narrowed her brow at her friend.

"I gathered that." I held out a hand. "I'm Nate by the way. Camille's boyfriend. It's Jin, right?"

"Uh, yeah. Boyfriend?" Her gaze shot to Camille. I didn't turn to see what silent girl gestures she was doing behind my back.

"Yes, her boyfriend," I assured her.

"O-kay." Her eyes widened as she clutched her robe tighter.

"Mommy, what's going on?" Another child's voice entered the conversation. I looked down and saw a black-haired Asian child clutching Jin's robe.

"Nothing, Zach. Auntie has a visitor. Go back to bed." The boy was the same height and size as Tanner.

"But he gets to stay up!" Zach wailed and stomped a foot.

"What?" She spotted Tanner hiding behind Camille. "Tanner, get your little booty over here right now. You know you're supposed to be in bed. Auntie Jin is getting ready for work, and Mommy has a visitor. Come on." Her arm pointed down the small hallway.

Camille leaned down, hugged her son, and then kissed his forehead. "I love you, baby. Sleep tight, okay. Mommy will be here when you wake up."

And there it was. *Mommy will be here when you wake up.* The reason why Camille left my bed. She had to get back to her son. Her four-year-old son. Four and a half. Oh shite. That meant…no. Fucking no! I stood and waited until the children were around the corner.

"Nice meeting you, Nate," Jin said over her shoulder and hustled the boys off. I turned and stared at Camille.

"He's four and a half?"

"Yes," Camille whispered.

"He's Tyler's son?" I asked the question knowing the answer. Camille nodded and closed her eyes on a heavy breath.

I stared at her. The most beautiful, kind, sweet, intelligent woman I had ever known. The only woman who had ever gotten under my skin. My *girlfriend*. The first woman I'd ever given that title to had a four-year-old son who belonged to my best mate. Sod all! If that wasn't enough, she could be pregnant with my own child.

151

"I have to go," I said through clenched teeth, not sure what to do but positive I couldn't be here right now.

"Yeah, it's best if you do. Good-bye, Nate." Tears slipped down her cheeks. I wanted nothing more than to catapult to her, kiss them away, and make it better for her, but she'd been lying to me. Lying for a couple weeks now. I needed time to process what happened and deal with it.

"I'll be in touch," I assured her placing my hand on the door handle.

"Whatever you say, Nate," she whispered. Her shoulders sagged as tears spilled down her cheeks and fell into tiny puddles on the wood floor next to her bare feet. I stormed over, pulled her body against mine, cupped the sides of her cheeks, and held her gaze.

"You're still mine. You wait for me to process this. Then we'll talk. Stop fucking running. Got it?"

Her lips trembled, and more tears poured from her emerald eyes. They were greener than any of the lush landscapes back home. She was undoubtedly breathtaking when she cried. I couldn't stop myself from kissing her. Her lips tasted of the salt from her tears and my sweet Camille.

"You'll wait. Say yes, precious," I urged, not willing to let her go until she agreed.

"Yes, precious." A tiny grin crooked at the corner of her mouth. Christ, she was heartbreakingly beautiful.

"I trust you," I said with finality and then kissed her once more.

"You shouldn't," she warned and closed her eyes.

"Don't make me regret it." I took one more taste of her lips, holding onto her far longer than I should. Having her close, my lips on hers, wasn't giving me the space I needed to deal with the shite storm that bore over us this evening. Another peck, a little nibble that gifted me the mewl, and I pulled away. "Christ, you're fucking delicious. I have to go. Later, we talk."

I left her standing dazed, teary-eyed, and so goddamned beautiful she made my eyes hurt and my heart bleed. I was royally screwed.

CHAPTER ELEVEN

Three days had passed. Three excruciating days filled with fear, uncertainty, and defeat. Nate didn't want me. If he did, he would have already come for me, made contact somehow.

Jin urged me to give it time. She explained that three days didn't mean it was over. It just meant that he wasn't done processing. No news is good news, she said. I didn't agree.

I untangled the strings of the bikini triangle-style bra. Only this wasn't your average triangle top bikini. Usually fabric covered the breast completely. This one did the exact opposite, encasing my full D-cup with half-inch satin strings that met at each point on the triangle and spider-webbed out into a perfect circle where my nipple could fit through. It drove the men absolutely wild, ensuring me a G-string full of stellar tips. Tonight the pick-me up to my confidence was warranted. I needed someone to want me. Even if it wasn't the man I wanted.

"Damn, you're going to rake in the cash tonight." Jin eyed the matching string bikini bottoms, garters, and fishnets. I grinned, more for her benefit then mine. It was all about playing up the dark side of erotic dancing this evening. Fit my mood perfectly.

Tonight, I'd be Mistress Black, smacking my own ass with a riding crop, making sure it turned nice and red before I turned it on a couple audience members. I always knew which ones were into the kink. The second my whip made an appearance their eyes would smolder. They were the heavy hitters, rich as could be, willing to pay a nice chunk for me to give them a couple solid swats from my crop. Half of them would try to disrobe so I could spank their bare fannies, even though it was forbidden. Employees were the only people permitted to take their clothes off. Gems was a gentlemen's club, not a brothel or a whore house. The owners made their money off the illusion of sex, not the real deal.

My cell phone rang as I applied a thick layer of candy-apple red, long-lasting lipstick.

"Aren't you going to answer that?" Jin asked looking at the screen.

"Nope. It's probably Oliver again." I rolled my eyes. "Aspen or Hank has a big mouth. Ever since the phone call at the office the other day, he's been all over me wanting the 'deets' as he calls it."

"Then why does it say Nate Walker is calling?" Jin grinned and answered. My mouth went dry, and I lost all ability to breathe. He finally called. A new fear splintered out my limbs like a windshield did upon taking on damage.

"Hey, Nate. Yeah, she's here. How are you?" What game was my friend playing? I held out my hand to take the phone, wiggling my fingers to hurry her. She shooed me away.

"Right now she's getting ready for work." Her eyes took in my barely dressed form. "Yeah, she works at the same club I work for. I've served a drink or two in my day... well, uh, it was nice chatting with you." I could tell that Nate's questioning took on a subject she wasn't prepared to answer. Mainly what we did at this "club". "Time to get the boys. Be good to our girl." She held out the phone and winked at me.

"It's Nate." She smiled wide.

"I gathered that." I held the phone to my chest. "You are so dead," I whispered.

"Not the first time you've said that, won't be the last." She flipped her shiny hair over her shoulder and left the room closing the door behind her. I took a deep breath then held the phone to my ear, needing to hear his voice but dreading what he had to say.

"Hey," I spoke quietly.

"Good evening, precious." His use of the much-loved endearment had my heart thudding in my chest. "I told you I'd call."

"So you did." I tried not to sound weak, but my voice shook.

"I missed you." His voice was smooth as silk and just as soft. I closed my eyes and took a breath, not capable of uttering a word. "I've had some time to think." He took a long breath. "Think about us. And you know what I've decided?"

Everything that *could be* depended on this decision. "Tell me," I whispered not trusting my voice. I held my hand to my heart. It thumped so loudly in my chest I worried he might be able to hear it.

"That you're the most beautiful woman I've ever known." I choked on the emotion his words hammered through my consciousness. He heard my reaction. "That I want to know you better. Every part of you. Including your wants, dreams, desires." His tone took on that gravelly sound that shot a bolt of pleasure between my thighs.

"I want to know and be a part of everything in your life, Camille, get to know Jin, and most importantly, Tanner." That was it. I couldn't stop them. The tears poured down my cheeks, ruining my makeup. I didn't care. He wanted to know Tanner. "How does that sound, precious?"

"Sounds…like a d-d-dream come t-true," I stuttered through my tears.

"Don't cry, love, I'm not there to kiss away your tears."

"I wish you were," I said without thinking.

"I can be there in fifteen minutes—"

I cut him off. "You can't. I have to work tonight."

A long drawn out inhale and exhale was the only sound I could hear through the line. "Then I'll come to the club where you work."

A cold sweat broke across my skin. Nate at Gems was not an option. "No! You can't!" I said too forcefully. An alpha like Nate didn't take too kindly to orders or boundaries for that matter. If his track record was anything to go by, if it involved me, he'd push his way in regardless of being invited. It's what made that place in me thrum and go molten all over.

"And why not?" His voice had a scary edge. One I hadn't heard before.

"I wouldn't be able to concentrate with you there." That wasn't exactly a lie. If Nate was there, all thoughts of dancing in front of other men for money would float away and disappear like a wish said into a breeze.

His laughter ringing through the receiver was glorious. The best sound I'd heard all week. "All right, love, you win. For now. I want to take you out. You and Tanner."

You and Tanner. Could any words ever sound sweeter? Nate Walker wanted to take me and my son out.

"I'd like nothing more," I said honestly.

"All right then. Saturday?"

I shook my head then realized he couldn't see. "I watch Zach on Saturday. How about Sunday?"

"You're going to make me wait three more days to see you? That's downright brutal."

I laughed, stood, and started to fiddle with my makeup, clearing away the remnants of smudged mascara.

"Lunch tomorrow?" he said with longing. If he were here, I'd wrap my arms around him and never let him go.

Unfortunately, he was going to hate my answer. "I have lunch plans with Aspen and Oliver."

"Not for long…" he deadpanned.

"How about you come with us? I'm sure they wouldn't mind." Actually, I was downright certain they'd be delighted. The entire reason for the lunch was so that Aspen and Oliver could grill me about Nate. With Nate there, they'd be on their best behaviors but could still enjoy watching me squirm.

"Smashing! I'll see you tomorrow, precious. Until then, I'll be thinking of your soft lips, and how I want to kiss them. About your sexy body lying under mine." He took a deep breath, and I could feel him exhale as if he *was* laying over me, my body naked, his breath skating over my feverish skin.

"Nate…not fair," I warned.

"It's not fair that I have to wait to touch you, wrap my arms around you, and show you exactly what I'm feeling."

"And what are you feeling?" I asked, racked with fear

of his answer.

"Love, precious." Hearing those words shook me to my core. No man had ever insinuated that he loved me. In the month I was with Tyler, he'd never once told me he loved me, though I'd believed I loved him. I was wrong. So, so wrong. Nothing compared to hearing the words from the man I was falling for.

Still it was too much, too soon. "Nate, you don't know that."

"Has to be. I've never felt anything like this for a woman. Ever. Only you."

"It's too soon. You barely know me."

He wasn't having it. "I know enough. I know that after three days without you, I don't want to be without you anymore. Not knowing if you were okay. What you were doing. How you were. Kiss your lips. Stare into those emerald eyes that make my heart pound." His voice calmed, slowed. "It hurt, Camille. No more. You're mine. We're seeing this thing through."

"Through what?" I asked, though uncertain I wanted to know the answer.

"Through forever. I'll accept nothing less."

★ ★ ★

Lunch turned into an event. When I texted Oliver that I was coming to lunch with them, he informed me Hank was coming along. Hank called me and gave me the weirdest third degree about not playing with Camille's heart. I assured him that my intentions were honorable even though my track record had not been.

He was shocked to hear that Camille had a child. I tried

to downplay it, even though I wasn't sure how I felt about it myself. I liked kids, but had no idea what it was going to be like to have one around all the time. It definitely added limitations on the times I could take Camille out, spend time alone with her, and get her back in my bed, for the love of God.

Once I arrived at The Place, the staple restaurant for our group, I was delighted to see Collier and his girlfriend, London, sitting at a table with Hank, Aspen, Oliver, Dean, Tripp, and my sister Emma. It looked like the whole gang was there. I made my way through the wrought iron patio gate and walked up behind Camille. She hadn't seen me yet. I knelt behind her, placed my hands on her shoulders, and nuzzled her neck. Her shoulders tightened for a second before I swept her hair away, and kissed the side of her neck where shoulder and head met. That spot on her body smelled wonderful and was incredibly addicting.

"Hello, love," I whispered against her ear. She turned toward me. Her eyes sparkled green with the bits of gold standing out against her yellow blouse. Her smile was a bright true ray of sunshine. I couldn't bear not kissing it. I leaned in and took her lips in a slow, lazy kiss. She hummed along my lips and placed a cool hand against my cheek. The gesture was so simple yet meant so much. It touched me, deep down where the hope that I'd ever find the woman for me was buried and forced it to the surface.

"Bugger all, you two! Get a room," Collier joked and then tossed a napkin, knocking me in the head. I pulled away, smiling. I petted my girl's perfect bottom lip, now reddened from my kiss.

"I missed you," I said, cupping her jaw.

"I missed you more." She smiled shyly. It was beautiful, lovely, and all for me. I was on top of the world. I took the seat next to her and clasped her hand, twining our fingers firmly together, then set them on my thigh. She grinned and swept a lock of unruly hair behind her ear. Christ, she was a vision.

My brother, Collier, caught my eye and nodded his head. He mouthed the word "stunning" and tilted his head toward her. I grinned wide, put my hand around her chair, and tugged Camille a little closer to kiss her temple. He shook his head with a huge smile. That's right, big brother, I've taken the plunge.

London's eyes darted to Collier's and then to mine. She clasped her hands in front of her and giggled with barely contained glee.

Over the next fifteen minutes, everyone ordered their food and boisterously talked over one another, as usual. I loved having Camille participate, being a part of what I considered my dearest friends. For the first time, I wasn't alone. I had someone to share in this joy. It was bloody awesome.

After the food was delivered, Collier and London kept winking at each other, sharing secrets in each other's ear in between bites of their lunch. Then I spotted something I never expected. London's left hand held a thin gold band on her ring finger. No diamond, nothing special about it, but the same flash of gold glinted on my brother's hand.

Holy fucking shite.

"Colly, you got something you want to share, brother mine?" I asked and then looked down at his hand. His jaw clenched, and he put his arm around London. The irritation in my voice could not be cooled. The entire table went dead silent. Forks and knives were set down, and all eyes were on the conspicuous couple across the table.

"Wanker," Collier gritted through his teeth and then grinned. "I guess now's as good a time as any. You all remember a couple weeks ago when London and I went to Atlantic City?" Most of the heads around the table nodded, back to taking bites of food, sipping their beverages as they paid attention. "You see, London and I had a wild hair—"

"Spit it out already, my food's gettin' cold," Hank encouraged, and then placed an arm around his wife. She leaned into his side automatically.

"Hmm, how do I say this…" Collier faltered.

"Oh honey, come on. Men!" She shook her head and rolled her eyes. "We got married!" London squealed and then held up her hand. The simple gold band gleamed in the sunlight.

Collective gasps ricocheted through the group. Tripp stood, walked around the table, and tapped Collier on the shoulder. He looked up at Tripp and then stood once he saw the menacing look on the man's puss.

"How could you, Bond!" He shoved Collier. London stood and got between the two. "I can't believe you'd do that. Not fucking cool!" he roared. Tripp, London, and Collier had a weird dynamic, especially after Tripp donated his kidney to save my brother's life. For the past few months though, they'd been the three amigos. I would never have expected him to have a violent reaction. My hackles rose, ready to get up and defend my brother.

"Tripp, sweetie, really, it's not his fault. It was my idea!" London yelled. He stared at her, his eyes showing a world of hurt.

"You fucking eloped, Bridge?" Tripp locked his jaw, and then turned around.

I hugged Camille to my side and watched the show. Standing behind Tripp, Aspen did not look pleased. With her hands on her hips, her giant pregnant belly protruded in front of her like a shield. She flicked her hair behind her and narrowed her eyes at London and Collier.

"What in the world would make you think it was okay to run off and elope?" The couple looked at one another, mouths opening and closing like fish out of water. "How could you not think about how that would make the rest of us feel?" The waterworks started. "That was incredibly selfish. Every single person here would have been honored to watch two people that we love bind themselves to one another. But no! You took the easy way out." She shook her head back and forth, then clutched at her stomach, and keeled over. Her expression turned pained.

Camille jumped up and ran to Aspen's side. "Where do you feel it? Back? Abdomen?"

"All over." Aspen gritted her teeth.

"No, no, no. It's too fuckin' early," Hank growled, and then escorted his wife back to her seat. "Deep breaths, darlin'."

Camille stood in front of Aspen, talking quietly. She asked if she could touch her belly, and Aspen nodded. Then she looked at Hank, waiting for his approval. He nodded and looked at her as if she was the sweetest woman in the whole world. Probably because she was.

She laid a hand on Aspen's belly. "Hold my hand, Aspen. When you feel a contraction, squeeze my hand, okay?"

Camille was all business. I loved watching her. The issue with my brother and London's untimely nuptials were forgotten in Aspen's obvious condition.

London was around the other side of Aspen, whispering in her ear, apologizing, kissing and nuzzling her hair. Aspen focused on her baby and squeezed Camille's hand when warranted. Camille looked at her watch. "Was it stronger, the same, or lighter?"

"It was lighter. It didn't hurt all over." Aspen took a deep breath. Hank watched, his sharp eyes flicking to Aspen and then to Camille. Oliver stood behind them pacing back and forth, his ear to a phone.

"Yes, contractions. We don't know!" he roared into the phone.

"Buddy, keep it down. You talking to the doctor?"

"Yeah," Oliver said, phone plastered to his ear. Camille shared some specifics with Oliver which he reiterated into the phone.

After thirty nail-biting minutes, it was determined that Aspen had been having Braxton-Hicks contractions, also known as false labor. Her breathing returned to normal, the baby settled down, and Hank hovered near his wife like a lion protecting his cubs.

"When's he ready?" Hank asked Oliver.

"Half an hour. Let's jet."

"Darlin', we're going to go to the doctor." Hank stopped his wife from speaking with a finger to her lips. "Angel, I swear by all that's holy, we're going, you're not arguing, and once we get a clean bill of health for you and our daughter, we're going home for the day."

"But…"

"No buts about it. I'm taking care of my girls and that's that. Oliver, you know what to do."

"Already done. Canceled everything. Nothing's more important than Pen," Oliver said to Hank while in the arms of Dean, Oliver's significant other.

Dean held Oliver's face and wiped his eyes with both thumbs. Oliver shoved his head in Dean's chest. Oliver truly loved Aspen, maybe even as much as Hank, only in an entirely different way. The same way the angered, brooding Tripp Devereux felt right now about London and Collier's eloping. Emma spoke quietly to Tripp as he stood in the corner. She whispered in his ear and slid her hand up and down his bicep in a soothing gesture. Made me wonder for the millionth time what the two had going. They claimed that they were just friends, but I wasn't so sure. Mentally, I noted I needed to have a chat with my baby sister.

Hank nodded at Oliver and then addressed Camille. "Cancel everything for the rest of the day, Cami. And"—he took a strained breath—"you proved yourself. I'm waiving the six months trial period. You're official starting Monday; benefits for you and your son start first of the month. And a raise. A big one!" He pulled her into an all-over hug, one only a man of his size could do without me want to take him out. As it was, it took extreme patience watching another man put his hands on my girlfriend.

"Really, Mr. Jensen…"

His eyes warned her.

"Hank," she corrected. He smiled. "I didn't expect anything. I've experienced Braxton Hicks before. They tend to start around thirty weeks and are often caused by unnecessary stress and strain."

Hank looked at London and Collier.

"Hank, mate," Collier started.

"Nothin' out of you. I'm pissed at both of you. You were selfish and can wallow in that guilt for the next few days. I don't care. The stress you caused my wife…unacceptable!" His words cut the tension raging through the group. Emma gasped, Tripp sneered, Dean and Oliver hugged, and London and Collier looked like puppies that had been kicked, left to starve, and shoved over the side of a bridge. As they should look for the stunt they pulled. Getting married, none being the wiser. Bollocks.

Hank and Aspen left with Oliver and Dean. I paid the bill and came back for Camille. "Let me walk you back to work." She nodded and then excused herself.

Collier came over and clasped my shoulder. "You brassed off, too?"

"Yeah, but I get why you did it. You didn't want to share her in that moment." And I did get it. If given the chance to whisk Camille away and make her mine for eternity, I'm not sure I'd make a different decision. Shite. I was getting way ahead of myself.

Collier pulled me into a tight embrace, the likes of which men didn't often do in public. "Brother mine, you know me too well. It's our second marriage. We didn't want to go through the rigmarole."

"I get it." I smiled and clasped his shoulder. "Plan a party. Let the rest of us celebrate with you. It will go a long way toward reestablishing the peace, mate. 'Sides, you still haven't told Mum. You think I'm brassed off? You're the nitwit that's never going to hear the end of it."

Emma chimed in as she hooked Collier in a hug. "You

are so dead, brother mine! D-E-A-D. I can't wait to see the fireworks. Can I tell Mum? Please…." She drew out the word and I laughed.

"Come on, precious, let's go. You have some engagements to cancel."

Camille held my hand in comfortable silence as we walked back to the AIR Bright building, both lost in our thoughts. "I can't believe all that happened. And you know what the best part was?"

I pulled her into my side and hooked a hand around her waist. "What's that, love?"

"None of your friends grilled us about our relationship or the fact that I have a son!" She laughed. Leave it to my sweet girl to find the silver lining.

After I escorted her to her building, I tugged her to the side of the glass doors and twirled her around, planting her up against the wall. Then I laid my lips over hers. She yelped and then moaned into my kiss. She was wet, sweet, and tasted of summer, all lemon and iced tea. Her tongue dipped into my mouth and swept alongside mine, taking as much as she was giving. I tunneled a hand in her hair and one on her hip, gripping her tightly, holding her just where I wanted her. She couldn't get away and I'd never let her.

After a few more slow pecks, her lips moved away and I chased them. "Nate, honey, I need to go to work. Hank has several things I need to cancel." She breathed into my mouth as I took her lips once more. She didn't seem in a hurry to get away. When we touched, I knew I held a power over her, the same power she held over me. It was all-encompassing and could make the grandest of plans disappear with one touch of her lips to mine.

"Two days, and you and the little one are mine. All day. Maybe even all night."

"Nate, don't push it…" she warned.

"I make no promises." I grinned. She rolled her eyes and pushed off me. She went back into work, and I watched her through the glass. Her yellow blouse moved with her body like a flag blowing delicately in the wind.

She settled at her desk, and then looked up at me through the glass. Her smile stretched wide, and the apples of her cheeks pinked prettily. I waved and entered the elevator. Our gazes held until the very last moment when the doors closed. Bliss. She was my bliss, and I couldn't wait to take her and her son out for the day.

If only I knew where I was going to take them. I'd call Mum. She'd have some ideas. Maybe I could get a call in before Collier's news broke.

That was not going to be fun. At least it would take the heat off me and my love life. Poor bastard. When Eleanor Walker got wind that her son eloped, she'd be more than angry. None of us would be safe. She'd likely get on a plane just to smack some sense into the bloke. When it came to her babies, you did not mess with Eleanor Walker. Collier was going to be in a world of hurt. I snickered.

"Better him than me."

CHAPTER TWELVE

"Mommy, why isn't he here yet?" Tanner looked through the blinds of our second-story apartment.

"He'll be here soon, honey. Relax." I mentally did a checklist. One change of clothes. An extra shirt, because you never know when he was going to spill an entire drink or fall in the mud. Food and toys…

"I'm gonna die if I don't find out where we're going." He slumped away from the window and into the thick cushions of our couch. "Do you think he'll like me?"

I stopped pulling things together. Snacks, sunblock, the extra clothes for Tanner and me for tomorrow just in case. I set the Capri Sun Roarin' Waters pouch in my hand down and watched my son worry his lip. His little fingers twisted together, and his brow was knitted in concentration.

"Baby, what's wrong?" I sat down next to him and pulled my guy into my lap. "Tell Mommy."

Tanner rubbed his face into my chest and clung to my arms. "What if he doesn't like me?"

"Why wouldn't he like you?" I asked, surprised. Tanner had always been confident and outspoken. What was it about Nate that had him acting so strange?

He shrugged. "Maybe if he likes me he could do big boy stuff with me. You know, play baseball and stuff."

In moments like these, I wanted to murder Tyler Thornton for leaving my son a fatherless boy. Every boy deserved to have their parents. Both of them. Like me, Tanner wished he had a complete family. My biggest worry about raising him alone was knowing he'd need a man in his life.

I didn't want to get my hopes up about Nate. He'd seemed okay with Tanner and was making an effort to get to know him. That could change in a moment. He may not want to be tied down by a child…and they tie you down. As in boat to a dock, anchor to the ocean floor. It's their world and you live in it kind of tied down.

Three hard raps came at the door, and Tanner's face lit up like he'd been handed a huge ice-cream sundae. I closed my eyes, took a deep breath, and said a silent prayer that today went well, that the man I adored would have space in his life and heart for my son.

"Hey there, sport." Nate entered, laid a large palm on Tanner's small head, and shuffled his hair. I needed to take him to get it cut. It was a bit shaggier than usual.

Tanner beamed at the bit of affection Nate bestowed.

I scoped out my *boyfriend* from head to toe. Nate was the epitome of male perfection. He wore a long sleeved Henley-style shirt in dark grey. It looked soft and well worn, something I'd love to snuggle into when I laid my head on his chest. The Henley sculpted perfectly to the incredible body I knew lay hidden beneath. His shirt went well with the dark designer jeans and trendy brown suede shoes. His slicked back hair was still wet from the shower.

Nate was doing his own perusal. "Like what you see?" I attempted to be coy.

"More than I should right now." He nodded down to Tanner, and a sexy grin stole across his face.

"I'm so 'cited, Mr. Nate. Where are we gonna go?" Tanner hopped from one foot to the other. He looked adorable in his blue overalls, yellow striped shirt, and red hooded sweatshirt. Slung over his shoulders was a little backpack with black-and-white checkers mimicking a race flag with a couple of red and blue racecars on the pockets.

Nate leaned down to eye level with Tanner. "I have a full day of fun planned, but first, I've got something for you." Tanner's eyes widened. Nate pulled a shiny gold circle from his pocket. *Next time I see you, I'll have a shiny gold coin for you,* he had said. He followed through. It was official. Nate was perfect.

"Oh my gosh! A gold coin. I'm rich!"

Nate chuckled and held up the coin. "It's not just any gold coin. It's a chocolate coin!"

Tanner's mouth opened as wide as his eyes. "I can eat it too?"

"If you want to. Sure. And just in case you want to, sport, I've got a few more. You can share with your best mate. Zach, is it?" Nate looked at me for verification, and I nodded.

My son jumped up and down holding his loot. "Where we going today, huh, Mr. Nate?"

"I thought we'd start with the Brooklyn Children's Museum."

Tanner tilted his head to the side and scrunched up his face. "What's a moz-u-liam?"

"That's where dead people rest," Nate said plain as day. I smacked my forehead with my hand while Tanner shrieked with laughter.

"We're gonna see dead people?"

"No, that's what a mausoleum is," Nate said very matter-of-fact. "We're going to the Children's Museum." He drew out the word so Tanner would hear the difference. "At the museum, we'll get to experience a variety of fun things including live performances, exhibits, pet some furry friends, and make our own pizzas!"

"I love pizza, and I love animals. Mom, can we go, can we go right now?" Tanner squealed.

"Let me say hi to your mum first. Then we'll shove off, yeah?" Nate held his hand up and Tanner smacked it in a high five.

"Go put your coins away, and go to the bathroom before we leave, baby. I don't want you having to go the second we get into Mr. Nate's car. Okay?" Translation: I don't want Tanner having an accident on Nate's pristine leather seats in his very expensive car.

Tanner scurried off, hollering and jumping down the hall to the bathroom.

I looked up as Nate stalked toward me. His blue eyes were the brightest I'd seen them, matching the color of the sky. His hands cupped my neck, his thumbs lifted my chin before his lips covered mine. He tasted of mint and English breakfast tea, two flavors that were quickly becoming my addiction. Nate pulled my body flush against him as he kissed me. I felt the kiss through every inch of my body, wanting more, but knowing I couldn't have it. Not right now. One of his hands sifted through my hair. Thank God I wore it down, or it would be a ratty mess the way he liked to maneuver my head this way and that. He took my mouth in long deep sweeps of his tongue and sharp tiny bites of his teeth. The man could kiss. He brought me right to the pinnacle of excitement in the time it took to light a match. He ignited desire just by saying my name in that gravelly "just woken up from a long sleep" tone of voice. Sexy as hell, and all mine.

He pulled back until our mouths were an inch apart. "Morning, precious. You look ravishing."

Really? I didn't agree with his sentiment, only wearing a simple light blue sweater, jeans, and ankle boots, but I felt good. He made me feel as though I was dressed to the nines and about to walk the red carpet.

"Morning. Thank you," I whispered against his lips. He licked them, which I took as my queue to lay one on him. Long sips from his lips would never be enough. I'd always want more, need to have more of him. His hand palmed my ass, and brought me flush against his body. I moaned into his mouth, feeling the ever-present thickness pressed against my belly.

"Isn't that gross?" a quiet small voice said not far behind us, followed by a giggle. My ears perked, knowing we had an audience.

"Girl cooties are sick," another voice said. Nate pulled away from my mouth and grinned like a loon, rubbing my nose with his.

"Looks like we got caught." Nate waggled his eyebrows.

"Guess so." Without warning, Nate yanked himself back, clutched his chest, and pretended to clumsily fall back on shaky legs.

"Oh, no, boys, save me. I was attacked by the cootie monster." He brought his hands to his face and fell to his knees in front of the boys, who were roaring with laughter. "N-n-eed water…must have water to kill the poison girl cooties." He fell to the ground in a heap of limbs and muscle. He made for one sexy area rug.

"Get the water!" Tanner yelled to Zach. Jin's son ran to the sink, grabbed a cup from the dish drainer, filled it with far too much water, and ran back, spilling almost all of it as he skidded to a stop in front of Nate's prone form.

"Mr. Nate, sit up. Drink this before you die!" Tanner grabbed the glass, which had maybe a half inch of water left in it and put it into Nate's hand. Nate leaned up as if it took every ounce of his strength, brought the cup to his lips and drank it all. Then—much to the boys' delight—bounced up to standing as if he was a supercharged action figure.

"You saved me!" He pointed at me. "That dastardly beautiful girl held me down and smothered me with girl cooties. You are my best mates having saved me from the heart-stealing, cootie kissing monster!"

I opened my mouth in shock. "Hey! I'm not a monster. And I did not steal any kisses!" I put my hands on my hips. "You gave them freely."

"Be careful, mates, you never know when the heart-stealing, cootie kissing monster will attack!" he warned.

"All right, all right, enough. Time to go. Be good for your mama, Zach."

"She's taking me to the park today!" he answered happily. I was grateful that Jin was taking Zach somewhere. It made it less awkward for Nate to take just Tanner, and not him. But we needed the time alone. In the future, we'd plan things with Jin and Zach. At least, I hoped we would.

"Okay, so when I get back we'll talk about our 'ventures!" Tanner exclaimed, smacking hands with his best friend.

"Yeah! Sounds awesome! Bye, Auntie Cami. Bye, Mr. Nate." Zach waved as I herded my two guys out the door. I loaded my arms with the stuff we might need and pulled the door closed.

"What's all this?" Nate looked at the four bags I was carrying. "You moving in?"

I pinched my lips together and knocked a hip out to the side. "No! One has a change of clothes, pj's, etc., for Tanner. One has the same for me. One is filled with snacks, a handful of toys, crayons, and coloring book," I rattled off all the items I could remember putting into the bag. "And the last one is my purse. I need that. Is that all right with you?"

"Blimey! Wee ones need a lot of things." He threw the items into his trunk.

"That's nothing compared to what you have to carry around for a baby," I said absently, not thinking of the can of worms I opened.

Nate's head shot up, reminding me of our little mishap last weekend. "How long until we know?" he asked softly, his mind going exactly where mine had. I studied my ankle boots.

"A couple more weeks. I'll let you know when I know." His gaze held mine and then finally he nodded. Conversation ended. For now.

Nate opened the car door and Tanner jumped into the waiting booster. "How did you know he needed a booster?"

"I called my mum. She gave me some ideas on what we should do today and told me to make sure I had an appropriate child restraint for the car. I based it on how many kilos I thought he was. This was the model that was suggested online."

My eyes misted as I realized how much thought he'd put into our day out. To make sure my son was in a booster made me realize that Tanner's safety meant as much to him as it did to me.

"Thank you." My words were filled with emotion. He leaned in, belted Tanner into his seat, closed the door, and then pulled me into a hug.

"There's nothing I wouldn't do for you, or your son by extension. The sooner you realize I'm not going anywhere, the better off we both are."

I nodded and climbed into the passenger side, ready to go wherever he wanted to take us.

★ ★ ★

"Mr. Nate, Mr. Nate!" Tanner pointed at the huge Ferris wheel at New York's iconic Coney Island. His eyes were filled with wonder and joy at the flashing lights, booths, and rides. It reminded me of Camille's look when I took her to the theatre district to see Chicago a couple of weeks ago. Christ. Was it only a couple weeks? It felt like ages ago, like I'd always been with her, with this small family.

Hank gave me a head's up that this was the place to take a child and my mum concurred. As I watched both mum and child's eyes light up and smiles widen, I knew I'd done well.

"Have you ever been here?" I gripped Camille's waist, holding her beside me. Tanner wanted to hold my hand which I found surprisingly comfortable aside from the constant swinging. The boy could not just walk. No, he skipped, jumped, hopped and swung my arm with purpose.

All of which I found increasingly adorable and trying in equal measure.

"I always wanted to go but you know…" She looked around then answered with a shrug. "Could never afford it."

It burned me up that Camille never had a normal childhood, one filled with a mum and dad to protect and love her, show her all the things the world had to offer. I'd bet a thousand quid she'd never been outside New York and New Jersey.

I would change that very soon. Come the holidays, I'd take her and Tanner home to England. She didn't have family and mine would adore her. When I spoke to my mum a couple days ago, she forced me to send a picture of my *girlfriend*. She was delighted to hear I'd finally committed to a woman enough to give her the prestigious title. I sent the picture I had as my personal background on my cell phone. It was Camille outside the theatre on our date, looking utterly magnificent in the green dress that matched her eyes.

As expected, Mum thought she was lovely. Dad said she was a fit bird, which she most certainly was. They couldn't wait to meet her and her son. My mum and dad didn't give two heaps about the fact that Camille was so young with a child. They just accepted that I knew what I wanted and supported me. That's the kind of family everyone should have.

I looked at Tanner, and he looked up at me, all smiles. His blue eyes could easily have matched my own, but they didn't. They actually were the same eyes as Tyler's. That was a facet of Camille's history we needed to discuss. Why wasn't Tyler in the picture? Why didn't he pay child support? Lastly, why didn't *he* ever mention having a child? A beautiful, intelligent, happy boy that any man would be proud to call his own. The pieces didn't add up.

As we walked through the crowds, we enjoyed cotton candy. We rode the Ferris wheel, which Tanner loved and Camille learned made her motion sick. After the ride, she stood sipping water and holding her stomach tentatively. I worried it was more than the ride that made her nauseous. I looked up early pregnancy symptoms, and sitting at the top of the list was morning sickness, which I also found out didn't happen in the morning. It happened at all bloody hours of the day. It had been a week. Maybe it didn't take too long to hit?

"Mr. Nate, can we go on the giant circle again!" Tanner held his arms out wide, hugging the sky, and then jumped around like only a little one filled with sugar and excitement could.

"Sure, sport. If your mum says so, I'll take you."

"Mom, Mom, can we pleeeasssseeee?" He drug out the word as if it had fifty letters.

"It's probably a good idea if I sit this one out." She clutched her hand over her stomach once more. I pulled both of them to a nearby bench in front of the ride.

I placed my hand her over stomach, not knowing what the hell was coming over me. She stiffened, and her green eyes locked with mine. They were unreadable.

"I'll take care of you, Camille. No matter what," I assured her, rubbing her flat stomach. She pulled my face to hers and kissed me. It was so much more than a simple kiss when our lips touched. It was filled with hope, her fear, and maybe even a little bit of love mixed in. She was falling for me. I knew it and craved it with every fiber of my being. I wanted her love and commitment even though I knew it was too soon to ask for it.

"You're such a good man," she whispered against my lips.

"I try, precious. I try. You okay here alone?" Tanner tugged on my arm, no longer capable of waiting patiently. "Come on, Mr. Nate. Let's hurry!" I stood up, grabbed him by the waist and twirled him onto my shoulders. He gripped the top of my head perfectly.

"Oh my, don't drop him!" Camille watched in amused horror. I gripped the boy's hands and held them out wide.

"I've got him. Trust me." I smiled and spun him in a circle. He giggled and clenched my hands firmly.

"I do, Nate. I so do. Wait." She came to me and put her hand on my back pocket where my phone was. She swiped her finger across the lock and her picture lit up. A saucy grin lifted her lips after seeing the photo. "I want to take a picture of you guys."

"Please! Mum wants one of sport here." I tickled Tanner's thighs with one hand and he laughed.

"Okay, ready. Say cheese." Camille snapped the shot.

I pulled a laughing boy off my shoulders and asked the bloke playing with his phone next to us if he'd do the honors and capture our first family date.

I held Tanner on my hip and tugged Camille to my other side. Tanner slung his arms around my neck, hugging me. It felt beyond right. Beyond just a smile. This was a jaw aching, cheek burning, eye squinting happiness that I would fight tooth and nail to keep. I was on top of the bloody world.

The man snapped a couple shots. Quickly, I sent the

snapshots to Mum, Camille, Collier, Emma, Ella, and my e-mail address with the caption, *This is my life, and it's perfect.*

I then took my little sport on the circle ride. While we were in the air, the wheel stopped for a panoramic view of New York. At the very top, Tanner hit me with a question I was nowhere near prepared for.

"Are you going to be my daddy?"

After a couple deep breaths, I formulated the answer to a question I had no answer to. I decided to just be honest.

"I don't know, sport."

He accepted that answer, and then asked, "Are you going to marry my mommy?"

Visions of Camille with a white dress hugging her long and curvy body, walking along the beach, a beautiful sunset behind her, a bouquet in her hands and a glorious smile on her face had the words clogged in my throat.

"Maybe one day. We're just starting out."

He nodded and bit his lip. "If you marry my mommy, will you be my daddy then?"

I laughed and pulled him close to my side. "Yeah, sport, if your mum and me get married, I'd be honored to be your daddy if that's what the future holds." Nothing like a kid to get right to the heart of it.

After a long silence, the ride ended, and I clasped his hand. As we were walking toward a revived Camille, Tanner yanked my hand and I stopped. "Mr. Nate?"

I went down on my hunches and looked into his baby blue eyes. "Yeah, sport?"

"I hope you marry my mommy."

I smiled as I replied. "Me too, sport. Me too."

He gave me the first real hug I'd ever received from

a child. He was warm, small, and fragile. Instantly, my protective side came out as I curled the boy to my chest and settled my chin on his head. He smelled of cotton candy and popcorn with subtle hints of the baby lotion I smelled on his mum. From here on out, I'd associate those smells with joy and happiness.

I closed my eyes and delighted in his embrace. It was gone far too quickly. It turned out that a day of fooling about with a four-year-old was as exhilarating as it was exhausting. I brought them both back to my flat where I had planned on making dinner. Tanner was asleep in the car five minutes after we left the theme park. When we got to my place, Camille pulled his sleeping body out of the car and put him over her shoulder.

"I can take him," I offered. He looked pretty heavy.

"I'm used to it." And I bet she was. A single mother. All alone. Not for long if things kept going as well as they had today.

We rode the elevator to my flat and I had her carry him into one of the spare rooms. This room was simple. Not much in the way of design with solid green walls, dark cherry furniture, and a white duvet. London was supposed to start on the redesign this week. I should have Camille talk with her about things she may like to see since I planned on having her here a lot more. With Camille here, that meant the little guy would be here, too. He needed his own space. There was no reason one of the four bedrooms couldn't be for him. I made a mental note to discuss my new idea with London.

In the kitchen, I pulled items to make a simple pasta dish. Mum made it very clear that children were often difficult eaters, and pasta was usually a sure thing. "Does Tanner like pasta?"

"Oh yes, he's not really a picky eater. As long as it doesn't have exotic things in it, he'll be fine. He can pick out anything he doesn't like." She poured herself a glass of crisp white wine. It was so easy, being with her, having her in my home. I turned on light classical music on the sound system in the nook off the kitchen. Chopin's lilting tones filled the kitchen through the surround sound speakers.

"Is the music okay for Tanner?"

"He'll sleep through an earthquake most of the time. Besides, he's tired. He may not even wake for dinner."

I grinned and pulled her against my body. "Really?" I was instantly aware of the possibilities that gave us. Slowly, I slid both hands from her waist up her back and down again. She sighed, tilting her head to the side and I took her pale lovely neck, dragging my teeth along the smooth surface until I heard her inhale of breath. That was the first sign she was aroused. Her breathing changed. Then her breasts pebbled. I could feel them tighten against the thin layer of my shirt. "How well does he usually sleep?" I asked while kissing my way down her neck to suck and nibble on the delectable spot where her neck and shoulder met, the space I loved.

"Oh…really well." She exhaled her breath as I explored the hem of her jumper, burrowing my hands under it to cup and squeeze her breasts. She moaned and came at me for a kiss. I pulled away, not allowing our lips to touch, wanting to watch her come undone before my eyes, preferring to wait until the last possible moment to take her succulent mouth.

"Do we have time?" I asked, rolling and twisting her

nipples. She trembled and bit her lip. Her eyes were closed, her mouth open. She was completely gone to the sensation of my hands on her body.

"Yeah…" She let her head fall back, arching her chest into my hands.

I lifted her jumper and pushed down the cups of her bra, exposing them to the warm air of my kitchen. Her tits were ripe, reddened like little berries plucked off the vine, only it was my fingers that had done the plucking. A carnal desire to take, to ravage and mark my woman almost split me in two. The need building in my loins, growing stronger with every sigh, moan, and tremble she gifted me with.

I palmed her arse, and pushed her to the counter. A quick flick of the wrist and the button of her jeans was undone. Her jeans were pushed down to her ankles and my hands were gripping bare flesh. Paradise. I nibbled and bit at her tightened peaks. Her breath came in harsh pants against my ear as she kicked her pants away.

In what felt like ages but was really only seconds, I yanked her up by her arse, and set her on the counter top, opened her legs wide and pressed against her center. I took her in a searing kiss I felt low in my back, pleasure expanding out through my chest, arms and fingertips. She clung to me, tilting her hips to rub along the ridged line of my erection.

"Christ, precious. I'm going to taste you now." I accentuated my words by trailing my tongue up the side of her neck. "You'll be my appetizer," I promised, running my hands up her legs, tugging at her knickers, and pulling them down her long limbs. Slowly, I made my way down her body, kissing each perfect tit, sucking the hardened nubs into my mouth, biting enough to mix pleasure with pain. A glance at her face showed me she was lost in passion. Her cheeks were rosy, eyes closed. Her teeth bit down on her plump bottom lip. I swirled my tongue around her naval and was rewarded with an all-over body shiver and the attempt to close her thighs.

"Ah ah, no closing your legs," I tsked.

Camille shook and opened her eyes. The green was almost completely black with only a sliver of color remaining. She watched me, her eyes heavy-lidded as I forced her legs open wider, exposing her feminine heat. The lips of her sex were moist, pink, and glistened like a juicy peach. I couldn't wait to take a bite. Her womanly scent filled my nose and made me salivate, honing me in on my woman's desire like a fox to its prey. Nothing but Camille and her weeping flesh existed in this perfect moment. I'd remember and revisit it in my memories forever.

I blew on her sensitive core and gloried in the quiver that ripped through her body. She placed her hands on the edge of the counter. Her knuckles whitened with the force of her grip. I pulled the lips of her sex apart with the pad of my thumbs, leaned against her thighs, and licked her from the bottom of her tiny rosette all the way up to the tight kernel of her clit. Her body shuddered as I sucked her clit hard into my mouth, swirling around the bump, lapping greedily.

When I dipped into her sex and pushed my tongue as far as it would go, her tangy essence coated my mouth, surrounding me with the pure womanly taste of my Camille. No man had ever gone to this place but me. The dizzy feeling of power and possession roared through me. I growled into her sex, held her arse to my face and ravished her. Licking and lapping, sucking and fucking until I felt her tighten her thighs. My hands deftly held her in place. Her body leaned out, arching into a beautiful rainbow shape, her mound pressing closer, her lush tits pointing to the ceiling. She was unearthly, gluttonous in her passion. Her need drove her to claw at my back and sink her hands into my hair as she ground into my searching mouth. I loved it. Every press of her hands made me mad with lust as she rode my face, driving her orgasm to the highest peak. When Camille hit that final plateau, I sucked her clit into my mouth, firmly planting my lips around the center of her pleasure. Then I surrounded the tight knot with my teeth and flicked at the sensitive flesh with the very tip of my tongue until she broke, crying my name.

"Nate! Oh God, Nate!" she practically screamed her release. Her juices trickled down her thighs, and I lapped up every last drop, pressing my tongue deep where her nectar was strongest. Her body tightened again as another orgasm took my sweet Camille into orbit. This one shocked her so much she flung her body back and slammed her head against the cupboard.

I pulled away from her delicious cunt and brought a hand behind her head. "Shite, precious. Be careful," I scolded, putting my forehead against hers.

She was dazed and unaffected by how hard she hit her head, but she'd likely feel it tomorrow. I licked my lips, still tasting her sweet honey on my tongue. My dick hardened even further at her taste. More. I needed so much more.

"Be careful? How can I?" She took a jagged breath. "How can I when you're doing that?" Then something changed, and she pulled her head away from mine, realizing where she was. "Oh my God. We can't do this here. Out in the open. Tanner could walk in." She placed a trembling hand over her lips, her eyes wild.

In moments faced with an extreme case of blue balls, you're capable of giant leaps in logic and improvisation. I hauled her body against mine. Her legs locked behind my lower back as I walked her right into my pantry. I couldn't take her to bed. We'd have to walk past Tanner's room. *Tanner's room?* Fuck, I was so gone for this woman and her kid.

Turning abruptly, I pushed her against the door of the panty. The thick gnarled wood was hard and unrelenting. It was also solid fucking wood, a good inch thick that would muffle, if not obliterate, any noise. "Hold on tight, precious. It's going to be a bumpy ride." I grinned, lifting her arse with one arm. She held onto my shoulders and squeezed her toned thighs against my ribs as I got my jeans unbuttoned and boxers pushed down enough to let out my cock. I was far too eager to sample her heat.

I kissed her hard, fast, and deep, and then took her body the same way. She cried out at the striking penetration. "Fuck, you're so"—I gritted my teeth—"so bloody tight." I accentuated my words with a hard thrust. Her eyes closed.

"Eyes, Camille. Give them to me. I want everything you have. When I'm inside you, I want everything you are right there with me."

CHAPTER THIRTEEN

His words held me against the pantry door as easily as his strong arms did. He didn't realize how much he seduced me with only a few simple directives. I was so far gone for this man I no longer knew which way was up, down, sideways, backward, forward. All I could do was *feel*. When Nate was inside me, joined in the most intimate way possible for a man and a woman, nothing else existed.

His rock-hard length pressed deep into me. The wide knob of his cock dragged along hyper-sensitive tissue, sending spikes of pleasure to every pore. I clung to my man as he slid his arms up my back to cup each shoulder with his palms. With this new leverage he plowed into me, bringing his hands down hard on my shoulders and jack-knifing his hips up, going impossibly deep.

"Christ, Camille. You're never bloody running from me again." Nate took my lips in a brutal kiss. I loved it. I loved the way he got possessive, accentuating his words with deep thrusts that sent me higher and higher, ready to take the plunge. I kissed him back. As hard as he gave, I gave in return. "Promise me," he said on a particularly hard drive into my core.

"Oh God, I'm going to...again!" My back arched as if a hot poker pressed into my lower spine and jolted me to move. The feelings were so strong. The way Nate built me up, smoothed his hands up and down my body, caressed, squeezed, manipulated—owned every response until my body gave him exactly what he wanted at his command surprised me.

"Promise me you'll be mine!" he roared, holding my hips in place, wedged between the door and his body. His cock rooted deep inside. He kept me there on the edge of release, swirling his hips around in dizzying tantalizing circles, stirring the pleasure, coaxing my body's response.

"Yes, Nate, yours. Baby, only yours."

"Oh, I love when you call me baby," he growled and picked up his pace, relentlessly pounding. His body was tight, his muscles strained beautifully as I clung to his thick biceps. The pleasure of my orgasm was such that I lost all connection to time, space, and matter. I drifted in the height of bliss for so long blackness swam around me.

When I came to, my body was spent though I was standing against the pantry door. The heavy weight of Nate's body surrounded me, his labored breaths puffed wildly against my neck.

"Shite, I love fucking you." His words broke through the sex-induced haze. He *loved* fucking me. That was not the same as saying he loved me, though I suspected things were more serious than I had ever dreamed possible.

"I love, um, you doing that to me."

His mouth moved into a grin I felt against the damp skin of my neck. "You can't say fucking?"

Heat suffused my cheeks. "I can. Just as a rule, I don't usually cuss."

"Too crude for my sweet American girl?" Nate chuckled and planted a line of kisses along my neck. I craned my head to the side to give him better access.

I inhaled, enjoying his lips on my skin. "No, just when you have a child at eighteen, you learn quickly to mind your words or your little parakeet will reiterate it. Speaking of little ones, I need to check on Tanner."

"Of course. It's easy to get carried away with this luscious body." His hands covered my breasts and squeezed. He looked at my chest lovingly as if he was loath to let me leave.

"You won't find me complaining." I looked down then back up. I cupped one of his cheeks, feeling the prickly stubble abrade my palm. He leaned into it warming my heart. "Nate, I never knew it could be this good. Feel like this with a man."

His gaze held mine. There was conviction and strength in the warm blue eyes. "Precious, it's always going to be like this. There's so much more to experience together. Years of it, in fact." He kissed me and then pulled out of my body. A trail of semen followed. We looked as the result of our lovemaking trailed down my leg.

"Fuck." I finally used profanity. Right now, it was warranted. Heat overtook my body and my heart pounded ferociously against my chest. My skin felt heightened and prickled at the edges as if someone was tickling me with a feather…everywhere. That scary buzzing sound hit my ears, and I clung to Nate's biceps to stay standing. I spent long moments taking deep breaths trying desperately to calm down.

Nate closed his eyes, licked his lips, took a deep breath, and held onto my shoulder. His eyes opened and locked on mine. "Don't run," he said as if his heart was breaking. I was having a panic attack about the fact that, once again, we acted like stupid sex-drugged teenagers who didn't know any better. And he was worried about me running off? Men really are from Mars.

"Twice!" I held up two fingers which could not to be mistaken for the peace symbol.

He shook his head. "Camille, I'm sorry. It's my fault. I didn't intend to shag you in the kitchen. Bloody hell, I didn't intend to shag you at all tonight. Not with Tanner here."

My eyes widened. "Oh. My. God." What if Tanner woke and didn't know where he was. He'd be frightened out of his mind. "I have to go to him." I pulled my sweater down and looked around for my jeans. Crap! I left them in the kitchen.

Nate opened the door and I rushed out. Grabbing a wad of napkins from the counter, I cleaned up the evidence of our pantry romp, threw on my undies and jeans, and was clasping the button as I rounded the door to the room that Tanner was sleeping in.

He was still dead to the world. That hit me like a crash dummy vehicle hits a test wall. He was comfortable here.

"Camille, leave him. Let's talk about this."

I rounded on Nate and then stomped off into the kitchen. Once there, I grabbed my glass of wine and downed it in a couple of gulps. "I can't believe we did that again! What are we sixteen? Can't keep our hands off one another long enough to put on a condom? We're playing with fire, Nate!"

"I know, I know. We'll figure it out. Whatever happens, I'm sorry." He looked so panicked, very unlike the normally overconfident, alpha male always in control. Right now he was just a man. A man who, along with his *girlfriend,* made a couple really bad errors in judgment that could affect the rest of our lives.

"It's not just you. I was there. Full participant right here." I raised my hand mockingly. "I... We cannot have a baby right now. We don't know each other well enough for that level of commitment. I'm just now on track with taking care of Tanner, my job, schooling."

Oh God, it could all be over from two stupid mistakes. Though they felt so incredibly right at the time, the consequences could last a lifetime. I doubted that Nate wanted to be shackled to me and a couple kids.

He rounded on me, pulling me into his warm chest. His hand held my head and I could hear the thud of his heart, strong and comforting. I rubbed my nose against the soft Henley he wore, doing exactly what I wanted to do earlier when he first showed up at my apartment.

"Camille, you listen and you listen good. You are not alone. Not now, not ever again. I know it's only been a short time but..." His words cracked and I looked up at him. "We're together and I don't see that ever changing. I want to be with you. I want to get to know Tanner. Spend more time as a threesome. Over the past few years, I've been floundering, focused on my career and nothing else. I've used women as mere shags." My body tightened hearing him speak of being intimate with other women. The hard edge of jealousy dug into my heart. He ran his arms up and down my back, relaxing me once more.

"Until you. This. Us. It's somehow better than anything I ever dreamed I'd have. I'm..." He took a deep breath, cupped my cheeks and kissed me softly. Then he pulled back. "I'm in love with you."

The entire world slowed, went silent, and then stopped

moving all together. Nate's eyes turned an indigo blue. "Did you hear me, Camille?"

I shook my head, feeling hot all over. Numbness filled my senses. If he hadn't been holding me so tightly I may have turned into mush and melted to the floor. A man loved me. No, not any man. This man. My Nate.

His lips quirked into a knowing grin. "I love you, precious."

"Again," I whispered wanting nothing more than to hear the most beautiful words ever said aloud.

"I love you, Camille Johnston." He kissed my cheeks.

"Again."

He kissed my forehead. "I love you." He kissed each of my closed eyelids. "I love you." He trailed his open mouth down the side of my cheek, along the edge of my chin. "I love you," he said one last time before his lips took mine in a hot open-mouthed kiss.

The man of my dreams loved me.

Only in my wildest fantasies did Prince Charming capture the peasant girl and make her his. I wasn't worthy of him, his love. He still didn't know about Gems. We hadn't figured out how to negotiate having a relationship with Tanner in the picture.

"Look, precious, I know this may come as a surprise to you, but I'm not the kind of man who bestows accolades of love, willy nilly." His gaze bore into mine. "I have never told a woman that I loved them, other than Mum and my sisters. Only you." Honesty, sincerity, and yes, love, permeated his words. My strong, confident, alpha male was professing his love for me.

Tears filled and blurred my vision and fell down my

cheeks. "Nate, I…"

He stopped me from continuing with the pad of his thumb over my lips.

"Don't. You don't have to say anything. Just know I love you. And if my voracious need to mate with you results in us having a wee one, well, then I'll do everything in my power to be the best father."

More tears. I could not hold them back any more than I could stop breathing. Nate pulled my face into the crook of his neck, holding me while I cried. He was the perfect man and he loved me. Me.

The orphan girl from New Jersey nobody ever wanted. I was so consumed with my own love for this man I was incapable of putting the feelings into words. Instead, I'd show him. Nate picked me up and walked me to his bedroom. This would only be the second time I'd lain in his bed, but this time, I'd stay. I wouldn't run.

In case I didn't believe Nate's profession of love, he spent hours showing me just how much he cared. He muffled my lustful cries with his mouth and swallowed the pleasure as easily as he gave it. Over and over, he proved to me how much he loved me, telling me repeatedly with his body, his kiss, his fevered touch and his words until I fell to sleep nestled in his arms.

★ ★ ★

I woke feeling hot. I was surrounded by warmth on all sides. Nuzzled into my chest were two dark heads. One had bright hues of chestnut and gold hair, layered over my naked chest with her cheek to my heart. Right where she should be.

Another smaller head with short hair was lying on my

other side. Little puffs of air escaped his small pout. A drop of drool coated my chest under his tiny mouth. At some time in the night, Tanner must have crawled into bed with us. Thank God Camille had enough sense to have me put on a pair of boxers. She wore knickers and one of my T-shirts. Currently my large hand was firmly planted on her rounded arse. I gave a little squeeze and she rocked her hip into my side. Her thigh rubbed along my morning wood delectably. If Tanner weren't here, I'd do something about that.

That would be something I'd need to get used to. What was the term my friends with kids used? Ah, cock-blocking. I snickered softly now fully appreciating their endearment when they called their children "CBs."

As I studied Camille's face in the soft golden light of morning, I fell more in love with her. She was impossibly beautiful. I watched her sleep and saw my future. With Tanner and potentially our wee one if that came to fruition. In the past I may have been more worried about an unplanned pregnancy. For some reason, being here with my girl, holding onto her, an arm around her boy I felt content. Blissfully and utterly happy in life. A foreign feeling but one I'd go to great lengths to keep.

Camille was a mystery, one I would thoroughly enjoy solving. I could have easily read the report my private investigator sent, detailing everything about her life. He was good at his job. Would have left no stone unturned, but I rather appreciated peeling back the layers of this fickle bird more and more. The bits of information she shared, finding out about Tanner, all added to her appeal. She wasn't the average young woman in her twenties. Camille was an old soul. She'd been through a lot, and it gave her a maturity others her age didn't have.

Looking at Tanner sleeping peacefully against my chest, his hand clasped over his mother's on my sternum was one of the most startling sights. I wanted this. A family. People counting on me for affection, comfort, and love. Watching them sleep, I was filled with a sense of protectiveness. These were now my charges. Camille and Tanner would be my family. Sooner rather than later. When I knew what I wanted, I didn't dabble in insecurity or uncertainty. No, I jumped—risks be damned.

It had worked smashingly well for Stone, Walker, & Associates. I had to believe with my whole heart that it would work with these two priceless souls.

Through my musings the little guy had woken and was now staring at me.

"Mr. Nate? Why is your pee pee standing up so big?"

I laughed, jostling Camille. She woke and rubbed her head along my chest like a baby kitten, stretching against my side and forcing my "pee pee" to harden further.

"Whoa, it just got even bigger!" Tanner said, his eyes staring at the huge erection I was sporting through my boxers and the sheet covering my lower half.

"Tanner, baby, what are you doing here?"

Tanner's little hand went to grab my prick. "Can I feel it?" he asked in awe.

I flung my hand over my dick and pressed away from his reach. "No, little man. You can't. You never touch a bloke's willy."

His eyebrows crunched up. "What's a willy?"

Camille laughed into my chest. I was glad someone thought this was funny. I was mortified. I took a deep breath and lay back down. He sat up cross-legged next to me, waiting patiently. Camille chuckled again.

"You gonna help me out here?" I asked her.

"With boy parts?" She sounded shocked and shook her head.

I ruffled a hand through my hair and sighed. "Okay, sport. Here goes it. When a boy…er…a *man* wakes up in the morning, sometime his 'pee pee'"—I used his word—"gets hard and stands up. It's normal and will go down in a few minutes."

He grabbed his lips with his hand and pinched them together, seeming to chew on what I'd said. "So will my pee pee get big like yours?" He stood up and pulled down his pants to show me his willy. "See, mine is little and yours is huge!"

"Tanner!" Camille scolded.

I closed my eyes and shook my head. "Put that thing away. You never show your private parts unless it's to a doctor, your mum, or me. And me only if it hurts or I'm helping you with a bath, okay?"

He nodded and jumped down from the bed. "I'm starving, Mommy. Can I have cereal?" Discussion over apparently. Would I ever get used to kid-speak? I hoped to hell I would.

Camille sat and pulled her hair off her neck. "Uh, honey, I don't know. We'll see what Mr. Nate has okay."

I cringed. I didn't have cereal. Never had a taste for it, but if I was going to have the lad here, I'd need to make some provisions. Maybe I could have Emma help? Camille got up and pulled on her jeans from yesterday, hiding her sweet arse. I groaned, and she winked at me over her shoulder. I'd had her so many different ways last night it was a wonder she could walk.

"Come on, Tan Man. Let's find something and get going home. I need to get ready for work. I'm going to be late." She sounded worried.

I got out of bed, pulled on my jeans and went after her, bare-chested. "You have your clothes here?" I asked.

She nodded. "Yeah, but I need to take him back to Jin."

"I can do that. And you can walk to work. You know how close AIR Bright is." I hugged her and placed a soft kiss on her lips.

"You don't have to do that. I don't want to burden you—"

I cut her off with a kiss. The giggling behind us stopped me from deepening the kiss. I cupped her cheeks and winked at the little guy happily waiting at the bar for breakfast. "I want to. It will give me time to get to know the lad," I added.

At that statement she melted, the line on her forehead disappeared, and her features softened. I kissed her once more. "Go get ready for work. I'll feed Tanner."

"You sure?" She seemed uncertain.

"Sport, tell your mum to get ready for work. Us men can get to cooking breakfast." I puffed my chest and hit it with my fists.

"Yeah, Mommy. Get going. Mr. Nate and I got this." He clapped his hands together.

I cooked him a plate of eggs and fruit. He gobbled them up so fast I worried he'd be sick, but his mum said that's the way he always ate…with gusto. I liked that. Made me feel good that he liked the meal. I kissed his mum good-bye and then dressed in a dark suit. I let him pick out a tie. He enjoyed my tie rack immensely, saying over and over that he couldn't believe how many I had. Finally he picked a deep red one that went well with the suit and crisp white shirt I chose.

As I was tying the knot, he sat on the bed, his little head down, deep in thought.

"What's up, sport?"

He looked at my suit and then down again. "I want to be like you," he said.

I got down on one knee in front of him and ruffled his hair. He looked up, a quiet sadness in his eyes. "How so?"

"I like your clothes. Never had clothes like that."

He gave me an idea. "Would you like to go to work with me today? My law office?"

Tanner's face lit, and a bright smile replaced the frown. He nodded fast and repeatedly.

"Right then. We best get you the proper attire. Come now. Let's get you a suit."

His eyes widened, and he grabbed my hand. Tanner's hand was pint-sized compared to mine and that overprotective feeling swept through me again. "For real?" he asked in that sweet boy timbre.

"Yes. Let's go."

I called Emma on the way to the car park. She told me where to go to purchase children's attire. Apparently Ralph Lauren had a children's line, which included very manly mini-sized suits for wee ones. We had a smashing time working with the sales attendant, finding him just the right suit. It looked so similar to mine, he could be my own son. The thought warmed me and gave me a gushy feeling

I'd experienced a lot lately.

We entered Stone, Walker, & Associates hand in hand. Emma's mouth dropped to the floor.

"And who is this little fella?" She crouched, her dark hair swinging over her shoulder.

"I'm Tanner," he answered, and then cowered into my leg just enough that I could feel his nervous energy.

Emma smiled. "And who is your mummy?" she asked, her English accent thicker than mine or Collier's since we'd been in the States for years and she'd just arrived months before.

Tanner's eyebrows scrunched together and he looked up at me. "What's a mummy?"

I laughed. "Well, it's a dead body that's been wrapped for preservation." His eyes widened.

"I don't have any mummies. Sorry," he answered, deadpan. I bit my tongue not to laugh out loud. Emma chuckled.

"Well, isn't he just precious," she said and eyed me speculatively.

"Sport, she means who is your mom. Camille Johnston is his mother, or mum, as we say in England." Tanner nodded and Emma's eyes widened.

"When the conversation went crazy at lunch the other day and she mentioned being pregnant, the two never connected." She shook her head. "Well it's lovely to meet you, Tanner. I really like your mum."

"She's the prettiest and nicest mommy in the whole world." He smiled. "And she likes to kiss and sleep with Mr. Nate a lot!" he continued, not realizing the bit of gossip he'd provided my sibling who would later torture me with it.

I smacked my forehead. Now I knew why Camille did this gesture so often in his presence. "What Tanner means is…"

Emma just laughed and waved it off. "No explanation needed. But this is too good. I can't wait to find out what Mum has to say."

My hackles rose, and I placed a hand on her shoulder. "Leave it be. This is new and Camille scares easily. Last thing I need is Mum getting involved." Besides, I was keeping Mum in the loop to some extent. No need for her to know about stay overs.

Emma bit her lip and tilted her head to the side. She looked at Tanner and then at me. "Fine. I won't meddle. You guys look adorable though. Let me take a picture." She pulled out her iPhone, and I placed Tanner in front of me, my hands on both his shoulders. We both smiled wide, and she captured the image.

"Send me a copy. While you're at it, have a couple copies printed and framed. I want that on my desk at work and one for Camille as a surprise." I pulled out my phone and sent her the image of the three of us together and the one of just Camille. "I just sent you two more. I'd like the same. Make sure the framed images are visible on my desk."

Emma shook her head and put a hand on her hip. "Wow, you're… I never thought I'd see the day when you'd be smitten. It's really quite fabulous."

"Don't you have work to do? Tanner and I have lots to do today. Right, sport?"

His eyes lit at the mention of his name, and he nodded excitedly. He was a really great kid. Kept quiet and only spoke when spoken to unless he was at home or in an environment that was familiar. Camille had done a wonderful job raising the boy alone.

She shouldn't have been alone. Tyler should have taken care of his responsibility. It seemed everyone had been right about the bloke. He was nothing but a womanizing bastard. I'd yet to deal with him, but that would have to come. I needed to set the record straight, and he needed to know he had a son.

CHAPTER FOURTEEN

Nothing prepared me for the vision that entered the office at closing time. Nate strode in holding Tanner's hand. They were both dressed in matching suits and smiles. If anyone had seen them, they would have assumed it was a proud father with his son.

I stood with my mouth open, taking in their matching attire.

"You look amazing," I whispered, my gaze eating up every inch of one the loveliest images.

"Mommy! Mr. Nate took me to work today. He's a liar!" he said happily.

Nate laughed and leaned against my desk. Full belly guffaws racked his tall muscled frame.

"Tanner, it's lawyer, not liar," I corrected, sighing. Nate still laughed hard.

"Mommy, mommy. Guess what I did?" He didn't let me answer. "I went to work. I saw Mr. Nate's office. He has this big window." Tanner stretched his arms out as wide as he could. "It's like a wall. And you could see the whole wide world!" he squealed, bouncing up and down. "He even let me color on the whole window with light highters!"

"Highlighters, sport." Nate smiled.

"Yeah! Light highters! I had yellow, and green, and pink, and blue! And I color-did all over the window wall! We took a picture you have to see." He tugged Nate's pocket and dug his hand in. He pulled out Nate's cell phone with no regard for personal boundaries. I worried my lip as Nate clicked a couple buttons and showed me the screen. As clear as day, you could see Tanner in front of his wall of art and the buildings and horizon through the glass. It seemed as though he traced the shapes of the skyscrapers with the bright colors. I was impressed that Nate would be so comfortable letting Tanner deface his office.

Tanner moved from foot to foot until I told him it was amazing. I loved watching his exuberance. Nate put his hand on the boy's head. Tanner calmed then looked up at Nate with an adoring smile across his little face. He was falling in love with Nate the same way I had.

"The lad was very helpful actually. He went to court with me, held my briefcase which was a very important job." Tanner nodded excitedly. "He sat perfectly quiet while I pleaded a case. We had lunch."

"We had the bestest ever tacos ever, Mommy! I love tacos! And I met his brother. I forgotted his name, but he talked funny like Mr. Nate and gave me ice cream!"

Nate laughed and pulled me into his chest. "Sorry I didn't tell you I had him for the day, but I couldn't bring myself to take him home. I did stop by your apartment to tell Jin I was keeping him for the day. She was surprised but okay with it. We wanted to surprise you."

"I am surprised, that's for sure. I can't believe you did this! You know he's going to get so attached…" I warned. I really wasn't sure how connected Nate wanted to be with Tanner. Sure, he said he loved me but I was a package deal. There was never going to be an "us" without Tanner included.

"As he should. I told you, precious. I'm not going anywhere. Get used to it. I want you both with me tonight." I planned on finding a way out of it, but he squashed that plan.

"Jin already told me you're not working tonight so you're free. I have London and Collier and Emma coming for dinner. I want you and Tanner to get to know my family." He went behind my desk, opened my drawer and pulled out my purse. "Let's go."

"Nate, I don't know if that's a good idea."

"Tanner? Would you like to spend the night at my house again? I have an Xbox and lots of games," he offered.

"Yes, oh, yes. Mommy, Mr. Nate promised to teach me a car racing game. We picked it up at the game store. It's Lego!"

"Low blow…" I whispered so only Nate could hear.

Nate shrugged and grinned. "Whatever it takes. I want you with me as often as possible. Both of you." He gestured to Tanner, and my heart filled with adoration and extreme love. He was pulling out all the stops and I couldn't understand why. I was a nobody, but with Nate, I *felt* like a somebody.

Later that evening, I worried my fingers and sipped my wine when Nate opened the door. I heard male laughter and a round of back slaps. I walked around the kitchen and into the living room. Collier removed London's coat as Nate removed Emma's. A handsome tall man with brown hair and light eyes that were green as my own came to me and put out his hand. He seemed familiar in a way that you recalled a long lost friend or schoolmate.

"I believe we met at lunch the other day but with all

the ruckus"—he tipped his head to London and Collier—"I didn't get to really make your acquaintance. I'm Tripp Devereaux, London and Collier's friend."

"It's good to meet you, Tripp. Camille Johnston. Everyone calls me Cami."

"Everyone except me." Nate grabbed my hips from behind, bringing me flush against his form while he nuzzled my neck. He laid a hot kiss on the spot he'd claimed as *his* and stuck his hand out to Tripp. "How goes it, mate? I see you've met my girlfriend, Camille. You going stag this evening?"

Tripp glanced at where Emma was chatting with Tanner. "I figured I'd keep Em company."

Nate's eyebrows rose and I smiled. Tripp's intent was clear, even if his words were clouded.

Nate set Tanner up with the new video game in the media room just off the kitchen. I could see him sitting quietly as he played the game two rooms away. It was the perfect set up. We'd fed him some chicken nuggets and fruit before the group came, so we'd have adult time. We planned on inviting him back for dessert before bed.

I was surprised at how easily Nate made Tanner and me part of his everyday life. He didn't seem bothered or burdened having a child around at all. Actually the very opposite seemed true. He made a point to include Tanner in conversations, joke with him, and overall connect with him on a "guy" level.

We finished the dinner I helped Nate cook. Everyone devoured the filet mignon in a red wine reduction, seasoned veggies, and a rice pilaf. "Hey, London, can I have word with you about the redesign? Camille, can you come over here, too? I have some ideas I've jotted down."

Both London and I excused ourselves from the group chatting around the living room table.

"You've finally looked at some of the specs? I'm shocked!" London laughed.

"Ha ha. I wanted to show you and Camille some ideas. Now that Camille and Tanner are going to be here regularly, I want to make some changes to the plan. This room—" He gestured to the room Tanner had used last night and would tonight.

"You mean the workout room?" she asked.

Nate shook his head. "Exactly. Gym's a no-go. I can use the building's facilities. I want this one changed into a room for Tanner. He loves race cars and race-inspired themes. I want you to go forward with that concept. That's what he likes. Right, precious?"

"That's his favorite thing but—"

"Perfect! You'll make the change, London? We need to make sure there are bunk beds or two beds in there. He has a best mate. I want him to have a place to sleep when we're child caring."

London grinned. She pulled a piece of long black hair into her hand and twirled it around a finger. Her eyes were see-through gray and sparkled like diamonds. "Of course I can make the change. A child's bedroom will be such fun. We'll start work this week. Camille, are there any changes to the plans you'd like to see? We could easily change things to reflect a family home."

"Uh…I don't know." I was freaked out and beyond capable of speaking. Nate was moving so fast. I felt like a top, spinning out of control, slamming into one thing after another.

"London, make whatever changes necessary to make sure Camille and Tanner are most comfortable here. Soon they'll be living with me and I want them to feel at home," Nate said.

It took a couple of moments for his words to sink in. *Living with me?*

"Excuse me. Nate, what?" My breath left my lungs in a whoosh. I was doing my best to not have a full-blown panic attack.

Nate pulled me into his arms. I went willingly, cuddling in his warmth. "Camille, you admitted you're mine. You agreed you wouldn't run. I told you I loved you. You don't think I'm going to let you live so far from me, do you?"

Confusion stole my breath. When he said it like that, it almost sounded logical. I composed myself in the comfort of his embrace. "We have to talk about this. There's so much we don't know about each other. Then there's Jin and Zach. She can't live without my half of the rent."

"Oh, my sweet. I will ensure Jin is well taken care of. I'll pay the rent for a year, more if you'd like. Whatever will make you happy. Whatever will make you say yes."

Now he was asking. The food I'd consumed churned in my stomach as acid set fire to my chest. My heart pounded and I clung to Nate, trying to press down the fear bubbling just under the surface.

"It's too soon. We've only known each other a few weeks. You're asking me to move in?" My voice rose, and the rest of the room stopped talking and focused on us.

"You wanker. You're moving Cami in and didn't mention it! Congrats, brother mine!" Collier came and clapped Nate on the back, his brown eyes dazzled with delight. I groaned and put my head in my hands.

Emma jumped up and down and hugged us painfully. "This is… It's just so perfect!" Her voice dispersed like a wave crashing against the shore.

"Nothing's been decided," I whispered into Nate's ear.

"I can be very persuasive, precious."

"And I can be very argumentative!" I shot back.

"That I know. I'll take my chances." He grinned and kissed my temple. "We'll discuss this later."

I nodded and crossed my arms over my chest defensively, annoyed that he got the last word and excited at the possibility of this actually happening. Living with the man I loved, Tanner with his own room, feeling the love of a man who cared for him… It was the stuff my dreams were made of. I just never expected it to ever happen to me.

★ ★ ★

Camille was quiet the rest of the evening. After I dropped the bomb that I intended for her and Tanner to move in, she'd withdrawn. Together, we went through the routine of putting Tanner to bed. There were many steps in the process including bath time, reading time, discussing the highs and lows of the day. For a moment in the hour-long process, I thought it would never end. Camille was thorough and didn't stray because she wasn't home. I appreciated that about her. It proved how stable she was, regardless of where she laid her head.

I pulled her into the bedroom after I turned down the lights and double-checked the locks on the doors.

"We have to talk," I said. She cut me off with her lips.

They were warm, inviting, and tasted of cherries. I licked the seam, deepening the kiss when she opened her mouth. Her arms came around me and her hands sank into my hair. She ran her fingers through the strands as she tugged and nipped my lips. Before I knew what was happening, she had me on my back and was straddling my lap.

"Precious, we need to talk…" I reminded her but quickly forgot when she unbuttoned my dress shirt and licked the flat discs of my nipples. It was a huge erogenous zone for me. My dick rose painfully against the fabric of my trousers. She continued licking, nipping, and sucking her way along my chest, over each muscle of my abdomen.

"You have an amazing body, Nate. I could lick you everywhere." She moaned and jutted her pelvis against my thigh rubbing her center along the muscled quad. This was the first time she took the lead physically. I forced myself to just enjoy the sensations of having her mouth and tongue all over me as long as I could.

Deft fingers unbuckled my belt then removed trousers and boxers in one swift move. My cock bobbed in front of her face, as if greeting her after being freed from the constricting garments. She slid her nose along the length then inhaled, moaning as she placed a hot opened mouth kiss at the base of my cock. With a tight fist she gripped the base and yanked up slowly. Chills ran from the bottom of my spine up and out every pore.

"What do you want me to do?" My cock wept at the tip, ready for her mouth to cover me.

"Suck me off. I need your mouth on my cock now, precious."

Camille responded by sucking my length into her

mouth and down to her throat where she started gagging. At first it felt magnificent having that tight ring of muscle hugging the wide crown. "So good…" I started but heard a muffled noise. I opened my eyes to see Camille and her sinful mouth completely surrounding my prick. It should have been the sexiest image I'd ever seen, but it wasn't. Tears streamed down her face as she gagged and choked. I softened at the sight of her struggling.

I pulled her off my cock, not knowing what the fuck that just was, unless possibly it was the worst blow job in the history of blow jobs.

"What's the matter? Aren't you going to fuck my face and force it down my throat?"

"What the fuck are you saying? No, I'm not going to fuck your face. You're not my whore. You're my girlfriend. I would never in a million sodding years force anything on you. If you want to share your love for me with oral sex, I'm honored. But not like this." My tone bordered on disgust. Her face crumpled, and tears poured down her cheeks.

"I'm sorry. I know I'm not any good. I never could take it down my throat well enough. Tyler told me to just stay still while he shoved it in. I practiced hard not to throw up. I promise I won't get sick on you. You can use me."

"Fuck! I'll kill the bloody prick with my bare hands." I tugged Camille up and over my naked body holding her close. "Precious, what he did, that's not love. That's not even respectful to a woman. I would never treat any woman like that."

"But I know men love, um…getting sucked on. I want to. I want you to be happy!" Her lip trembled.

I shook my head and gripped her arse. She moaned,

still turned on even though I was having trouble keeping it up, due to visions of Tyler forcing Camille to take his puny cock down her throat.

She kissed me. "Please, let me try again. I can make it good. I know I can."

I nodded. "Okay, but let me guide you. You should never feel pain, cry, or feel the need to stave off vomiting. This should be mutually enjoyable. If you don't like it, you don't ever have to do it. Understand?" She nodded and kissed me deep. Her tongue and mouth were sweet and sugary, just like candy. We kissed for long moments, getting back the excitement before we were sidetracked by her past.

"Take your clothes off," I told her. She sat up, straddling my hips, and pulled her dress over her head. She was clad only in a navy-blue lace bra and matching knickers. "So bloody gorgeous. I'm never letting another man see what's mine ever again." Her eyes widened and she bit her lip. I was too distracted by her glorious tits and arse to worry over my possessiveness. I pulled the cups of her bra down, exposing each globe, then leaned up and sucked a perfect pink tip into my mouth, rolling my tongue around the pert flesh. She moaned and jerked her hips against my groin bringing my cock back to full mast instantly. For long minutes she rubbed her sex along my length as I toyed with her tits. She moaned and gasped as I sucked and nibbled until finally she tipped her head back, ground down on my dick, crushing her clit against my rock-hard erection and came. Christ, the woman was uninhibited in bed and all fucking mine.

Once she came down from her high, I kissed her and then yanked the edge of her knickers, ripping them easily. "Hey, I liked those!"

"I'll buy you more. Tons more! Now I have an idea." I swooped in for another tangle of tongues. I could drown in her taste, but I had something far more delectable I wanted to sample. "Turn around and hover that pretty pussy over my face."

Her cheeks reddened, and she bit her lip nervously. Another position she never enjoyed with the cocksucker. All the better. I wanted to introduce Camille to all the possible ways I could pleasure her. "Come on now, precious, don't be shy. Turn around and let me have at that arse." She giggled when I said arse. It was adorable how Americans seemed to love an English accent. As long as my Camille thought it was sexy, I couldn't care less about anyone else. Finally, she turned around, and instead of backing up, she stayed still. There was no way she was getting out of this due to nerves.

I gripped her arse and tugged her back, settling her pretty cunt over my face. I could feel the heat coming off her center like waves of energy. Her scent was musky after coming against my body. My mouth salivated at the nearness and smell. With my thumbs, I parted her slowly and looked at her pink flesh. So perfect and ready to be taken by me, and only me. Instead of licking her clit which I knew she'd expect, wanted even, I flattened my tongue and went deep, tasting her softness, licking along each wall, pressing her arse hard against my face so I could get an inch deeper. Her essence was thick, rich and coated in sweetness. Like the syrup of the gods.

"Oh, oh, oh," she called out on each drive of my tongue, her hips thrusting forward to push me deeper.

I pulled back and breathed her in, my eyes rolled to the back of my head in pure bliss. I could die a happy man if I could wake daily with this pussy at my disposal, ready to be licked and sucked before starting the day. It made me painfully hard thinking about our future.

"Now take my cock into your mouth, baby, just slowly. Lick and suck it however you feel comfortable." She stilled and leaned down. I felt a soft kiss on just the head and then her tongue swirled around the tip.

I moaned, not for her benefit, but because it felt so damned good. Her mouth came around the crown, and she sucked in about an inch and let it go with a plop. "Fuck that's good!" I encouraged so she'd know what worked. For a moment I didn't feel anything until I felt a wetness at the very base and then the sensation moved up my length inch by slow inch as she licked my length. "Yeah, precious. Perfect," I said as she finished the journey and then put the front half of my cock into her mouth. Her little tongue swirled around the flesh as she sucked. I saw bright lights flashing along the edges of my vision as the mother of all orgasms rolled and built in my body.

"You got it, baby. Keep going like that and I'll come so bloody hard." She moaned and the vibrations sent spikes of pleasure down my shaft to rest heavily in my balls. They tightened and swelled as she lapped at the tender tip of my dick, pressing her tongue into the slit at the top.

As Camille sucked and treated me to an oral loving, I buried my face between her thighs. She jerked when I sucked her clit into my mouth and then retaliated by sucking my dick farther into hers. Camille got the hang of what she was doing and started bobbing up and down over my shaft, sucking, licking, and kissing every inch, driving me completely wild. While she sucked, I made sure to give just as good as I was getting. I tongue fucked her over and over until she was crying out, my dick lodged deep in her throat.

I wanted more, so much more. I kept going, bearing down, eating her as if I'd never get another chance. She howled around my dick and then sucked me so hard I didn't have the time to warn her, spurting hotly into her mouth. Stream after stream left my aching cock as she sucked it down, taking it all as I licked and tongued the cream of her third release. Fucking ambrosia.

Physically spent, I turned her around and cuddled her to my side, her head on my chest where I needed her. "Think about moving in with me. I'm in love with you and want to make this a home for you, me and Tanner and possibly any little ones we may have accidentally made along the way."

She groaned and all the breath left her lungs. Finally she responded, "I'll think about it." It wasn't a no, but it wasn't a yes either.

"How long?"

"How long what?" she asked.

"How much time do you need to decide? A couple days?"

"Nate," she warned.

"Okay, okay." I kissed her temple. "A week?"

She shook her head against my chest.

"No, huh, well how about a fortnight then?"

"How long's that?" she asked.

"About two weeks." I waited in silence. I thought possibly she'd fallen asleep when she finally answered. "Okay, I'll have my answer for you in two weeks."

I hugged her then tipped her chin up to kiss her swollen lips. "That was a mighty fine blow job by the way." I grinned and waggled my eyebrows at her. She smacked my chest and buried her face into my skin. Her cheeks were flushed that rosy pink I adored.

"I enjoyed what we did. That was…"

"Mind–blowing? Worship worthy?" I added.

She giggled and bit down on my peck then sucked the skin, finishing with a soft kiss. There would be a mark left there. She didn't realize the velocity of her sucking capability. I didn't care, I wanted marks from her love bites all over me as reminders. "I was going to say fun, but that sounds so paltry now."

We both laughed and I hugged her to me. She draped a naked thigh over my groin. "What happened with Ty, Camille?"

She groaned and pushed her hair out of her face. I gripped her waist and hauled her completely on top of me. Skin to skin. She clasped her hands on my chest and leaned her chin down. "What do you want to know?"

So many things, I wanted to reply. Instead I started with the burning question. "Why doesn't he know about Tanner?"

"It's not a pretty story, Nate. I'd hoped to save you from it."

"I need to know if we're ever going to move forward."

She nodded and leaned in for a kiss. I returned her kiss then settled back down to wait.

"A couple days after I turned eighteen, I met Tyler. We hit it off right away. I was taken by his looks and he seemed nice, interested in me. He talked me into bed after only two dates, and took my virginity roughly in a hotel room. We only ever met in a hotel. At the time I didn't think much of it as I was trying to find a job, figure out what to do with my life. I didn't have much to my name and no friends. He made me feel cared for and wanted."

I let her think about the past and figure out how she wanted to share it.

"Then I missed my period. After a week of waiting for it, I finally took a test. It said I was pregnant. I went to Tyler's office because I couldn't wait any longer. I was scared but excited about bringing a life into the world with the man I thought I loved. I was so wrong."

Her eyes misted, but her tears never fell. I hoped she was done crying for the prat.

"I told him I was pregnant and he claimed it wasn't his. He knew I had been a virgin but didn't care. He called me a whore and manhandled me a little."

My arms tightened around her and I gritted my teeth, ready to throw some clothes on and go beat the living hell out of the bastard.

"You were so fucking young. He took advantage of you!" I was unable to keep my opinions to myself.

Camille put her fingers to my lips. "Let me finish. You don't know everything. What I say next may change your opinion of him and me." Her lip quivered.

I sucked her lip into my mouth soothing the ache. "Nothing will make me not love you."

She took a deep breath. "He told me to get rid of it, that he didn't care what I did. And then…"

Anger filled all the little pockets of my soul, and I wished he were here right now, so I could tear him apart the way he had my sweet Camille all those years ago.

"…he gave me ten thousand dollars. Told me that's all I

was ever going to get, to leave and deal with the issue."

"Christ! Rat fucking bastard! He should have taken care of you, Camille. Helped you." Now I knew why she'd never had a relationship after Ty, and why she'd run from one between us. It was likely the same reason she hadn't told me she loved me.

I wouldn't pressure her for the words. She told me in the way she looked at me, the way she smiled when I entered a room and the way she made love to me with her whole body, heart, and soul.

"Don't you hate me for taking the money?" Her face was tight, her bottom lip tucked tight between her teeth.

"No, no, I don't. The opposite, in fact. He gave you that money to keep you quiet and to dispose of his responsibility. You *needed* that money to survive. I could never think poorly of you. I love you, Camille. Nothing you say or do is going to change that. I love you. Do you hear me?"

She nodded.

"Can you feel how much you mean to me?"

Her hands cupped my cheeks. I turned my head and kissed each palm. "I love you so much, Nate. I'm so sorry I haven't said so. I'm just so scared to love you and lose you. There's still so much we need to get through." Tears trickled down her cheeks again. At least this time they were because of her love, not because of her fear.

"We have time. We have all the time in the world." I hugged her and kissed her more times than I could count. Slowly I pulled back and held her gaze with mine. I wiped the tears from the apples of her lovely cheeks. "Knowing you love me…it's everything, Camille. It's all I need."

CHAPTER FIFTEEN

The better part of two weeks passed by in complete harmony. For once in my life, I felt everything was moving as it should. After three years of dancing, I was leaving Justice, my alter ego behind.

I wouldn't miss her or the various men who adored her. I'd be heading out on a high note, too. Tonight, I would work my regular stage shift and a private booking. The owners said it would be a real money maker. Apparently, a group of Richie Riches heard their favorite dancer was leaving and booked a private show. Since it was my last night, the owners made sure they paid double for the privilege of having me all to themselves. It would be my highest earning night ever. I couldn't wait to use that money to pay off my next set of online courses. It would put me ahead of the curve and back on track with my studies.

True to his word, Mr. Jensen signed me on full-time, and Tanner and I had full medical benefits now. I couldn't be happier. A heavy burden lifted knowing I'd be saving that expense and Tanner was protected.

Aside from Nate's near constant prods about moving in with him, things were going so well I hesitated to change it. He wanted Tanner and me with him, officially, period, end of discussion. I still wasn't convinced it was a good idea. We'd only known each other for a few weeks and most of those were tumultuous. Things had recently been beyond amazing but that didn't change the newness. I'd agreed to stay with him on the evenings I didn't work at Gems, but so far I still had my space. I worried about what to tell Jin. I was concerned that she'd be devastated if I told her I was moving in with my boyfriend. It turned out I was wrong. Nate told her.

The man would drive a perfectly sane woman to the loony bin. Half the time I didn't know what to do with my alpha, overly possessive boyfriend. He didn't waste time talking to Jin about the prospect. Jin admitted being sad but knew that neither of us wanted to live the rest of our lives as we were now. Once she found out Nate would be paying a year's rent in advance and that we'd pay her to watch Tanner while I worked, she knew it was a win–win situation. She wouldn't have to worry about a roommate and she'd make extra money caring for Tanner during the day. She might consider leaving Gems, too.

Nate still hadn't mentioned Tyler since our discussion and for that I was grateful. It seems as though what he found out about his friend had irreparably ruined his friendship. It was a catch-22. As much as I hated Tyler, I didn't want to ruin anything for Nate. I loved him and wanted him to be happy. The situation with his friend and me weighed heavily on him. I wished I could make it better.

Leaving those thoughts behind, I focused on the fact that it was my last night at Gems. I planned to go out with a bang. The owners informed me that the "suits," as they called them, were ready for me to go on.

I checked the clock and splayed my fingers to express my need for five more minutes. One last look in the mirror and my black *Pulp Fiction*–inspired wig was snugly in place, the blood-red corset with black trim held tightly together by crisscrossing black satin ribbon. I turned to check my booty. G-string perfectly placed, garters running down the middle of my thighs nicely, just a little nudge here and one there, and I was ready for my last performance.

Gems had been a home of sorts for the past three years, but I wasn't sad to leave. I had a future so bright it blinded me in its golden rays. After almost two full weeks, I'd decided I would move in with Nate at the end of the month. I'd thought of nothing else the last couple weeks, running over the pros and cons. All the cons related to the newness of our relationship and leaving Jin and Zachery. The pros were so many it filled an entire lined yellow sheet of paper. The biggest pro? I loved him. And over the past few weeks we had been together, he'd proven he loved me. Nothing was going to get in between that love. He promised he'd always love me and I believed him.

I planned on telling him the big news tomorrow morning. Tanner would be ecstatic.

London had made a fantasy room for him at Nate's apartment. He called it a flat, New Yorkers called it an apartment. In my mind, it was big enough to be a mansion. It had more rooms than he needed and lacked for nothing in the way of amenities. The building had a pool, a gym, and a restaurant. A busy professional working virtually would never have to leave the building.

Nate took advantage of the pool most nights. Watching him swim was like watching a moving piece of art. His lines, the movement of his toned muscles stretching and propelling him through the water was breathtaking. Tanner loved the pool like any four-year-old would but hadn't had much experience in water. Nate worked with him on learning to swim and said once we moved in, he'd take him each night to ensure he was safe around water. Another pro according to Tanner.

I made my way slowly up the stairs and onto the stage. A black velvet curtain hid me from view. Sounds of male laughter, clinking of glasses, and whistles started the second the lights dimmed and my music started. I let the heavy tones of the base sweep across my senses, thrum against my chest, and rumble into my heels. Music and movement helped me escape the reality of what I was actually doing. When I followed the melody with fluid movements and gymnastic inspired pole work, I was usually able to forget that a crowd of horny men were watching and often times touching themselves while I worked.

I took a deep breath in as the curtain rose. My hands gripped the pole above my head, and I faced the back wall, allowing the men to see my bare ass pressed against the pole, my back arched. I knew without needing a mirror that the picture I presented was every man's fantasy. Using this as a tool, I pulled high, swung my legs into the air, and curved around the pole to the floor. When I looked up to assess the men, my eyes caught a pair of familiar blues, ones I did not look forward to seeing.

Tyler Thornton.

His grin was wide, and he held a hand loosely in front of his face as he took in my body. He licked his lips and I turned my head. The odds were he wouldn't recognize me. I was wearing a wig, and frankly, it had been a long time since he'd seen this body. It was different, matured, and changed after having a child. Sweat prickled at the edges of my hairline. Usually I didn't perspire. I was in excellent shape, long and toned, yet still curvy. The presence of my ex, Tanner's biological father, put my nerves into overdrive.

I took long yoga-style breaths, bent at the waist, and shook my moneymaker. Several of the men whistled. Some threw money on the stage. A few didn't even pay attention, they were so busy talking business in the back to notice the half-naked girl on a stage fifteen feet in front of them.

Tyler was laser-focused on my body as I undulated, undoing the first few eye hooks of my corset, giving my ample bosom additional space. I needed the extra space to suck in the air I was having trouble keeping. With a saucy step, I sauntered to a black glossy chair that had only a seatback but no arms. In a move I stole from Jin, I straddled the chair, giving the men a nice healthy view of my satin-clad center and then leaned back, balancing on the chair, putting my legs out in a wide air split. That caught the men's attention. With a twirl of my legs, I flipped and straddled the chair reverse cowgirl, bumping and grinding along with the music as they cheered.

"Take it off, baby!" one man yelled.

"Let's see that rack!" another cheered.

Turning to face the men, I grinned and slid my hand down the front of the corset and over my sex, mimicking touching myself. The men went wild! Money seemed to come from nowhere, littering the glossy stage with the color green. It was the surge of bills I planned on cashing in tonight. Sucking my dry finger into my mouth, I heard a collective groan. Men were so damn easy it was ridiculous. I hadn't even touched myself, just pretended to, and they went brain-dead.

I bent my body over the back of the chair, my head hanging upside down, blood rushing to the crown. That's when my worst nightmare occurred. I didn't fall, didn't lose my wig. A man didn't try to touch me. The chair didn't break. No, it was so much worse. A man with long even steps entered the room. I would recognize that gait anywhere. My gaze went from his large feet, covered by well-defined quads in black tailored slacks up to a pinched in waist, broad chest and shoulders, and finally up to the most stunning face I'd ever known.

Nate.

With a swing of my body, I covered my face and turned around.

"Boooooo, baby, get to the good stuff! Show us your titties!" one man hollered. His tone bordered on angry.

I swung my hips from side to side and went back to the pole. If I was dancing, maybe I could figure out a quick exit. The music changed once more. It was the last song of my time on the stage, and these men expected a show. If I didn't take my clothes off, there would be mutiny. If I did, I ran the risk of Nate noticing me. So far he hadn't glanced at the stage. I loved him even more for that. He was talking quietly to Tyler. It was obvious the moment things got heated between them because Nate stood abruptly and his chair fell to the floor. Tyler stood next to him, hands on Nate's forearms trying to calm him down. Rage plastered Nate's features.

The song came closer to the end, and I removed hook after hook of my corset. At the highest beat, I undid the last hook and splayed open the corset, showing off my bare breasts.

"Damn, girl, I could suck on those tits all damned day!" a deep voice rose above the crowd of applause and howls.

"Yeah, baby, come over here and sit on my lap. I'll make it worth your while," another man yelled, holding up what looked to be a fifty-dollar bill. As much as I'd like the money, there would be no lap dances. Typically in the private room anything but touching the dancer and removing your thong was allowed. Not tonight. It would hinder my big payout. Right then, all I could think about was getting the hell out of there before Nate recognized me.

I closed my eyes, letting the men look their fill. Whoops and hollers of joy and excitement filled the room as I massaged and cupped the heavy weight of my breasts. All seemed fine and I was about to flip over and make my final exit when I opened my eyes and held the gaze of the man I loved and adored.

His mouth locked in a grimace, teeth clenched. Even from a distance, I saw his jaw so tight he could cut leather between his teeth. His gaze swept across my mostly naked body from my head to each bared breast to my miniscule panties, down each leg and back up again. I felt the heat of his anger palpitating in waves in my direction.

I closed my eyes, swirled around on my butt, and made to leave the stage. The lights dimmed, and the music went back to normal club-style tunes.

"What. The. Fuck!" I heard the very distinct English accent as Nate roared his disapproval. I heard his loud footsteps over the beat of the music as he stomped to the stage. I'd almost made it to the steps when his hand encircled my wrist and spun me around.

★ ★ ★

Naked. My precious Camille was stark naked, and every man here was drooling and looking their fill. I reached a shaky hand out to the black wig and pushed the offensive thing off her head. It fell to the floor, and her glorious brown locks fell in spirals over her breasts and bare shoulders.

"Camille, no." My voice was hard to hear over the loud techno music. Her eyes widened and her gaze lifted over my shoulder. A quick glance and I saw Tyler, only he wasn't looking at me. His eyes were devouring every inch of my girlfriend. He licked his lips, and I threw off my suit coat, spun Camille toward the back wall, and covered as much of her naked body as I could. In seconds, I had my jacket covering her lady bits.

"Well, well, well. What did I tell you, buddy? She's nothing but a skanky whore." He tsk-tsked. His hand clasped my shoulder. In the past, I would have been comforted by the action. If this had been a whore, and not the love of my life, I could have let it slide. I was no longer that man, and he was no longer my best mate. Instead of shrugging him off, I turned on a heel and slugged the bugger right in the kisser.

"Shut the fuck up, Tyler. I've had it with you and your shite!" The bouncer caught up with us and prevented me from getting additional shots in. The giant black man held me and gestured for Camille to leave the stage through the back exit.

"Camille, meet me outside!" I yelled. The bouncer said something into an ear piece and before too long, both Tyler and I were out on our collective assess in front of the club.

"Don't come back, or you'll get more than a sore ass

for your trouble!" The bouncer shoved me to the ground. My knees bit into sharp gravel, but I didn't feel the pain. My anger had taken over all rational thought.

Tyler stood and shook dirt and rocks off his own knees and suit jacket. He looked at me and shook his head. "You punched me over her?" His voice shook with rage. "For a fucking stripper!"

I lunged at him. My body was hot, muscles primed and ready to strike. A fight was what I needed, and I was going to take a pound of flesh. Tyler fell to the ground, and we rolled, gravel and dirt crunching around us. Eventually I got the advantage and straddled him, slamming his head into the dirt.

"You cocksucking piece of shite! Do you know what you did to her? This is your fault!" I roared, planting my fist firmly into his jaw. The sickening sound of knuckles meeting bone filled the air. Blood poured from Tyler's nose, and he spit a spray of blood in my face. His fist shot out and caught the side of my face and eye socket. Pain sent me back a step but not enough to let go of the arsehole.

"Nate, Nate! Get off him! He's not worth it!" Camille tugged at my biceps. "Please. You can't go to jail for this!" Her words finally entered my brain, and I pulled away and jumped off him.

He rolled to the side and spit out more blood, and then wiped his nose on the sleeve of his suit.

"Motherfucker, you ruined our friendship. Five years of brotherhood for this whore! Believe me, her pussy is not worth losing your best friend, Nate." He scowled. "I know. I've had it!"

He gutted me with those words, the reality sickening

me. I made to go at him again. Camille jumped in front of me.

"It doesn't matter what he thinks, Nate. I don't care. He can call me whatever he wants. He means nothing to me," she cried as tears filled in her eyes.

Tyler groaned and looked up at the sky.

"I came here tonight, Ty, not because you invited me, but to tell you the truth."

Camille's eyes widened in horror. "No, Nate, please don't." A tear slipped down the side of her face. "He doesn't care," she tried, but I was ending this right here.

"You have a son! A beautiful four-year-old boy named Tanner."

Tyler rolled his eyes and put his hands on his hips. "Is that what she told you? That the kid is mine? And you believe her?" He shook his head.

"Of course I believe her. The boy looks exactly like you!"

"And probably a handful of other johns she fucked to pay the bills. You saw her. You think she shakes that ass just for you? Did you even know that she was spreading her goodies all over town?"

His words sank in and hit a point in my heart that I couldn't deny. Camille had lied to me repeatedly. Lies of omission, but still lies. She stripped however many nights a week, baring her beautiful body to the highest bidder. My mouth watered with the sour sickness you get right before you vomit. I pushed it down and took a few deep breaths.

"The boy is yours. I've met him. He's perfect. You can request a paternity test—"

"I don't want anything to do with the little bastard.

Even if the kid is mine, he's the spawn of a two-bit skank. I've paid my dues. I gave her money to do away with the pregnancy. I should have known the stupid fucking cunt would screw me over one day." The words he used to describe the woman I loved filled me with a rage so dark it spilled out of every pore controlling all my instincts. I was about to rush him again when he grabbed Camille's wrist, lifted his hand, and backhanded her. "That's for not doing what I told you, you dumb bitch!" he said as my body plowed into his.

"Don't you ever fucking put a hand to my woman again!" I shoved him down and cinched his neck in a chokehold. My knees held his biceps and effectively restricted any defense from him. I squeezed with every ounce of hurt and anger I had. Time blurred and faded as I held his life in my hands.

Eventually I realized that Camille was beating my back with her fists, screaming for me to let him go, that he was turning blue.

I flung myself off him, my arse hitting the ground hard. My entire body shook with uncontrollable rage. Camille sobbed, her forehead against my back. "I'm sorry," she whispered over and over, a hollowed chant against my back.

Tyler turned over and lifted himself to his hands and knees. His breathing was labored. When he stood, his face was bloody and unrecognizable. "I don't ever want to see you or your bitch again," he croaked in a raspy voice. "And if you come at me again, Nate, I swear to fucking God I will crucify you. Feel fucking lucky I'm not pressing assault charges." He was right. I was lucky. Even if he did, I wouldn't care. It would have been worth it.

"And what about your son?" Emotion filling me as

Tanner's innocent face entered my vision.

Tyler wiped his bloody face and spit more of it on the ground in a pool of crimson sludge. "What of it? I have no desire to see or be a part of this bitch's life. She's been doing fine on her own, and she can continue to do so."

Camille whimpered and shook behind me. Her sorrow was palpable and matched my anger.

"You'll sign your parental rights away?"

"Draw up the papers, asshole. Have them on my desk Monday morning. It will be the highlight of my fucking week," he grated through his teeth and then grinned as I looked at the man I had once called my friend. Did I ever really know this person? His face was smeared with blood, and his cheeks and chin were swelling more prominently.

He'd gotten in a couple good hits of his own. My chin and the skin around my right eye were tender and swollen. A cut on my lip stung as I licked it and tasted copper. "Done," I said with finality.

"Yes, we are. Have a nice life with your whore." He left with that one last potshot. Again, my muscles flexed, wanting to defend and defile.

"No more, Nate. No more," Camille said, her voice laced with sadness and regret. I nodded and ushered her to the BMW. She got in without a word.

Ten minutes from home, I addressed her coolly, "Call Jin and tell her you're staying with me tonight. We need to talk." She nodded, pulled out her phone, and texted her friend.

I parked in the car park and led Camille to my apartment and the master bathroom. She didn't say anything and I didn't speak. I needed silence for what I had to do right now. Thoughts of her lies and betrayal spun in a vortex of mistrust through my mind. I had to cleanse them and the situation forever.

Without speaking, I peeled off her clothes. Her breathing was shallow, and she seemed to be only sucking in air when she had to. Once I removed her clothing and had her bare in front of me, I winced, knowing so many other men had seen what was mine, masturbated to images of her beautiful body. It hurt as if needles were being poked into my eyes.

"It's still me," she whispered. "I'm still the woman you love." Her voice broke on the last word. "The woman who loves you."

I searched her face. The swelling around her cheekbone where Tyler had hit her was red and would be purple tomorrow. A low growl of hurt, anger, and remorse ripped from my throat. I slid my hands over each breast and cupped their weight. "How many men have touched these?"

She shivered as I tweaked each nipple. "Only you since I had Tanner," she said with conviction. So the stripping didn't include touching. Thank Christ for that.

I gripped her hips, pressing her into my hardened cock through my trousers. I wanted her to feel the effect she had on my body. She groaned and closed her eyes. I palmed her arse, digging into the fleshy, rounded globes. "And this? Who's touched your pretty arse?"

She shook her head. "No one but you…" She licked her lips.

I pushed her back and cupped her mound. "And this perfect pussy. Who, Camille? Who owns this cunt?" I ground out the words so forcibly she gasped. Her gaze locked with mine.

"You, Nate. The only man I've ever loved." I sank two fingers into her heat. She moaned, her body tightening instinctively around the intrusion. She was ready for me. Slick and hot, just the way I liked her.

I licked my lips and hovered near her face. Still fully clothed, I palmed a tit and rolled the nipple. Her cries filled the room as I finger fucked her good and hard. I added a third finger into her slick pussy and zeroed in on that spot deep within her, the one that made her insane with need.

"Oh, Oh, God, Nate…" She started her worship and I grinned with twisted pleasure. I was making a point. She was going to accept it or this relationship was over.

"No man gets to see, touch, kiss, lick, or fuck what is mine. Got that, Camille?" She nodded, her head jerking up and down. "I own your tits, your arse, and your sweet fucking cunt. It's all mine. Do you understand?"

"I want to be yours, Nate." She moaned as I pressed high and deep with my three fingers. Her back arched, offering her pretty knockers up for the taking. I sucked one hard and then bit the tip. She cried out.

"Your pleasure…bloody everything is mine. Do you give it freely?" This was her one opportunity to say no.

"Yes, please, Nate. Oh God…" She whimpered as I tickled the bumpy patch of skin within her that I knew could make her come in seconds. Her green eyes were misty as I massaged her deep, fucking her hard and fast with my fingers. She made that little mewl sound at the back of her throat as I plunged high. The sound made my prick hard as a hammer and ready to nail her.

"Will you ever bare this body?" I sucked a nipple into

my mouth flicking the tip. "The body you now gave me freely?" I moved to the other tit and sealed my lips over the erect flesh. "Will you ever show it off again to anyone but me?" Biting her nipple, she screamed and climaxed. It pounded through her body and her sex clenched down on my fingers milking her release.

"No, only you. Only you!"

I manipulated her G-spot, fucking her hard and fast, forcing her to soar into another orgasm. She flailed wildly. When she calmed down, I shed my clothes and pressed her against the bathroom wall. I kissed her, taking her mouth in bottomless penetrating licks. With my free hand, I grasped the shower handle, turning on the water to the right temperature, never letting up on devouring my woman's lips.

"Shower time. I'm not fucking you until you're cleaned of every man's eyes that were on you tonight." She nodded and then put her head down in shame. "No more, precious. You will never take off your clothes and bare your body for anyone but me. When you strip, it's for my eyes only!"

"I love you, Nate," Tears spilled down her cheeks. "I needed the money, I couldn't afford life with Tanner and medical coverage and food…"

I cut off her words with my mouth, sucking and licking as I led her into the shower. Camille stood stock still as I poured soap onto a washcloth and washed every inch of her magnificent body.

Finally, I'd cleaned enough, enough to sooth my frustration and the heavy weight of her past. This cleansing symbolized the end. The end of her trials, loneliness, and the nonstop worry for herself and her son. For me, it symbolized rebirth. That our time together would never be tainted again by our past transgressions. I wasn't a saint in my past. I didn't treat women as kindly as I could have, never gave even an inch of my heart, but with Camille, I would give my all.

"Precious, I know why. I could gather that. Just know that you will never have to again. I forbid it. It is my job now to take care of you and Tanner. You *will* move in with me and you will never ever worry about money again." I held her chin up and watched as her lips trembled, her body shaking, the shame powerfully visible in her gaze.

"You still want me?" she said so lightly I could barely hear her over the sound of the shower.

I tugged her against my naked body, her arms wrapped tightly around my back. She pulled so hard against me it was as if she could meld our bodies into one by sheer will alone.

"I've told you before. I'll always want you. I'm hurt, upset, and angry over what took place tonight, but I will heal. We will heal together."

CHAPTER SIXTEEN

My life was perfect. An uneventful two weeks had passed since Nate caught me stripping at Gems. In that time, he'd moved Tanner and me into his newly redecorated apartment.

London pushed through the huge changes to make the place more inviting and conducive to a family. It helped her timeline considerably and allowed her a couple of free weeks between clients, which Collier appreciated.

Nate and I decided when the time was right, we'd get a house, something perfect for our little family with the room for growth.

My job at Jensen Construction couldn't be any better. I was officially a full-time, salaried employee with my own medical benefits. I made quite a bit more money with the raise. Now that I was living with Nate, I had extra going to my school tuition.

He had London set up his-and-her desks in the office so that I could work on my studies in the evenings while he pored over his current caseload. It was almost frightening how easily everything fell into place.

Tanner was adjusting well and adored Nate. Nate was teaching him how to swim and included him in anything we discussed. Currently they were building a giant battle base out of Legos for the new army figures Nate had bought for him. Everything seemed heavenly.

I thought about how much my life had changed over

the past five years. From foster child to single mother to stripping to working in an office in downtown New York City, to going back to school and now living with the man of my dreams. The man not only loved me, but loved my son. Life couldn't be better.

"Hey, precious, I've got something for you." Nate padded into our den barefoot, wearing faded jeans and a V-neck white T-shirt that stretched delectably across his muscled chest. I licked my lips and looked my fill. He leaned a hip against the bookcase and crossed his arms over his chest. That didn't help my instant desire at all. The T-shirt rode up on his biceps and the fabric expanded over his bulky biceps. "You keep looking at me like that and I'm going to have to do something about it."

I grinned. "Whatever do you mean?" I answered coyly and twirled a lock of my hair. I leaned back in the high back leather chair and continued my appraisal. Nate was a feast for the eyes and looked incredible in a suit, but casual Nate was something special. From the tips of his bare toes, to his messy finger swept hair, he could make any woman swoon. He looked that good.

His gaze held mine as he presented me with the sexy smile I coveted. "Come here." He set down a file on his desk and pulled at my hands. In one tug, he had me wrapped in his arms, with his lips devouring mine. His tongue swept in and licked away all thoughts of schoolwork and pop quizzes and replaced it with lust and need.

The man was maddening. He could take me from zero to sixty in the time it took to blink. One of his hands slid down my back, sending shivers skittering along my pores as he palmed and pulled me closer by the seat of my ass. I felt the steely ridge of his hardening erection and my core clenched, tightening, ready for anything he would give.

Nate walked me back to the big double sided desk. With quick movements he had my yoga pants on the floor and my ass on the desk, legs spread wide. "Tan Man is in the bath. We have a little time."

Vaguely I heard Tanner down the hall, splashing away in the bath. We never filled the water high enough that he could hurt himself and always kept an ear to the door. "Mmmm, then I better be quiet." I yanked at the button and zipper of his jeans.

Nate pushed his jeans down. His thick cock sprung out, deliciously hard and moist at the tip. I wanted to taste his excitement but that would take a lot longer than we had and I needed him inside of me. His lips covered mine, our tongues danced to our own sensual rhythm while he nestled his cock right at my entrance. He pulled back, held my legs wide, and rubbed the tip of his cock over my wetness.

"Love to watch when I take you, precious. Going deep in your body, coming out slick with your arousal, fucking Christ…nothing is better." He moaned as we both watched him slowly press his thick cock inch by inch into me. The lips of my sex spread impossibly wide around his girth. Every time it felt and looked more beautiful than the last. When he was wedged so deep I swore I could feel him touching my heart. I shook with barely controlled desire. It happened more often when we were close like this, the emotions overwhelming me in their beauty.

"Oh, baby, I love how you *feel* me." He gripped my ass. Nate instinctively knew what having us completely joined did to me. It was magical every time. He held me, buried deep, kissing my neck, hairline, chin until finally, his mouth landed on my lips. When he opened my pout with his tongue, he pulled out and thrust sharply. It stole my breath, forcing a weighted gasp that he swallowed into his own mouth on a growl. Nate slowly picked up the pace, pulling out, letting his hard shaft grate sweetly along every nerve inside me then plowing back home. Over and over, he made quiet love to me, sucking down gasps and moans, preventing me from calling out like I usually did when we made love.

"I love to love you, Camille," he whispered into my ear. His thrusts quickened, tipping up and slamming home at the edge of each ridged jerk of his hips.

"Oh Nate, it's always so good. I love you so much, baby. Oh God…" I whispered against his ear, the orgasm building between my legs fast and furious, spreading pleasure out my limbs, filling me with light, love, and extreme pleasure.

"Don't hold back…give it to me." He bit down on the spot where my neck met my shoulder, brightening his mark from the other day. Pain shot through me as if lighting a stick of dynamite.

"Baby, now. Come in me now!" I yelled, but he covered my words with his lips, softening the high-pitched tone.

Nate gripped my hips and pulled me deep. The muscles in his arms tightened and his veins strained against tanned skin as he held onto me, digging into my flesh.

I wrapped my arms around his neck and held the back of his head, sealing our lips as we flew together over the edge into beautiful oblivion. Hot spurts of his essence poured into me in long washes of heat, warming me from the inside, matching the fire that prickled along the surface of my skin.

He held us together for long moments.

"Mom! Nate! I'm ready to get out!" Tanner screamed from the other room. Nate laid his forehead against mine and chuckled as we both tried to catch our breath.

"Perfect timing the lad has. At least we were finished this time." He pulled out and looked down. His body went completely ridged, and his fingers tightened against my hips.

"What's the matter?" I followed his gaze to his softening penis. It was covered with smears of blood.

"I hurt you, Camille." He sounded choked up as his eyes widened in horror.

"Baby, no. No, you didn't. I was due any day, but with our unprotected sex over the last three or four weeks, I wasn't sure. Now we know." I looked down, shrugged, and hopped off the desk, not wanting him to see me have my mental freak-out. Seeing the blood reminded me of my first time with Tyler. That experience tore a hole in my heart. He had roughly taken my virginity, rutted like a beast, and then got up to shower, leaving me bleeding and in pain.

Nate's shoulders slumped as he pulled up his pants.

"I'll go get Tanner," he said quietly.

I rushed to our master bath and pulled out the tampons. After washing up and taking care of my womanly needs, I put my mental state back in check and went to help get Tanner ready for bed.

We usually went through Tanner's routine together. Nate had picked it up and added a few flairs of his own, preferring to tackle my son into bed and tickle him until he called for help. Nate was unbelievably good with Tanner. He genuinely seemed to enjoy this new role of father figure.

I watched Nate clothe Tanner in pajamas and tuck him into bed with less exuberance than he had these past two weeks since we'd moved in.

"Baby, I got this. Why don't you get us a drink?" Nate nodded and I caught a glimpse of something in his eyes. "Hey." I grabbed his arm. There was something in his eyes I didn't recognize. "What's the matter?" I asked.

"Nothing, it's fine. I'm going to get a drink." He left the room.

I went through Tanner's routine quicker than normal, wanting to find out what was going on with the man I loved. I kissed my little man, turned off the light, and went to find my big man.

He was on the patio, the sounds of the city all around him. He had a large scotch in his hand and was sipping it. I sat down next to him in the two-seater lounge, sending a silent thank you to London for thinking of "couple friendly" patio furniture.

Snuggling into Nate's side, I blew out a nervous breath as his arm came around me and pulled me to his side. My knees were up on the lounger, leaning into his thighs. I sat and waited while he drank half of his drink.

"I wanted you to be pregnant," he said.

Those were the last possible words I expected to hear slip from his lips. "But it's too soon. We just moved in. We are getting over some pretty crazy stuff and trying to learn to live together as a family."

"That's just it. If you were pregnant with a wee one, we'd be a family for real. I want that, Camille." His hand tightened around my shoulder and he turned to look at me. His eyes were soft and so blue I could drown in them.

"I want that with you. Marriage, a house, more babies, the whole kit and caboodle."

I grasped his hand. "And we can have that. Whenever we want. When we're ready."

"I don't want to wait. I'm ready now. I want you as my wife. I want you pregnant with my child and I want to adopt Tanner as my own son. And I want it all yesterday," he said with the passion I thought he reserved for fighting a court case.

"Baby, it's too soon."

"Why? Give me one good reason why I shouldn't make you mine as soon as possible. Make Tanner mine officially?"

I licked my lips and held his hand tighter. "Well, we've only been together for a couple months. Weeks really. It's all so sudden."

"When you know what you want, Camille, and you feel what's right, it doesn't matter how long we've had it. We get to have it for the rest of our lives. He sighed. "I brought home the papers to start the adoption of Tanner. The moment Tyler's rights are officially removed by the state of New York, I want my name on a fresh new birth certificate for our boy."

Our boy.

Nate thinks of Tanner as his. He claims my son the way a dad should. The way a real father does. Tears filled my eyes and he held my face. Tanner was going to have everything I didn't. And it was me giving it to him. Me and the most amazing man. It was a true justice for all the hell I'd gone through as a child and as a single mother.

"You really want Tanner to be yours?" My voice betrayed my emotions.

"Precious, he already is mine. The day I met him and looked into his eyes, I saw my future. In him and in you, the woman I was meant to love."

"Okay." I let everything go. The fear, the worry, the past. Nate and Tanner were my future, and it was staring me in the face. For once, I wasn't going to be scared. I was just going to fall.

"Okay what?" Nate cupped my face and wiped away my tears with his thumbs.

"Okay to everything. To it all. Marriage. A family but most of all to you being Tanner's father. I couldn't have picked a better man if God had given me the chance to mold you myself."

Nate's smile was the biggest I'd seen. He jumped up, pulled me into his arms, and swung me in a huge circle. "You mean it, love?"

"Yes," I laughed, meaning every word.

"You're making me the happiest man. I'm going to treat you and Tanner so well. And we'll have a baby of our own right away!" He squeezed me.

I laughed and hugged him back. "I'm actually rather shocked we aren't already pregnant with as many times as you have 'conveniently' forgotten to use protection." I grinned.

"I didn't forget. I just bloody didn't use them. Nothing comes between me and my woman. If we get pregnant, all the better."

My eyes widened. "You were trying to get me pregnant?" I smacked his arm.

"Not exactly trying. I just figured if you got pregnant with my babe we'd have a wee one and move things along.

Now you're saying we can anyway. Works smashingly for me!" He kissed away my response with a toe-curling kiss.

I moved out of his arms. "So, when do you want to start all of this?"

His look turned predatory. I knew that look. I saw it not an hour ago when he took me to heaven and back on our desk. Slowly I backed up. He followed. "No time like the present, precious. You better run because I'm going to shag the shite out of you!"

"You can't!" I stopped when my back hit the French doors. I found the handle behind me. "I'm on my cycle, remember?"

"I don't give a damn, my love."

"What if I do?" I tilted my head to the side as he caught me around the waist.

"You'll get over it." He took my lips with his own.

★ ★ ★

"I'm going to marry Camille," I said, entering Collier's office. He was on the phone.

"Beauty, I'm afraid I'll have to call you back. It seems as though my brother's a stone's throw from going off the trolley. Call you soon, *wife*." He smiled and hung up the phone. "Now what is this about getting hitched?"

"I'm doing it. I picked out the ring this morning." I laid the blue velvet box on the table, and Collier grabbed it. He opened it and saw the princess-cut diamond set in antiqued white gold with baguettes on the sides. A long whistle escaped his lips.

"That's a mighty fine ring you've got there." Collier

242

looked at the ring and then back at me. His lips twisted into a grin. "She pregnant?"

"No, you old sod! She's not pregnant…unfortunately," I grumbled and took a seat across from him.

My brother's eyes widened. "You mean you want her to be with child?"

"I wouldn't be against her carrying my lad, no. With Camille, Colly, everything has changed. I want to be with her all the time. I need her to have my name and for every man on this earth to know she is taken. And I'm going to adopt Tanner, too."

Collier's hands steepled under his chin. "That's a lot of change in a short amount of time. Why the rush?"

"Pot, meet kettle…would you like a spot of tea, brother mine?" Coming from a man who shacked up and married his woman in less than a year, I couldn't believe he'd spit that weak argument.

"Touché."

I grabbed the ring and put it back in my pocket. "It's not a rush. I just know Camille is it for me. Something about her and her son drew me in and made me never want to leave. I have a fierce need to protect them. Did you ever feel that?"

Collier nodded and blew out a breath. "Right away, yes. I wanted to lock up London and never let her out of my sight. Only now can I go a day without speaking with her, but in truth, it's still torture."

I smiled and stood. "Well, I can't wait to make her my wife. Only I'm going to give her the wedding of her dreams."

"Bloody hell, please do. At least you'll get Mum off my

arse. She says now that I've taken away her opportunity to see me get married, she wants a grandchild posthaste."

I grinned. "Well, brother, maybe I can take care of that, too." I winked and he slumped back in his seat, shaking his head.

"My, have you changed. It looks good on you."

"It's the love of a good woman. Makes me want to do crazy things." I headed to the door. "You'll be my best man, right?"

Collier walked over to me with a hand out. "Try to stop me." He shook my hand and then pulled me into a hug. "I'm proud of you, mate. Never thought I'd see the day that the great ladies' man would fall for a sweet bird like Camille, but I'm so glad you did. I like her. A lot. She's a perfect addition to our family."

"Now I just have to ask her and set a date. Best be on my way. I've got a woman to woo."

"That you do. But don't forget you have two cases in court to win."

I laughed. "Shite. I almost forgot I had to work today. I'll win those two cases with my bloody eyes closed!" And I could as on top of the world as I was.

Ring in my pocket. Two cases won. And the perfect location chosen. Everything was set and ready.

"Where are we going?" Camille asked for the hundredth time.

"Yeah, where we going?" Tanner asked. The lad was just as impatient as his mum.

I shook my head, finding it hilarious that these two could not handle a surprise. "You'll just have to wait and see."

The limo pulled over to the curb. Camille's eyes widened as we got out of the car. Tanner looked around at all the sparkling lights and started hopping up and down.

Right in the center of the theatre district sat a table with a red-and-white checkered tablecloth. A red rope surrounded it with a bottle of champagne and apple cider waiting on the table that was set for three. I ushered Camille and Tanner into their seats. A pizza delivery man opened boxes and dished out cheese pizza onto Tanner's plate and a couple loaded slices on mine and Camille's.

"Pizza is my very favorite!" Tanner shoveled a huge chunk of pizza into his mouth. Camille was in awe as I poured glasses of champagne, and then a glass of cider for Tanner. The lights from the theatre signs sparkled and bounced off the crystal glasses, breaking the light all around us into rainbows of color.

"This is… There aren't words. Why?" She looked around and petted her son's hair.

I tinkled our glasses together and looked into her eyes. "Because this, precious, is where I fell in love with you. Right here where you spun around in a circle and looked at me as if I was the man of your dreams."

"You are the man of my dreams," she confirmed.

"And you're the woman of mine. That's why I wanted to bring you here to make it official." I got down on one knee. Her eyes immediately filled with tears as she put her fingers to her lips. She looked around at all the bystanders that were stopping to watch the show.

I pulled the ring from my breast coat pocket and opened it. Her eyes took in the size of the ring. "Camille, I have loved you almost since I laid eyes on you. I want to live my life parallel to yours. I want to raise your son and make him my own. Will you do me the honor of becoming my wife?"

"Oh my God, Nate. Are you sure?" She never ceased to amaze me, always asking if I was sure I wanted her.

"I have never been more sure of anything in my life. I love you and want you to marry me. Say you'll be my wife?"

Tears spilled down her cheeks as she got down on her own knees, cupping my face. "It would make me the happiest woman in the world to call you my husband. I love you, Nathaniel Walker. I always will."

I placed the ring on her finger and she gasped. It seemed large on her finger, but I didn't care. I wanted every bloke within a ten foot radius to be blinded by my undying love for her. With a flourish, I pulled her up to standing and kissed her. In that kiss, I left all the loneliness of the past and proved that she alone was the only woman for me.

"Yippee. Mommy's going to be marry-did!" Tanner squealed and hugged our legs. I held onto his little shoulder and kissed my girl one more time. She made that little mewl sound that I knew was solely for me. Then I crouched down again.

"Remember, when you asked me if I was going to marry your mum and I said I didn't know?"

He nodded, head bouncing up and down.

"Well, I am. And you remember when you asked me if I was going to be your daddy if I married your mum?"

He nodded again, his big bright blue eyes misted over.

"Well, sport, I'm going to be your daddy. Would you like that?"

"Really?" Tears fell down his little cheeks, and his nose

reddened.

"Oh, baby," Camille cried and hugged her son. His eyes never left mine.

"Yes, Tanner. I want to be your dad if you'll let me. What do you say?"

"Can I call you Dad?"

My voice choked. I had to be strong. I swallowed, pushing the lump down my throat at the sincere hope I heard in this little one's voice. "You can call me whatever you want."

"I want to call you Dad." His voice broke and tears ran down his cheeks. I pulled him into my arms, making sure not to hug him too tight.

"I love you, Tanner. I'm going to be the best father to you and husband to your mum. Okay? I promise."

"Okay, Dad." Camille gasped, and I choked back the tears at hearing him use my new title. "Can I have more pizza now?" he asked and wiped his nose along his shirt sleeve.

Camille and I laughed as did the half of New York that had stopped to watch us.

"Yes, son. You can have more pizza now." I fluffed his hair and served my boy another slice.

The three of us sat as one little family. Camille stared at her ring and picked up her glass. I picked up my own and Tanner held his up. "What should we toast to?" Camille asked.

"To us. Mum, Dad, and my son."

Tanner beamed and we all clinked our glasses, sealing the toast with love and a bright future.

CHAPTER SEVENTEEN

When a woman becomes engaged, something changes. A confidence that you didn't have before fills your essence, adds a bounce to your step, and seals a smile to your face. That's how I felt. Like a confident, happily-in-love woman who had the whole world ahead of her. Nate gave me that last week when he put a shiny diamond ring on my finger, declared his love for me on the streets of New York, and asked me to be his wife. As if that wasn't enough, he even asked Tanner if he could be his father.

I hummed along with a tune I had playing on my iPod as I dusted our desks. Nate and Tanner were playing soldiers in his room down the hall. Tanner's squeals of laughter were music to my ears. In the past three weeks, he'd changed so much. No longer was he timid with Nate. He, too, seemed to be filled with a confidence driven by a secure and stable home life.

Smiling happily as I cleaned, I shifted the mess of papers and files on Nate's desk, trying to put them in some semblance of order. Something caught my eye. My name. I sat down in his leather chair and tugged the bright red folder from the messy stack of files. Yep, Camille Johnston— Full Investigative Report was neatly typed on the flap. On the top of the file was a yellow sticky note with a Spark Investigations logo and a Manhattan address, phone, number, and website.

In almost illegible writing, I made out the following:

Walker—

Hope this info gets you the girl.

—Jonny

What the hell was this? Nate had me investigated? Why? When? So many questions ran through my mind as I opened the file. Inside were approximately ten to fifteen sheets of information. The first was a summary of the rest. I scanned the first page noting my name, address, a picture of my driver's license, my employment history, however brief. Page two had a copy of my high school transcripts, my current college coursework and grades. The next couple pages were marked "confidential" and were a history of my foster care. It clearly showed each home I'd been placed in from birth through age eighteen. A social worker's commentary about removing me from abusive homes was noted.

As I read the pages, the memories of that life slammed into me. My heartbeat sped up as I read through each account of abuse and the corresponding hospital or child psychology visit. It was worse when I was younger. I didn't remember the broken arms, legs, and bruises. There was even a full written statement from my Kindergarten teacher. She was convinced I was being beaten and called child protective services, who paid a visit to the home. The home turned out to have ten foster kids living there and two sisters who were prostitutes.

Jesus. It was shocking how little I recalled. The pages included doctors' reports after I was pulled from each home, confirming I was still a virgin, my hymen intact. Reading this part particularly turned my stomach. A heavy ache in my gut, chest, and heart made me feel weighted, rooted to the chair. I was barely able to move as memories poured over me. Years of abuse, regret, and sadness came back in a thunderous wave that choked me. My stomach churned, and I grabbed the trash can and retched the remains of my breakfast into the can. Dry heaves racked my body. As I came back to the here and now, I felt a cool cloth on my forehead.

"It's okay, love. You're okay." Nate's voice broke through the terror of reliving my past. I gripped him to me, holding on so tightly I may have bruised him. He didn't care. He held me tighter, whispering sweet nothings, petting my hair, back and sides until I calmed down. I grabbed a tissue off his desk, blew my nose, then slumped back into the chair.

"What happened? Why did you get sick?"

I took a deep breath and searched his eyes. Nothing but concern and love stared back.

"How could you?" I grabbed the file and shook it in his face. He looked at it as if he'd never seen it before.

He grabbed the folder, read the name and saw the note. His eyes widened. "Precious, this is not what it looks like."

"Really? Because it looks like you had me investigated. Why? Why would you do that?"

His hands curled around my biceps and he brought his face close to mine. "Listen to me. Yes, I had you investigated. That was right when we met." I stiffened in his arms and tried to pull away. "No, no way. You are not running. You are going to listen."

"Talk fast," I grated through my teeth, anger and hurt filling my tone.

"I admit to having you investigated. Only it was when we first met. You didn't want to go out with me. Christ, I had to chase you at every turn. And I…shite, Camille. I really wanted to know you."

"So you had my privacy exploited. Betrayed my trust? Why didn't you just ask me what you wanted to know instead of reading my entire life in here?" I tapped the red folder.

"I didn't. I swear. I haven't read it. Jonny delivered it months ago. It's been sitting on my desk this whole time and I'd forgotten about it. I swear to you on all that's holy I didn't read it!" His tone was pleading and laced with fear. "Camille, I promise on our love, on Tanner's life that I did not read that file."

I held his gaze. He didn't flinch, twitch, or anything that would lead me to believe he was lying.

"I'm not okay with this!" I shoved against his chest. He stepped back giving me the space I desperately needed. I picked up the file. "I need some time alone. Either you can leave or I can."

Nate's eyes widened. "Just for a time. Not forever. I won't let you leave me forever. Not for something so bloody asinine. It was a mistake, Camille. A stupid fucking mistake. I regret it! I didn't know I'd fall in love with you. I didn't know!" he roared hands in the air. Then his shoulders slumped and he took a deep breath. "Tell me you're not leaving me?"

The wealth of sadness in his eyes almost destroyed me. "I'm not leaving you. But I need some space to think about this. To read this file alone. Do you understand?"

He nodded solemnly. "If you want me to leave, I will, but I'd rather stay here with Tanner. I can't bear to be away from both of you right now." His words broke me. I went to him cupped his cheek and kissed him briefly. A small touch to let him know I still loved him.

"I'll be back later."

"When?" His request sounded desperate, uncertain.

"When I'm ready. When I'm not so angry with you. When I have perspective again."

"Fine. Your men will be here when you come home, waiting for you. I love you more than anything, Camille. Please don't make this more than it is. A sodding mistake. Okay?"

I nodded, not trusting myself to respond. I needed time to think, to understand and forgive. My whole life I'd spent running. Right now, I planned on taking a step away with every intention of coming back.

With a heavy heart, I went into Tanner's room and told him Mommy had an errand to run. Then I went to the bathroom, brushed my teeth, and cleaned up after my vomiting spell. When I got to the living room, Nate stood with the door open, holding my coat. God, I loved him to insanity, but I was angry with him.

When I walked to the front door, he pulled me to him and covered my lips with his own. He didn't allow me to pull away. Instead, he dived deep with his tongue, pressed our bodies together tightly, and kissed the daylights out of me. My entire body filled with light, connected to his. Without him, life was dark. In his arms, the sun shone so bright I needed shades. He patched all the doubt, worry, and concern I had about his love, his intentions with one simple kiss. I pulled away.

"I love you, Nate. I will come home. I just need a little time."

"Take the time you need, just…come back." His soft

blue eyes were bursting with sadness. "I love you."

"I love you more. I'll be home soon." I turned and left.

Instead of hailing a cab, I decided to walk the streets of New York until I came upon Central Park. There, I sat on a bench and looked out over the wide expanse of green. It was a lovely spring day in the City. There were people playing catch, throwing a Frisbee, and walking their tiny dogs. Most were pint-size. You didn't see a lot of big dogs in New York. If we got a dog, we'd get a *dog*. A large one, like Butch, Hank and Aspen's dog.

After spending a few minutes talking myself down and taking in the scenery, I pulled out the file.

Nate said he didn't read it and I believed him. I had to. What was a relationship without trust? Besides, we'd survived bigger betrayals than this. My stripping, for example, and keeping Tanner a secret. Those were pretty large secrets, and Nate had been hurt. We'd survived those trials and tribulations and come out on top. We'd get past this one too.

I looked down at my left hand. The huge reminder of Nate's love sparkled and glowed on my finger.

Nate loved me. I knew it with my whole heart. I was not going to let his stupid mistake take our happiness away from us. What was done was done. Re-living my childhood through a variety of medical reports and social worker comments wasn't pleasant, but it was my past. It wasn't possible to change it. I needed to get over my childhood and start anew.

My life now was far removed from the broken orphan I was. I had a job, was going to school, had a beautiful son and a man who loved me for me. The future was now, and I was happier than I'd ever been.

With a renewed confidence, I opened the file, and flipped to the last few pages. One was my hospital stay when I gave birth to Tanner and a copy of his birth certificate.

The last two documents were an absolute shock. My birth certificate with my real parents' names filled in, not blacked out.

I held my breath as I read my mother's name.

Name: Constance Camille Johnston, Age: 19, Status: Deceased

My mother had died the same day I was born. I flipped the page and saw another certificate. It was her death certificate. Cause of death: Complications during childbirth.

A tear dropped onto the sheet. I hadn't realized I was crying. My mother, just a year older than I was when I had Tanner, had died giving birth to me. My father, or someone, had given me her name. It gave me a warm feeling, knowing I shared a name with her. A picture of her driver's license was attached to the report. Her long brown hair was wavy like mine and parted down the middle. Her eyes were hazel, but it was hard to see in the small picture. Her smile was mine, big and toothy. She was beautiful.

I took a deep breath and wondered what it would have been like to have been raised by this woman. What was her life like? Her family? Anything? I read her death certificate and found the names of my grandparents. Both were listed as deceased. My shoulders slumped.

Then I realized I hadn't looked at my father's information. I flipped back a couple pages and read the name.

Father: William Robert Devereaux, Age: 30, Status:

Living

That would make my biological father fifty-three now. I scoured the page showing my father's last known address. He was in New Jersey of all places. Same city I grew up in. Why would he not have raised me? I scanned the information about William Devereaux, noting he had the same name as my new friend Tripp. Small world.

As I continued reading, that world got a whole helluva lot smaller. William Devereux was married when I was born and had two additional children now. Marcus Devereaux was currently playing football at Michigan State University, present age 20. Tripp Devereux was working as a model for AIR Bright Enterprises and bartending, present age 26. Last known address, downtown Manhattan.

Holy shit.

My body tingled. Panic ripped through the edges of my vision, turning the once blue sky a faded black. My eyes rolled back into my head. The last thought I had before the world went black was that Tripp Devereux was my half-brother.

★ ★ ★

I slammed through the hospital doors into the emergency department. "Camille Johnston, my fiancée! Where is she?" I roared to anyone and everyone who would listen.

A petite mousy woman dressed in scrubs came up to me. "Calm down. Right this way." The nurse led me and Tanner through throngs of emergency personnel and beds separated by drapes. His little feet tripped in my haste to get to Camille. I pulled him up and onto my hip. He clung to my neck but kept silent. Finally, the woman pulled a pink drape back, and I saw my girl.

"Precious, baby, what happened?"

"Mommy!" Tanner cried, reaching out his little arms to his mum. I set Tanner on the bed, and he scrambled into her arms. She held him tight and kissed the crown of his head. I cupped her face and she smiled. She looked fine until I grabbed the back of her head and she winced.

"What happened?" I barely contained my rage. If someone hit my girl, they were going to be dead.

"I fainted. Hit my head on a park bench in Central Park."

"Why?" I shook my head, not understanding. "Why did you faint?"

She shrugged. "I think I had a panic attack." The words hit me like a punch to the gut. She was so stressed out about what I did, the files on her, that she couldn't handle it. I knew I shouldn't have let her leave alone.

"I'm so sorry. Camille." I kissed her lips. "It's all my fault. I should have never had Jonny investigate you."

My sweet girl shook her head and then grabbed at the back of her head. I looked behind her and felt the nasty bump she had.

"I'm fine. Really. It wasn't what happened. It…uh…it was what I read in the reports that overwhelmed me." She bit her lip and I sat on the side of the bed.

I slid my hand along her calf and knee. "What was it?"

"You're never going to believe this. I'm still not sure I believe it." She shook her head.

"Try me."

She licked her lips again, and I got the cup of water sitting on a table near the bed and poured her a glass. She took a sip. "I have two siblings."

My eyes widened. "Really? Did you find out who your parents were?" I knew that was something she'd always wanted to know but could never get the information.

A sad smile stole across her face. "Yeah. My mom is deceased. Died while giving birth to me. She was young, only nineteen." I could tell the information had wounded her. Even when you didn't know your family, finding out they were gone before you could know them had to hurt.

"I'm sorry about your mum. What of your dad?"

Camille nodded and pinched her lips together. "That's the crazy part. He's alive and living in New Jersey."

"That's bloody fantastic! We'll look him up, ring him!" I said happily.

She shook her head. "I don't know. Maybe. There's more. His name is William Devereaux."

I scratched at my goatee and the scruff on my cheeks. I hadn't had a chance to shave before our argument, and I was beside myself while she was gone. The name was familiar though. Our mate shared the last name, but that was pretty common. "What else?"

"I have two brothers."

"And how is that a problem? Precious, this is amazing news! You wanted siblings. Now we can find them." I didn't understand why her face seemed so concerned.

"Nate, one of my brother's names is Marcus. He's a college football player in Michigan."

"Excellent sport! We can go see one of his games. What of the other brother?" She didn't seem quite herself. I would have expected this news to have her shouting through the rooftops not sulking in a hospital bed. And why did she have a panic attack? This was incredible news not something to panic over.

Camille took a deep breath. "Nate, my other brother is Tripp Devereaux." At that moment, my head literally spun on its axis.

"No fucking way!"

"Daddy! You promise-did no more cusses. Mom says those are f-bombs and you cannot have any bombs. No a-bombs, b-bombs…" He kept going until he got to the right letter in the alphabet. Our little man was a true comedian. "Mommy says f-bombs are the worstest ever!"

I ruffled Tanner's hair. "You're right, sport. No more f-bombs." I grinned. He smiled and continued hugging his mum.

"That's insane! I mean…" I shook my head as the doctor entered.

"Ms. Johnston, your X ray looks good. No damage, just a nice size goose egg. It will go down with ice and time. Take it easy a few days, take ibuprofen, and let me know if you feel any dizziness. You the husband?" the doctor asked me.

"Yes," I said without a second thought. It wasn't his business if it was official or not. It would be soon enough.

"Wake her every four hours tonight, just in case. She didn't incur a concussion, but you can never be too careful when it comes to head trauma."

I saluted the doctor. "Will do. But she's okay?"

"Yes. Just needs to rest. Says here you have a history of panic attacks?"

Camille nodded. "I used to have them a lot when I was a kid. Hadn't had one since bringing this guy into the world though." She hugged Tan Man to her chest and he giggled. "I'll be fine. Just some really shocking news. I'll be more careful."

The doctor handed her discharge papers.

We checked out of the hospital and hailed a cab home. Once I had her back in our flat and cuddled up in bed, I tended to Tanner, putting him down for his afternoon nap. He went out like a light. It blew me away how well the kid slept.

I made tea, put together some chicken salad sandwiches I'd prepared while Camille was out, and took them to the bedroom. I set the tray down on the side of the bed and kissed my girl's forehead.

"How you doing, love?"

She smiled sleepily. It made my heartbeat quicken. Seeing her cuddled under the covers in *our* bed was the most beautiful sight. I never wanted her to leave again. Even if it was for the afternoon. Had I told her in advance about the file, she wouldn't have hurt herself or been alone when she found out this startling information. I could have supported her through it.

"I'm fine. You don't have to hover. Really. Just processing it all," she said drowsily.

"Yeah. It is quite a lot to take in. I do want to apologize again. I feel responsible for what happened. If I told you earlier…"

"Stop, Nate. We make mistakes. I should have told you right away about Tanner and Gems. But I didn't. Sometimes we make bad choices. Surviving them together, that's what makes us stronger."

God, I loved her.

"I'd do anything to make you happy. You know that right?"

"Oh Nate, I do know that, and, baby, you do make me happy. I've never been happier in my life. Soon we'll married and adding to our family. But I still have to figure out how to deal with this information. Especially about Tripp. I mean, he's our friend." She put her hand to her forehead and shook her head. "He's your brother's best friend. So weird."

I nodded. "Yeah, it is unusual, but now that I think about it, the two of you look a lot alike. Dark hair, the same exact eyes. Your smiles are different and obviously he's manlier." I tickled her knee and she laughed. "But yeah, I can see it clearly now."

I laid the tray of small sandwiches and tea on her lap and then grabbed my own plate and sat cross-legged across from her. We ate and sipped our tea in silence, both of us content with our own thoughts.

"What do you think he'll say when I show him this information?" She worried her lip.

I looked at her nervous face and pondered it. "I can't say. Only way to find out is to tell him. Want me to invite him over?"

"Yeah, but not right away. Let me process this first. Think about the best way to bring it up."

I respected her decision to wait. She needed to accept the information and figure out how she wanted to handle it. When we were done with our food, her eyes got heavy, and it was hard for her to keep them open.

"Will you hold me?" she asked.

I slipped off my jeans and got into bed in my underwear

and T-shirt. She snuggled into my chest. Best feeling ever. Having my woman in my arms, right where she should be. "Whatever you decide to do with this information, I'm here for you. To talk, vent, cry, laugh, whatever it is you need, you can count on me, love."

"I know I can. Thank you."

I pulled back and looked at her. "Why are you thanking me?"

"For loving me," she whispered and snuggled closer into my chest. Her eyes closed, her breath left her lips in a soft puff.

"And I always will, precious. Always."

CHAPTER EIGHTEEN

Secrets sucked. Having them, knowing them, spreading them, and telling them all made for a giant knot of tension swirling and festering in my gut. I'd known Tripp was my brother for the better part of a week, and I still hadn't figured out what to do with the information.

Worse, I'd avoided Collier and London all together for fear I'd accidentally slip and mention the secret I'd been harboring all week.

Nate had been wonderful about it all. He hadn't pushed, though I knew he worried about me. We agreed it was my problem but he'd be there to get me through whatever I decided. He thought it was best to just schedule a time to meet with Tripp as if it was that easy. I'd gone almost twenty-four years not having one soul to call my own besides Tanner. Now to find out I had not one brother but two? What would it do to Marcus? The last thing he probably needed during schooling and sports work was for me to show up unannounced and say, *"Hey, I'm your big sister, Cami. Want to hang out and get to know one another?"* It sounded incredibly lame. I couldn't bring myself to even call the number the private investigator had supplied for him.

Calling William Devereaux was also out. The man's name was on my birth certificate, but in two wet swipes of a pen, he'd given me my name and signed away his rights as a parent. He probably assumed I'd been adopted. Maybe

I would have been if the young couple I'd been given to hadn't divorced and then turned me over to the courts at two years old. Who knows? It was all so far in the past, yet it kept bubbling to the surface like an overflowing pot of boiling water.

I looked up at the clock and noticed it was close to lunch time. Just as I was about to grab my purse and head to the little sandwich shop down the block, the doors to the office opened and Oliver followed by a very pregnant Aspen walked in. I'd rarely seen them the past month as I focused on getting my life with Nate in order.

"Hey, sweetie." Oliver waved. "You're coming to lunch with us."

I set my purse on my shoulder. "I am?"

"You are." Aspen rubbed her protruding belly. It was huge. It looked like a perfectly round beach ball had been shoved under her formfitting dress. Even with the added weight, the slight woman still looked amazing, not a hair out of place.

"Did I miss something?" I asked, walking around my desk.

Oliver shook his head. "Nope. We're just ready to celebrate." He looked at his nails, analyzing his fingers.

"Celebrate? The baby?" I asked cheerfully.

Aspen was in her last trimester and I hadn't been invited to a baby shower. Maybe the obscenely wealthy didn't have baby showers. Then again, even though I was extremely poor, I didn't have a baby shower. At the time, there was no one in my life who cared, aside from Jin.

"Baby showers are so last decade. We're going to have a party after our girl here is born. Aspen has bought everything under the sun for the little one and she doesn't need any more pink outfits. I swear, if I open one more package with a pink dress in it, I'm going to hurl." He stuck his finger in his mouth and made a fake gagging sound. "Newborns in pink look like old chewed-up pieces of bubblegum." His face contorted into a look of horror as he shivered.

Aspen smiled. "He's funny, but right. You should see how many pink dresses have been sent. As if a newborn could wear forty pink party dresses? I donated them all to the local women's center. Hank has already nixed the idea of taking her anywhere but to close friends and family the first month. Says he read it in one of the books." She rolled her blue eyes and her lips twitched.

"He has both of your best interests at heart, and the first month you just want to get to know your baby. Learn her likes, dislikes, little sounds." I took in a deep breath and remembered when I had Tanner. He was the most beautiful angel baby. I looked forward to that again. To feel a baby move within my stomach, this time sharing it with the father and Tanner would make it all the more special.

"So back to grubbing. Our girl here"—he rubbed Aspen's belly and she sighed—"is hungry, and we want to celebrate your pending nuptials to my Gandy Candy doppelgänger. Yummo!"

Aspen shook her head. "You're not supposed to crush on other people's fiancés, Ollie. How many times do I have to tell you that?"

"One hundred and forty-five might do the trick," he quipped.

I laughed. These two were straight crazy, but I adored their relationship and appreciated my new friendship with them. Then an idea hit. Maybe I could talk to them about what to do about Tripp without telling them it was Tripp?

"What would you like to have?" I asked as we entered Aspen's private elevator.

"I'm dying for breakfast. I could really go for some eggs and bacon right now."

Oliver snorted and covered his laugh with his hand.

"What?" I enjoyed the unending banter and bickering between the two.

"It's just that she's said that every day this week. Ollie, order me some breakfast. Hank, let's have breakfast for dinner. If we're not careful, that baby's going to come out yellow and with feathers as many eggs as she's been feeding her."

Aspen huffed. "Eggs and bacon are the most amazing food in the entire universe." She closed her eyes and licked her lips. "God, it's so good. I can almost taste it now." She rubbed her belly. The sound of Ollie and I chuckling bounced off the elevator walls as the door opened.

"What's so funny?" a deep voice asked as we exited.

My heart stopped. Standing there smiling was a bright-faced, incredibly handsome man with eyes the colors of emeralds.

"Hey, Tripp. We're just about to go to lunch. Come join us?" Aspen grabbed his arm. He patted her forearm.

"I thought we were meeting at noon?" He looked at his watch.

Oliver's eyes narrowed as he put a hand on his hip and stomped his foot.

"You didn't get my text then." Aspen grinned.

"You said Tripp changed our twelve to one?" Oliver

twisted his lips, his pointed features showed his annoyance.

"Did I say that? I don't remember saying that?" Aspen flipped her hair over her shoulder and gripped Tripp's arm.

I stayed completely silent. Tripp looked over his shoulder and winked at me, showing that he'd noticed me.

"Don't try to change the subject, missy. You purposely changed our meeting! I hate when you mess with my schedule."

Aspen inhaled and continued bickering all the way into a shiny black limo.

Wow. This I would never get used to. My friends rode around in limos when I had never even owned a car. Public transportation had always been my mode of getting from point A to point B. Oliver spoke to the driver. "Take us to the same damn place for lunch we've been going all week," he huffed.

The driver smirked and pulled out into traffic.

"So I take it you're hungry," Tripp said lightly.

Aspen rubbed her belly and cringed for a second. I noticed, but she covered it easily. Maybe it was a twinge or her back hurting. I know in my last trimester, everything was uncomfortable. "If you must know, I am craving eggs, okay? Lots and lots of eggs with a side of crispy bacon. I have no idea why. It's not something I usually eat."

"I remember when I was pregnant with Tanner I ate so many pineapples I ended up with canker sores in my mouth from all the acid. It didn't stop me. I ate through the pain. Now, I rarely eat the stuff. I'm convinced babies tell their moms what they need in utero. Maybe baby Jensen needs protein?"

Oliver laughed. "I'm not sure how! She's getting a side

of beefcake every night from my hunky cowboy!"

Aspen shoved Oliver, and he fell over in the seat, howling with laughter.

Oliver laughed and snorted, practically spitting while trying to speak. "Hank's been hiding at my place! Damn girl is so horny he said his dick is broken and about to fall off!"

Damn. I remember that phase, being so horny and not having a man to help me through it. Poor Hank.

"Is he complaining?" Tripp laughed. "I can't wait to give him a ration of shit the size of AIR Bright. What man hides out from sex?"

Aspen clenched her teeth and sucked in a breath. "To be fair, I have been a little needy lately."

"Needy! A homeless man is needy, princess. According to the cowboy, she's hopping on pop every hour on the hour! Poor guy has to come to our house to give his baby maker a rest." Oliver snickered and the three of us laughed. I couldn't help it. It was pretty funny.

We made it to the restaurant and feasted on a variety of breakfast foods. Aspen had a dreamy look on her face, and if it were up to me, I'd give the poor thing eggs until she'd had her fill. She looked exhausted but beautiful.

"How much time do you have left?" I asked.

"Four more weeks. Seems like an eternity." She frowned.

I grasped her hand. "It will go by fast."

She smiled, but her smile turned into a thin line and her lips went white with tension. A soft hiss escaped her mouth. Her eyes widened and her face went deathly pale.

"What's the matter?" I clenched her hand. She squeezed tight, and then I felt something wet touch my hand as I moved closer to her.

"Um, I don't, uh, I don't know." She gripped her stomach and pulled my hand to her belly. It went from slightly hard to downright tight. "I think I peed," she whispered in my ear. I looked down and noticed the wetness along her royal-blue skirt. It was much larger than a little pee.

Her hand tightened on mine, and her head dropped to her chest. She breathed hard and moaned in pain.

"Oh no, Aspen. I think you're in labor!"

The two men's eyes flew to mine, sharing the shocked look I'm sure I had. Oliver jumped up and started dialing. Tripp and I helped her out of the booth. Oliver threw a hundred-dollar bill on the table. I knew that was double what our lunch cost, but didn't say anything as we ushered Aspen out of the building and into the limo.

"Fuck! I can't get Hank. Where the hell is he?" Oliver tapped frantically on his phone.

Mentally, I ran through his schedule. "He's in a meeting giving a presentation with a couple of the investors. It's going to be a few hours. The presentation I pulled together was slated for two hours. Then they were going to spend the afternoon in the conference room going over the numbers."

"Jesus Christ, what are we going to do?" Oliver's eyes misted as he held Aspen's hand. "She's gonna break my goddamned fingers!"

Oliver was not the person you wanted to handle a traumatic situation.

I pulled out my phone. "I'll handle this." I dialed Nate and put him on speaker phone so I could tend to Aspen while talking.

"Hey, precious—"

"Nate, I need you to do me a favor." I cut him off.

"Just breathe. That's a good girl. In and out slowly." Behind me, Tripp mimicked what I'd told him to do.

"Who the fuck is that in the background?" My alpha male heard another male voice and instantly reacted. I couldn't stop the eye roll, but secretly I loved how possessive he was of me. It made me feel special and desirable.

"It's Tripp. We're in Aspen's limo…"

"Brilliant! So you've finally decided to talk to Tripp about being his long lost sister?" Oh Jesus! Nate can't shut up for two damn minutes. Why the hell did I put him on speaker phone?

The entire car went completely silent except for Aspen's low moans of pain. Ollie groaned when she mangled his hand during the next contraction. Tripp's gaze bored into mine. I looked away, not knowing what to do or how to respond.

"What the fuck is he talking about, Cami?"

★ ★ ★

"Later, Tripp. We'll talk," I heard Camille say. Shite, I didn't realize I was on speaker. Christ. I ruined it for her. She was going to be brassed off. I could see her withholding the bonking for the foreseeable future over this bloody mess-up.

"Shite, love. I'm sorry," I spoke softly.

A commotion and a long groan was accompanied by a man's girly scream. "She's hurting me! Aspen, you're fucking hurting me!" I heard Oliver shout.

"What's going on?" I asked.

"Aspen's gone into labor. Her water broke, and we can't get hold of Hank. I need you to go get him and meet us at the hospital."

I put on my blazer and shuffled the phone from ear to ear as I put on my coat. "Where is he?"

"He's actually not far from your office." She read off the name of the company. I pulled it up on my laptop and stuffed everything in my briefcase that I might have needed for the rest of the afternoon.

"Okay. Got it. I'll get the bloke. We'll meet you at the hospital. Tell the wee one to hold off until his dad arrives!" A loud scream tore through the phone line.

"I gotta go." Another loud moan tore through the phone. "Love you."

"I love you," I said and rang off.

I headed out of the office and ran into Collier. "Aspen's in labor. Got to go find Hank across the way. Call London," I said as the lift doors closed.

Collier didn't ask how I knew Aspen was in labor or why I was the one running to get Hank. He just agreed. That's the kind of partnership we had. Often times fewer words were better than a long rant.

In fifteen minutes, I'd made it to the black glass building a few city blocks from ours, hopped on the lift, and pressed floor twenty-five. A text sounded on my phone. I pulled it out and read the screen.

From: Aspen Reynolds-Jensen
To: Nate Walker
Where the fuck is the cowboy? Aspen's killing me! We'll be at Lenox Hill Hospital in ten.

It must have been Oliver. The lift doors opened, and

I figured I'd have Hank call as soon as I got him out of here. Quickly, I found the right office and went to the receptionist. She was a mean-looking woman. Thin, pinched tight skin sucked her face like fondant over a skeleton. Her sharp blond bob and blood-red lipstick added to her fierce features.

She talked as I paced. Finally, I put my hand over the button on her phone, cutting off her call. "I need Hank Jensen. Now!" I growled, leaving no room for argument. Her entire face frowned. I didn't think it was possible, but I guess if you're a woman made of plastic, using one muscle pushes them all into motion. "Look, he's in a meeting here somewhere and his wife is in labor. She's on her way to the hospital. Can you help me or do I need to cause a *fucking* scene?"

Her face lightened a speck, a barely noticeable twitch. "Come with me." She scowled, then stood, and walked on the highest spiked heels I'd seen this side of a strip club.

She knocked on a door and waited, then pressed her ear to the door.

"Oh sodding hell." I gripped the handle and opened the door. Four men in suits and my man, Hank Jensen, turned their heads from the giant LCD screen and projector.

"Nate, partner?"

"We gotta go. Your wife is on her way to Lenox Hill Hospital. She's in labor!"

Hank didn't bother to say anything to the people in the room. "It's too early! She's not due for another month." His voice sounded frightened.

"I know. Let's go."

We made it into a taxi in record time. Hank dialed his

wife and Oliver must have picked up.

"Buddy, no, I can't understand you. Fucking hell! Give me my wife. She's what? Jesus, give me Cami then."

"What's going on, Cami?" He must have got my girl on the phone. He blew out a slow breath. "Okay, water broke, dilated to a six, and eighty percent effaced." Hank pushed a rushed hand through his sandy hair. Tension filled every surface of his face and body. "What's the doctor say?" He took a deep breath and leaned his head back on the car seat. "We'll be there in twenty. Stay with my girl. Ollie loves her, but he's a fucking drama queen. Take care of her till I get there. Okay, sweetie?"

For a moment, my hackles rose at his endearment but I knew Hank and his heart. He genuinely cared for Camille and I'd heard him call London sweetie as well. It was his old-fashioned Texan nature. They seemed to have the honey, baby, sweetie thing down pat.

He hung up and smacked a heavy hand against the seat back. "Get us to the hospital in ten minutes and there's an extra hundred bucks in it for ya," Hank said to the driver. "Got me?"

"You got it, mister!" The young-looking bloke pressed his foot on the gas.

In ten minutes flat, we were in front of the hospital. Hank threw a hundred and thirty bucks to the driver, probably making his day. We ran into the hospital and asked for labor and delivery.

I'd never run through a hospital so fast in my life, including seven months ago when my own brother was admitted. People only did this shite in the movies. Not Hank. He ran those stark white halls like a man running over hot coals. I wasn't sure his feet hit the ground. I could barely keep up with him.

When we got to the right place, I was breathing hard, but Hank was no worse for the wear. Blooming hell, how much did the bloke work out?

"Aspen Jensen! My wife!" he roared to a little thing in pink scrubs with flowers all over them.

"Room 5, one floor up in the private labor and delivery suites," the nurse called as Hank was already on the stairs, not willing to wait for the elevator. I followed him in my slick shoes and caught myself on the railing. We had to look like a couple of bank robbers the way we busted through the stairwell door and into the top floor.

Hank found the room and heard his wife scream. "God dammit. I fucking need Hank, right the fuck now!" she screamed at Oliver.

It was the most profanity I'd ever heard Aspen use... ever.

My lovely Camille rushed to her side with a cold cloth.

"Oh, God, that's good. Thank you, Cami," Aspen said, breathless.

"Angel." The word was laced with love. Hank and his wife reached for each other. Tears poured down her face.

"Hank, she's coming early. I don't know why." Aspen's head shook from side to side, and fear filled her voice. "I did everything right," she cried.

He kissed her face over and over and finally her lips.

Camille moved off to the side with her hands over her mouth. Her own tears fell down her cheeks. My girl was such a softy.

Oliver was at the window pacing. Tripp hung outside

the room, sitting in a waiting chair, twiddling his thumbs.

"Camille, love, I'm here when you're ready," I whispered.

She looked up. Her eyes were bright with love and happiness. She met me, grabbing her purse.

"No! Hank, no. I need her!" Aspen reached for Camille. My girl ran over and clasped both of hers around one of Aspen's.

"It's okay. Hank's here," Camille assured the suffering woman.

"Darlin', would you feel better if you had a woman with us?" Hank asked.

She nodded and Camille smiled. "I'd be honored to stay if that's what you want."

"You help me so much. Please don't leave," Aspen begged. Another painful contraction took her over. Immediately, Camille jumped to her aid and looked over to some machine that seemed to be attached to a cord under Aspen's gown.

"Okay, Aspen, it's peaking." Aspen grabbed Camille's hand and held both hers and Hank's. "Okay you've got this. Breathe in for five, out for five… That's it. You're coming down, it's lessening, and almost gone." She drug out the last word. "Really great job on that one. You barely cringed."

Aspen returned a weak smile. Camille looked at me over her shoulder.

"Baby, I'll be right outside if you need anything. I'll have Jin keep our son tonight, okay?"

She nodded and smiled. It was the prettiest smile on the most beautiful woman. She was in her element, helping a friend.

I looked over at the empty seat next to Tripp and sat

down.

"Crazy, huh?" I said. Tripp nodded but kept silent. Finally he turned and looked at me.

"Cami's my sister?"

CHAPTER NINETEEN

I thought the ten hours I was in labor was long. Those ten hours passed during Aspen's labor in what felt like an eternity of wading through a hurricane in five feet of snow wearing a pair of shorts. The last five hours were worse, utter torture on the mama and her support team. Not one to complain, but finally, mercifully, she got an epidural. It was as if the clouds opened up, the sky turned gold, and the heavens rained down love and light on us.

Two different doctors had been in and out, consulting about the premature baby and whether or not they should do a C-section. The second doctor thought Aspen was a week or so further along in her gestation than her regular OB-GYN. Whatever the case, she was finally at ten centimeters dilated and pushing to bring her daughter into the world.

At this stage, I stayed back and allowed Hank and Oliver to each hold a leg as I stood on the sidelines with London. We hugged one another as Aspen bore down, screamed with a mighty roar, and forced her daughter's appearance.

"Oh my God, angel," Hank said as they laid a doll-sized infant on Aspen's belly, rubbing and wiping her down while the three of them looked on in awe. Hank cut the cord as the doctor directed. Pride and tears filled the big man's eyes in equal measure as he looked at his wife and daughter.

"She's so...gross. What is that all over her?" Oliver asked.

Aspen laughed and Hank pushed Oliver's forehead with his palm, moving him out of the way. Oliver cringed and came over to us, his arms spread wide. The three of us hugged.

"She's perfect, angel. Just like her mama," Hank said, petting his daughter's hair with one finger. "Our baby girl, Hannah." The three of us turned and smiled. Hannah. Such a lovely name.

London went to her sister and looked over Hank's shoulders at their daughter, now free of all the gunk. Oliver and I peeked as well. She was lovely.

"Oh, she's stunning!" Oliver clapped. "Baby Hannah is a supermodel baby already," he gushed. "Look at her perfect pout." I grinned and looked at the precious angel given to this wonderful couple.

"Darlin', you did mighty fine." Hank petted his wife's hair and then kissed her.

"Hold your daughter," Aspen whispered, emotion thick in her tone.

He cradled the small bundle into his arms. "Daddy's perfect girl. I love you, Hannah." Hank kissed his daughter's little tufts of golden hair just on the crown of her head.

I watched in awe as the huge man rocked and bonded with his daughter. I snapped a picture with the camera they'd laid on the side table. I didn't have any pictures of Tanner this early because it was just Jin and me in the delivery room. I wanted to make sure they had some for their own memories.

"Oliver, buddy. Come meet your niece. Hannah Olivia Jensen." Oliver looked at Aspen and she smiled. A tear slipped down his cheek. She wiped it away.

"You named her after me?"

"We love you and all your pieces. It's our gift to you," she told Oliver.

Oliver choked on a sob and then hugged Aspen, kissing her cheeks, then her forehead, and briefly her lips. "Thank you. I don't know what to say?"

"Say you'll love her for eternity and always be there for her, like you are with me," Aspen whispered. The room was so quiet we could all hear them.

"Until my last breath," he promised, leaning his forehead against Aspen's. Their bond was forged in steel and deep affection for one another. Very much like a brother and sister.

"Now let me see our baby girl all cleaned up and perfect!" He sashayed to Hank, wiping at his eyes.

"You want to hold her?" Hank offered.

Oliver looked stricken. "No, I don't want to hold her! I will do that when I'm seated on a very cushy spot, preferably a bed, with pillows all around so that she is the most safe—" Hank held his arms out and led Oliver to the chair.

"Hold your niece and shut up already," Hank said sternly but with a huge smile.

"Such a brute," Oliver said and then cooed to the bundle in his arms.

I walked to Aspen as they finished up with the placenta and stitching. London was hugging her and gushing on how perfect the baby's aura was.

London's eyes caught mine. "You helped Pen so much. You really know your stuff," she said.

I shrugged. "I've done it before. That helps."

Aspen held out her hand and grasped mine. "Thank

you. for everything," she said weakly, thoroughly exhausted.

I hugged her palm to my cheek. "I loved every second. Thank you for sharing this moment with me. I'll remember it always."

London stayed with Aspen as Hank, Oliver, and I returned to the waiting room. Hank held his daughter close to his chest. The room was filled with waiting family and friends. I could see my guy in the corner, his smile wide as he noticed me. Hank's brood of Texans were all there, smiling and waiting patiently. All save for who I assumed was Julia Jensen, who jumped up the second Hank entered, arms out wide.

"You just set that perfect bundle right in my arms. I need to bond with my first granddaughter. What's her name, son?"

"Aspen and I are excited to introduce all of our friends and family to Hannah Olivia Jensen. Six pounds, ten ounces, twenty inches long." He kissed his daughter on the head once more and let his mother take hold.

Julia looked at her granddaughter then back up to her son. Pride and joy filled her gaze. "You and Aspen did mighty fine young man. She's an angel from heaven. Our Hannah girl. The name fits her beautifully and keeps with the H names." Behind Julia, Henry puffed his chest with pride at hearing his granddaughter's name. I so wanted traditions like that with Nate. One day.

"You done well, son." Henry Jensen clapped his son on the back and smiled. His features were a lot like Hank's.

Manly back slaps followed by a round of congratulations were doted on Hank. I snapped a picture of Julia holding her grandchild as Hank's father looked over her shoulder.

Finally, a couple dressed to the nines came up to Julia. "May I hold my first grandchild?" the man in a suit asked, his voice filled with emotion. The woman standing to the side looked exactly like an older, unhappy version of Aspen but looked on with wonder.

"Is the baby's name hyphenated Reynolds-Jensen?" The upturned face of Aspen's mother assessed Hank shrewdly. Her eyebrow was pointed into a fierce triangle as her lips twisted into a tight pout.

Hank shook his head. "Nope. She's all Jensen, just like her mama," Hank puffed with pride.

Aspen's mother rolled her eyes and sighed. "Well, she looks just like my daughter. She's very beautiful."

"That she is, ma'am."

After a few minutes of introductions, Hank took his precious bundle and announced that he had to get back to his wife. He thanked everyone for coming. He'd be in touch when they were home and settled in.

Hank stopped me as he was heading out the door. "I can't thank you enough for what you did." I put my fingers against the dewy hair of Hannah's head. She snuffled toward her dad's chest, rooting around.

"You're welcome." I laughed, watching the little face, mouth opening and closing against her dad's chest. "You better get her to her mother. She's a hungry girl. Check in with the office when you have a chance. I'll text you anything crucial, but I think we can hold down the fort for a while."

Hank nodded and left. Two arms circled my waist and tugged me back into a hard wall of muscle. "Precious, are you ready to go home? You look dead on your feet." I closed my eyes and let his words rumble through my taxed brain.

I nodded. "How's Tanner?" I leaned against his chest. The labor and delivery reminded me of my own experience having Tanner. I missed my little man.

"Enjoying his time with Jin and Zach. They'll keep him again tonight so you can rest. Come, my love. I need to get you to bed."

We started to leave, but were stopped by a heavy hand on my shoulder. I turned and stared into the green eyes of my brother. I took a deep breath and looked at the ground. My shoes the most interesting things ever.

"We have to talk," Tripp said. "I know this is weird. It's beyond strange for me, but Nate updated me on the investigation he had done into your family." Tripp shoved his hands into his pockets and looked around the room. Anywhere but at me. My heart thudded in my chest.

"Tripp, I don't know what to say. I meant to tell you privately in a setting a little less…dramatic, but I'm glad it's out. At least now you know. I'm your half-sister. We share the same father." I exhaled the breath I was holding.

Nate squeezed me to his side and released me when Tripp grasped my hand and tugged me into his chest. His arms came around me. His hand held the back of my neck. All the tears I'd been storing, the misery of my childhood, the lack of family tumbled out. As I sobbed, my brother held me. He whispered, "It's okay," into my hairline, over and over. What he said next blew me away. "I'm so happy you found me."

I leaned away from him. "What do you mean?"

"Our dad's a drunken philanderer. One night when he was three sheets to the wind, he confided in me. Said he lost the love of his life when she gave birth to his daughter. He was back with my mom for a spell then. I was twelve or thirteen. He said his daughter would have been nine or ten. Then, he passed out." His eyes were haunted by the misery of that memory. It didn't sound like his childhood was all roses and rainbows either. Later, I hoped he would share more with me.

I cupped his cheek and looked into the misty eyes that matched my own. I smoothed his hair with my fingers. Our hair was also similar, not exactly the same, but the eyes didn't lie. The shape, color, and intensity were the same. Our noses were, too. "I always wanted you. A big brother," I whispered. He swallowed hard, then put his forehead to mine.

"I want to know you better. Spend time together. Would that be okay?"

"That would be," I choked and shuddered, overwhelmed with the feeling of finding my family for the first time. Nate's warmth permeated the back of my shirt as he put a hand on my lower back.

"It would be amazing. You know you have a nephew now." Tripp's eyes widened, and a huge toothy grin split his face. "Tanner will be ecstatic to meet his Uncle Tripp."

Tripp placed one last kiss on my cheek as London came to our little huddle. She placed a hand on his shoulder. Collier was close behind. "Everything okay, mate?" he addressed Tripp. "Brother?" he questioned Nate.

"Never better. I was just meeting my sister for the first time." Both Collier and London's face sported matching shocked expressions. "Can I call you?" Tripp pulled out his phone.

"Anytime you want." I smiled and gave him my

number. He tapped several buttons on his phone, and I heard a buzzing in my purse.

"That's me. You have my contact information now. I'll call you tomorrow," he added excitedly.

Nate grumbled and pulled me into his chest. "How about you call her in a couple days, mate? We'll have you over for supper. My girl is tired, needs a good night's sleep, food, and time with our son."

Tripp's eyes widened, and he ran a hand through his already messy hair. "Okay, yeah. You're right. Sorry." He grinned. "I got a little ahead of myself. This news, it's probably..." He took a huge breath and stared at me. "It's probably the best news I've ever gotten."

I melted and flung myself back into his arms, hugging him tight. He returned the hug and spun me around. "My brother," I whispered against his ear. "I have a brother." I laughed when he put me down.

When we finally pulled apart, we both were beaming. "See you soon...sister," he quipped.

"After a while, brother!" I called as Nate tugged me away, chuckling. I waved good-bye one last time and then hugged my fiancé.

"My life is perfect!" I said as he whirled me around and kissed me long and deep against the hospital wall.

"It's only going to get better," he promised.

"You're right, because I'm marrying you."

★ ★ ★

Camille slept for half a day and was still zonked. I picked up Tanner and brought him home.

"Okay, son, I'm going to teach you how to make

breakfast for your mum."

Tanner dragged a stool, the legs grating along the expensive pine wood floor before he hopped up. I shook my head but figured I'd let it go for now.

"All right, you crack an egg like so." I cracked the egg tapping it on the edge of the stainless steel bowl. I tossed the shell in the sink. "Now you have a go of it."

Tanner's little tongue came out of his mouth as he focused. It took him a while to crack the egg. Finally I covered his hand with my own and wacked it hard enough to break the shell.

"Now pull it apart here," I pressed his thumbs into the middle, opened it, and let the egg drop into the bowl. His eyes lit up.

"I did it, I did it! Did you see that, Dad? I'm so a good chef!" His little chest puffed with pride.

"You are doing a brilliant job!" I cracked the rest of the eggs and let him mix them up. He enjoyed that part immensely, though I think he got more on the counter than was left in the bowl.

For good measure, I cracked a few more and finished pouring them into the pan. I fried some bacon and potatoes and let him add the fruit I'd cut up to the plate.

"Mom is going to love this breakfast!" he squealed, running down the hall.

"No, sport, wait!" I tried to whisper loud enough for him to hear but not to wake Camille. He stopped just at the door. I handed him a bright yellow sunflower. The rest of the bunch was in a vase on the kitchen table. One thing I learned about Camille, she loved flowers. She seemed to adore them all, but her favorite were sunflowers. I had flowers delivered every week to our flat so she could enjoy them every day. Seeing her lean her delectable arse over the table in her tiny bed shorts and sniff them each morning was thank you enough. I loved starting my day with a shot of Camille-cheek with my tea.

I held my fingers up to my lips, mimicking quiet. He giggled and held his hands over his mouth. The boy could hardly contain his excitement. We entered as silently as possible for a four-year-old who couldn't be quiet. He crawled along the side of his mum and held the flower to her nose. I chuckled and she smiled, obviously aware of our sneak attack.

"Mmm, something smells divine."

"It's this flower, Mommy." Tanner shoved the flower into her nose. Her eyes opened and she tried to move her face as he continued to press it against her nose. "Smell it! Stop moving so you can get a good sniff," he said seriously.

She stopped and noisily sniffed the flower, then pushed it away, and sat up.

"It's great, baby. Thank you." Her sleepy eyes caught mine and the tray I held. "What's this?"

"Breakfast in bed, my love. You deserve it."

Tanner jumped on the bed. "I helped, I did it. I cook-did and cracked up the eggs!" he said with pride.

"You did? Well, I'm starving, and I will eat them all up!" she assured him.

"Okay, little man, stop jumping. I can't set down Mummy's food." He jumped down and crossed his legs.

"Can I have cartoons and cereal?"

I laughed. "We just made breakfast. You don't want that?" I asked, completely astounded. He normally ate everything.

"Today I want Lucky Charms and Batman!" He ran out of the room screaming the batman theme. We put the cereal and bowls at a low level in the kitchen so he could serve himself. He actually did a great job not spilling the milk.

I set the tray over Camille's lap and watched as she ate. She was ravenous, not having eaten a proper meal in more than a day. Once she was done, I moved the tray and snuggled into her side, kissing her sweet lips. She tasted of tea and butter.

"Mmm, that kiss was the perfect ending to my meal."

"Is that right? Well, I'll just have to kiss you after every meal, my love."

"You promise? Every day?"

"I do. And that brings me to something we haven't spoke of."

Her eyebrows knit together. "What's that?"

"The wedding. Mum called and wants to make travel plans to the States."

Camille bit her lip. "We could always just do something really simple. Like Justice of the Peace? I'm sure you know a couple judges who could marry us. We can pick any ole day and it would be fine. I don't really care. I just want to be your wife." That answer, sandwiched with ambivalence and lack of excitement, were not what I expected from a soon-to-be bride.

"Do you not want a wedding?"

She shrugged. "I don't really have any friends or family, besides Jin and now Tripp. What's the point, really? There's no one to walk me down the aisle. We could just elope like

Collier did. That would be fine."

"My mum would have a heart attack if we did not have some form of ceremony. How about this? We have a small wedding with close friends and family? We'll each have one attendant. You could have Jin. I'll have Colly. Tanner will be our ring bearer. Wouldn't you like to see him in a little tux that matches mine?"

A huge smile lit her face. Now that was the excited bride I needed to see. "I do love when you boys are twinsies. He'd love that, too."

"And you could pick the dress of your dreams. No budget. Which reminds me." I hopped out of bed, pulled out my wallet, and handed her two cards. One was a new debit card, the other was a Visa with her name on it."

"What are these?"

"The new cards to our banking accounts. I had your name added. You can keep your own account or merge it with mine. We're getting married soon. I want everything in both our names starting now."

"But, I figured you'd want a prenup?"

My head swung around to hers. "Whatever would give you that sodding idea? What's mine is yours, precious. And what's yours is mine. Just like Tanner. When you're officially a Walker, he will be too. We'll sign a wedding license and the official adoption papers at the same time." She needed to understand that there wasn't ever going to be anything between us ever again. No lies, secrets, no broken pasts, just the three of us making our life and home together.

Camille flew out of bed and into my arms. She wrapped her legs around my waist and sat in my lap. "I love you, Nathaniel Walker. You're the best thing that ever happened to me or Tanner. We will wear your family name with such pride." She kissed me for all she was worth. I pressed my arms to her back, surrounding myself with the thing that made me the happiest man on earth.

EPILOGUE

One year later…

I stared at the wedding photo of Nate, Tanner, and me. It sat in a position of honor on my desk at Jensen Construction. Thinking back to that day six months ago filled me with incredible joy. Our Caribbean cruise ship wedding was utterly magical. Nate and Tanner wore matching tuxes, as promised, each with a dark eggplant-colored vest and tie. Jin wore a stunning strapless, purple tea-length gown that matched. Collier looked handsome in a similar tux standing as best man. The helm of the cruise ship was decorated with hydrangeas, and a white metal arch was fashioned with ribbon and filled in with giant bursts of sunflowers. Hank walked me down the aisle, wearing a dark grey suit with a lavender tie. I could have had Tripp walk me down, but I didn't want Marcus to feel slighted. Besides, Hank had been there for me from the very beginning, and we shared a deep concern and respect for one another. The same way a father and daughter would, even though he was only eleven years my senior.

The sky had been a pristine blue and the ocean waters calm as we vowed to love, honor, and cherish one another all the days of our lives. We added a section to the ceremony where Tanner officially accepted Nate as his father. We signed our marriage certificate and Tanner's adoptions papers in front of God and everyone.

All the people we loved and cared about were in attendance. The Jensens, the Stones, Dean and Oliver, and my two brothers, Tripp and Marcus. Nate's family flew in from England.

After the ceremony, we spent ten days with our friends and family cruising along the Caribbean islands. After the ten days, everyone went their separate ways, and Nate and I spent an additional week in Jamaica for our private honeymoon. It was the first time in five years I had been away from my son, but Jin and Tripp assured me they had it covered. We received text messages and funny pics of Tanner daily. My brothers and I had gotten to know each other pretty well. Marcus had another year of college, but kept in touch. He had a lovely girlfriend he was smitten with and planned to marry one day. When school was over, they agreed to move to New York to be closer to Tripp and me.

Tripp still lived in London's condo and offered them a home with him. He said he hated being in the apartment alone.

Tripp and I were now the best of friends. We lunched every Wednesday and he attended family dinners every Sunday night at my home with Nate. Dinners were a standing invitation to whomever could make it. That included Collier, London, Emma, as well as our extended family of friends—Hank, Aspen, little Hannah, Dean, Oliver, Jin and Zach. Tanner adored Hannah and treated her like his cousin. We left it that way. In my world, friends were the family you chose.

"What are you still doing here? Let's go get the kids," Hank said as we closed up the office. It was our usual routine.

We entered the private elevator. Yep, I had been upgraded to special status and now had use of the private elevator. It felt incredibly "Mission Impossible-esque" to have my own code. I entered the number and pressed the button to go down to the fifth floor. We exited and pressed another few buttons on the door outside the office. Security in this part of the building had been expanded. Oliver wouldn't have it any other way.

As we entered, several squeals could be heard. Hannah toddled over to her father, arms open wide as she gibber-jabbered. Drool escaped her mouth in a long string of slime as Hank scooped her into his arms. "How's my Hannah Banana today?" Hank asked as he peppered her face with kisses. She slobbered and held her dad's neck, smacking his face repeatedly. Her golden blond hair curled around her neck and ears. A bright red bow held up a tiny bunch of curls, reminding me of Pebbles from the Flintstones.

A whoosh hit my side. "Mommy!" Tanner hugged me tight and then brought his ear to my belly. "What's my baby doing in there?"

I leaned over and hugged my son. "Sleeping." He concentrated on my stomach and frowned. "My brother sure sleeps a lot." He sighed and his little shoulders slumped. From behind me, I heard two more voices.

"Hey, precious, I thought I was picking up our guy today?" He hugged me and kissed my neck, nibbling a little. The spark sent chills down my spine to settle heavily between my thighs, softening my sex, making it wet and ready to be taken. He growled into my neck. "I know that look. Don't make me take you to the nursing room to shag the shite out of my wife."

"Please do," I murmured back, my need building stronger with each second. Damn hormones were insane. I wanted him morning, noon, and night. A few times the past few weeks, I'd begged him to meet me at the apartment for an afternoon delight. He always obliged. Such a good husband.

"Later, love." He kissed me one last time, gave the baby belly a rub, and crouched to hug Tanner.

Aspen must have entered behind him because she had Hannah on her hip and was talking to Jin about weaning Hannah off nursing and switching to cow's milk. Above Jin's head, the sign AIR Bright Children's Center sparkled. I smiled widely, truly enjoying how life came full circle.

When Aspen had Hannah, she and Hank couldn't bear to be away from their daughter, but neither of them would agree to leave their job. The issue of a nanny was born. Oliver suggested they open a daycare instead. Nate came up with the idea of hiring Jin as the director for the center. She had spent the last year going back to school getting her certifications and was ready when the center opened. I loved seeing Jin so content.

She was dating one of the attorneys at Stone, Walker, & Associates, which brought us all together even more often. Now she ran the entire daycare center, made a high-dollar wage, and had moved into one of Nate and Collier's apartments in downtown New York.

The entire fifth floor of the AIR Bright building boasted the full daycare and children's services for kids between four months to twelve years of age. There was one adult to every five children and only allowed a handful of babies. Those spots were dedicated to our small group.

Oliver interviewed, background checked, and called every reference for the personnel himself. He was dedicated to making the center the safest place for AIR Bright's children. I believed it was because of Hannah and his and Dean's daughter, Isabella.

That was another big change. It occurred after Hank and Aspen had Hannah. He and Dean had a simple wedding, hyphenated both their names, and found a surrogate who went through in vitro for them. They'd talked about it a lot during Aspen's pregnancy. When Hannah was born, they decided that they were ready. No one knows which dad is the "real" biological father, but they both take their role very seriously and as far as we were told, they don't plan to ever find out.

The best part about the children's center was that if you made over a certain amount, you paid tuition. If you earned less than the threshold but worked for AIR Bright, daycare was free for up to two children.

Aspen was adamant that having a child should not be a hindrance to her staff. Since the addition of the daycare, every facet, including her revenue streams, had increased twenty percent and staff turnaround was at an all-time low.

London and Collier entered and surprised both Nate and I.

"Hey, mate, what are you doing here?"

"I thought Aspen and Hank had a date tonight? Weren't we supposed to pick up Hannah?" London asked while furiously rubbing her swollen belly. It turned out our honeymoon was very fruitful. Both London and I were due a couple days apart, though her bump was expectedly a bit larger.

Hank slapped Collier on the back and then made a grab for London's belly. She rolled her eyes. "Go ahead."

He grinned and placed his giant paws on each side of her huge belly. We were both six months, and I'd just found out we were having a boy. Her visit had been this week.

"So? What are you having?" I asked excitedly.

London looked at Collier. "A boy!" he said and looked at London.

"A girl!" she said.

Hank's eyes widened and Aspen entered, rubbing London's belly. "A boy and a girl? Oh, how perfect!" She hugged her sister. The twins news wasn't new, but the sex was. The couple looked thrilled. Originally, London beyond freaked out at being pregnant. When she found out she was having twins, she accepted her fate and went with it. For a woman who had been so open and free, she now had everything dialed in and organized. I had to believe that was Collier's effect on his wife.

"Angel, we need to catch up." Hank gripped Aspen's hips and rubbed up against her like a cat on a scratching pole. "Let's start tonight after our date! I want another baby."

Aspen looked at her husband's face. "Are you serious? I just got my body back!" She pouted. He pulled her against his chest and palmed her ass.

"Yeah and it's fuckin' to die for. I want to put a baby in it!" He jerked his hips against hers and she grinned, clasping her hands around his neck.

I shook my head and laughed. Their little display reminded me of the heavy ache between my own thighs.

"Okay, okay, that's enough, mate. Christ! Too much info!" Nate scowled and hugged me to his side. I tickled his lower back and then grabbed his bum to remind him of my plight. His gaze shot to mine and turned a swirly navy-blue color. He nipped my lips. "Behave," he said and then gave me another peck. It wasn't nearly enough.

I took a breath, trying to calm my libido, and focused on London and Collier. "We're having a boy, you two are having one of each, and we already have Hannah, Isabella, Zach, and Tanner. Our family is growing and I for one couldn't be happier."

Collective murmurs of "hear, hear" and "Amen" were heard. Nate snuggled into my neck once more. "My girl is such a softy."

The group said their good-byes and shuffled out of the daycare, everyone content in where their life was. I had Nate, Tanner, and our little one on the way. I was finishing my school work in the evenings, and would soon be teaching grade school. It just proved how much your life could change if you love and let yourself be loved.

Hank and his angel, Aspen, were two people from completely different worlds, but love brought them together and made those differences seem very small. From what Nate told me, Collier pursued London relentlessly until she finally gave up her guilt and grief over falling in love again after losing her husband. For Nate and me, our story was no different than theirs. I didn't believe I was worthy of love. In the end, justice and love prevailed over my insecurities and the heavy weight of my past. All in all, each of us had beaten the odds, falling deeply in love forevermore.

FOR THE READERS

I can't thank you enough for sticking with me through the creation and release of the Falling Series. So many of you have reached out to me with loving, open arms, and for that, I'm so grateful. I was surprised when you fell in love with Hank and Aspen's journey as much as I did and continued to stay with me through London and Collier and now Nate and Camille's love story. I'm so honored to have had even one person read my books. Writing this series was a dream come true, and each and every one of you helped make that dream reality.

Many of you have asked for Tripp's story and one day I think I will write it, but right now my muse is kicking and screaming to spread her wings into the other love stories I have spinning a wickedly hot web in my brain.

If you liked the Falling Series, please consider leaving a review on Amazon and Goodreads. Those reviews mean the absolute world to an indie like me.

Authors, please check out the list of people I thanked and the "badass blogs" that I noted. Each and every one of them is incredible and could very well help you reach your dreams too.

Thank you all. Until next time…Namaste.

Audrey

Namaste
The light in me, bows to the light in you.
When I am in that place in me,
and you are in that place in you…
we are one.

ALSO BY AUDREY CARLAN

The Calendar Girl Series

January (Book 1)
February (Book 2)
March (Book 3)
April (Book 4)
May (Book 5)
June (Book 6)

July (Book 7)
August (Book 8)
September (Book 9)
October (Book 10)
November (Book 11)
December (Book 12)

The Falling Series

Angel Falling
London Falling
Justice Falling

The Trinity Trilogy

Body (Book 1)
Mind (Book 2)
Soul (Book 3)

ACKNOWLEDGEMENTS

To my husband Eric—I will always love you more. Thank you for your unending support and encouraging me to chase after my dreams.

To my mentor Jess Dee—You will forever be a beautiful part of my journey in this crazy world of writing romance. I have such an incredible author to look up to. Read her books. You won't be sorry people! www.jessdee.com.

To my critique partner, Sarah Saunders—I had no idea that when you offered to critique that you'd be so damn good at it. This book wouldn't be my best had I not had you there to provide such thoughtful criticism, funny comments, and overall character evaluation. You kept me honest and knew when a past character was falling out of their personality. This book is as much for you as it is for me. I love you girl! Can't wait to do it again!

To my soul sisters, Nikki, Dyani, and Carrie—Without the three of you well, I just wouldn't be me. I don't think I would have taken the leap had my girls not pushed and prodded. Trinity Trilogy is up next…prepare to be blown away by your doppelgangers Maria, Bree, and Kathleen. BESOS for life!

To my editor, Alfie Thompson—Thank you for always fitting me into your schedule and finding all my mistakes. Let's do this writer/editor thing again sometime.

To my sisters Jeana, Michele, and Denise—Thank you for reading and loving my books and spreading the word to all your friends and pretty much anyone that will listen. I'll love you forever.

To my beta readers:

Jeananna Goodall—After I send my chapters to my critique partner I send them to you and wait patiently (or not so patiently) to hear your opinion. I love the way you experience my stories. It's beyond what I could ever hope for. You're my biggest cheerleader and loving supporter. I have come to count on your thoughts and feedback and I will never take you for granted. Thank you for being you girlie. I love all your pieces!

Ginelle Blanch—You blow me away with your ability to catch errors after it's been reviewed, critiqued, edited and edited again! You make my books better and my heart bigger by sharing your experience from the readers perspective. I "heart" you hard.

Niki Davis—I still can't get over that you randomly wanted to beta and that you live down the street from me. I look forward to getting to know you better. Thank you for reading and reviewing Justice and sharing your experience. I can only hope that readers fall in love with my stories the way you have.

Additional special thanks to the following:

To Audrey's Angels—My official Audrey Carlan Street Team. I'm shocked, humbled, and so damn glad I have the most amazing women to lift me up and cheer me on. I dreaded starting a team because I was so worried that there wouldn't be anyone who wanted to join. I was floored by the outpouring of your kindness, love, and support. I owe you all some serious prezzies.

To Clista Seals—You're a beautiful human being and

I rarely meet someone whose spirit is as lovely and kind as yours. Thank you for your friendship and support.

To Emily Hemmer—Your guidance and friendship knows no bounds. I love who you are, your passion about the written word, and your bitchy muse who brings the world the most beautiful stories I've ever read. Namaste my friend. www.emilyhemmer.com

To Drue Hoffman—Best blog tour chick in the universe! She does incredible book promoting services for authors with a special love for helping out the indies. Visit her site to view pricing and service offerings. You be sorry you did. www.druesrandomchatter.com

To Carol Ray—Your support and love of indie authors is beautiful. Thank you for "pimping" me every chance you get, spreading the word far and wide about my books. <smooches girlie>

ABOUT AUDREY CARLAN

Audrey Carlan lives in the sunny California Valley two hours away from the city, the beach, the mountains and the precious…the vineyards. She has been married to the love of her life for over a decade and has two young children that live up to their title of "Monster Madness" on a daily basis. When she's not writing wickedly hot romances, doing yoga, or sipping wine with her "soul sisters," three incredibly different and unique voices in her life, she can be found with her nose stuck in book or her Kindle. A hot, smutty, romantic book to be exact!

Any and all feedback is greatly appreciated and feeds the soul. You can contact Audrey below:

E-mail: carlan.audrey@gmail.com
Facebook: facebook.com/AudreyCarlan
Website: www.audreycarlan.com